MASK
— OF —
SHADOWS

MASK OF

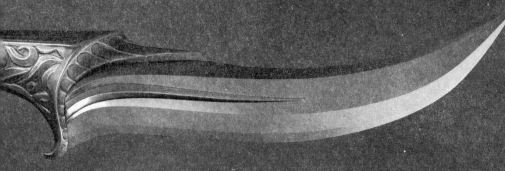

SHADOWS

LINSEY MILLER

sourcebooks
fire

Published by Sourcebooks Fire, an imprint of Sourcebooks, Inc.
P.O. Box 4410, Naperville, Illinois 60567-4410
(630) 961-3900
Fax: (630) 961-2168
www.sourcebooks.com

Library of Congress Cataloging-in-Publication Data

Names: Miller, Linsey, author.
Title: Mask of shadows / Linsey Miller.
Description: Naperville, Illinois : Sourcebooks Fire, [2017] | Summary: The
    gender fluid thief Sal Leon enters a competition to become a replacement
    member of the Left Hand--a quartet of the Queen's personal assassins--but
    must first survive the training and the contests while putting the reason
    for auditioning into motion--revenge.
Identifiers: LCCN 2016050928 | (alk. paper)
Subjects: | CYAC: Gender identity--Fiction.
Classification: LCC PZ7.1.M582 Mas 2017
LC record available at https://lccn.loc.gov/2016050928

Printed and bound in the United States of America.
WOZ 10 9 8 7 6 5 4 3 2 1

To my father.

It's not a picture book about a figure-skating alligator like we planned, but I think you would've liked this one.

CHAPTER
ONE

The thick, briny scent of sweat-soaked leather seeped through my cloth mask. A guarded carriage rattled down the road upwind of me. I leaned out of my tree and caught a flicker of light from a carriage lamp. The carriage's blue paint shone, gilded and mud-splattered.

I groaned. "Nobles."

The branches beneath me creaked as footsteps scraped along the bark. I flipped a knife into my palm. The sentence for robbing nobles was hanging.

But only if they caught you.

"Lords, Sal! Where you at?" Rath burst through the leaves and tripped over my perch.

"Point of hiding is to stay hid." I shoved him backward and yanked his mask down over his face. "What do you want?"

Rath tapped my nose with his baton. "You up to robbing Erlends?"

Erlends were stiff and cold as the lands they ruled and merciless as death. They'd hold a picnic at the gallows.

I tightened the knots at the back of my mask. "You up to keeping quiet?"

Rath slapped a hand over his mouth and nodded toward the carriage below us. I crept along my branch far as I dared, eyeing the coach's window. If I had no shoulders, I'd fit through easy.

"This'll be fun." I shook my head.

This would hurt.

"*Fun*-fun?" Rath rubbed the stump where his little finger had been. "Or 'you miss and we all get hanged' fun?"

"Fun."

Rath huffed, scrambling out of my tree. His footsteps whispered over the deadfall, and a long, low bird whistle echoed between the trees. One call, one carriage, and one shot at meeting our quota.

Horses clomped over the dirt, carrying the soldiers closer to our nets hidden in the trees. Ten mounted and armored guards circled the coach. They looked right and left, but they never glanced up. I exhaled and tightened my grip on the branch. The carriage rolled beneath me.

We dropped the nets. The soldiers howled, spears and arms tangling in the lines, and the driver jerked the coach to a stop. Rath whistled.

I flung myself from the tree. My boots tore through the carriage's curtain and took out a passenger with a sharp heel to the head. My shoulders scraped both sides of the window frame as I slid into the carriage. I waved my knife.

"Your money or your lives?" I asked, twisting round to the noble.

"Money." The noble was barely older than me and half a head

shorter, but she squared her slim shoulders and glared at me over wire-rimmed spectacles. She nodded to the unconscious servant I'd kicked aside. "For her too."

I swallowed my usual command of "hush and drop your knives" and nodded. "Deal—jewelry, money, and all manner of fancy things in your lap."

Finally, someone smart enough to know they weren't winning this fight.

She yanked the rings from her fingers. I rid the servant of her purse with one hand and held my knife to the noble with the other. Clever as she seemed, I didn't trust a noble not to plant a hatpin in my back. She cleared her throat.

"Problem, Erlend?" I glanced at her.

"No." She stared at my knife. "And you may call me 'my lady' or nothing at all."

I grinned and bowed. How Erlend of her—better than screaming and fighting though. "Of course, my lady."

She shifted. Her jewelry was a puddle of silver in her lap, with her purse half-closed over crumpled paper. She'd laced her fingers together to hide her trembling.

"You missed one." I lifted a small locket from her neck, doing my best not to scare her. Wasn't like I enjoyed scaring people, especially not the ones being smart when I robbed them. Being efficient got the same results as being mean. "And I'm not going to stab you unless you stab me first."

"You're robbing me at knifepoint." She jerked away. A sneer twisted her pleasant face into the Erlend expression I knew so well. "It's not valuable."

"It's got real rubies." I turned it over. Twisted-copper rose petals with inlaid ruby slivers adorned the front of the locket. I snapped open the clasp. Two portraits were glued inside—one of a child with chubby cheeks and the other of a woman veiled in blue who shared this lady's long nose. I slid my knife into the sheath on my belt and dropped the necklace. "Take it off."

Her hands flew to her throat. "It's not valuable."

"Shush. I'm not going to take it, but you need to hide it."

Wouldn't do for Rath to bust in and find the lady with jewels still around her neck. He'd laugh at me for days and take the necklace.

She fumbled with the clasp and hissed when her hair tangled in the chain.

"Quiet! Hold still." A dark curl was knotted around the thin chain. I tugged it free, inhaling a deep breath of her rosewater perfume and stumbling over my words. "My boss finds out I let you keep this, he'll take my hand."

"I'll try to keep your mercy out of the warrant description." She smiled. Barely. "But thank you."

First time anyone thanked me for robbing them. She was frightfully pretty too, with her dark curls and confident chin, standing up to me without fighting. Talking someone down took nerve and smarts.

She pulled away and her warm scent went with her.

"Hide it. Sorry I mucked up your hair." I gestured to the curls behind her ears. Lusting after Erlends would get me nowhere but dead.

"Well, I am being robbed." She slipped the locket up her sleeve into a hidden pocket and patted down her hair. "You're young for a road agent and nicer than the stories I've heard."

"And you're young for a member of the queen's court. Bet that pissed off all your old Erlend friends." I held up her silver ring stamped with Our Queen's entwined lightning bolts. She couldn't have been more than a year older than me. "You piss them off too much and they might send you out here with too few guards and refuse to pay your ransom."

I'd not put it past those warlords to turn on their own for profit.

A scream ripped through the window as the scuffle outside pitched into shouts and clashing swords, and the lady lurched away from me.

"Sorry—not kidnapping you. Only joking." I pocketed her ring and bowed. "Apologies for scaring you, my lady."

She wrinkled her nose. "Not for the robbery?"

"Only for scaring you." I whistled once—I was done, time to go—and nudged the servant with my toe. "And for kicking her. Tell her I'm sorry for that."

"And the robbery?" She didn't even flinch, just lifted her chin.

"Lords, girl, and the robbery. You harass everyone?" I twisted round, memorizing the line of her jaw, the fall of hair over her light-brown cheeks, and the smear of freckles along her nose. Least I'd have one bright light among my list of bad, bloody memories.

"Only the ones robbing me." She smiled, lips closed and eyes narrowed. "You're not one of those who've been kidnapping, are you?"

"No, they're vicious as cottonmouths and running the southern roads. Stay clear of there." I gestured at her, waiting for Rath's answering whistle. "But tell them I was mean. For my warrant."

Those fools kidnapping nobles would steer clear of our roads if they thought we were meaner than them.

"Terrifying," she said with a mock gasp. "A giant, monstrous beast with knives and a mask as hideous as their manners. It'll save my guards their egos."

I opened my mouth to make her take back the manners jab when the carriage door flew open. Rath ripped the top hinge clear off.

"More guards," he hollered, shaking his head and flinging blood across the carriage.

Fast as he'd appeared, he'd vanished into the trees. Outside the carriage, soldiers and thieves flailed in the darkness, a tangle of limbs and blades. I glanced at the lady.

"You want that warrant, then you have to escape." She shoved me out the door. "Go."

I leapt out of the coach and into the night, her image scorched into my mind.

CHAPTER
TWO

R oad patrols swapped routes." Rath tore through the underbrush, stolen spears slung across his shoulder and bouncing
on his back. "I nicked their reins, but they might follow. Most
loyal guards I've ever seen."

"You get much off them?" I stopped and turned an ear to the
forest behind us. Nothing coming.

Even if the guards chased us, they'd pass out from heat sick-
ness. I could barely stand the humid air in trousers and a shirt.
Armor was sweaty torture.

"Not enough." He skidded through mud at the edge of a lake
and jumped onto a rock, leaving a track straight into the water.
He leapt from stone to stone along the water's edge. "Think
having only eight fingers is acceptable?"

Grell da Sousa—our gang leader who ran every street fight,
robbery, and gambling house in the district of Kursk—took
Rath's little finger when we were nine. Rath had only skimmed

enough for room and board, but that day, we'd dropped below quota. We hadn't missed quota since.

"Who needs fingers?" I ripped off my mask, timing each breath with my strides. Breathing through linen was like gasping underwater. "I lifted some pearls and gems. Should be enough to cover us. Let's go."

Rath veered right back onto the bank.

I followed. I had to. Grell had sucked me into this profession when I was eight. He gave me the option of either paying him a tribute or losing a finger for every coin I stole in his district. Eight-year-old me liked my fingers. Rath and I worked together, saving wisely and rigging bets liberally, but I'd no sooner trust him to guard my back as Grell. Least Grell was upfront about clipping fingers.

Grell had lost his own finger in a fight, learned from it, and saw no wrong in teaching us how to live by breaking us down piece by piece.

I slipped my hand into the lady's purse and pulled out her small silver ring. The band scraped over my busted knuckles, but it was prettier than anything I'd ever owned.

"You're dawdling." Rath turned to me, now running backward. A tree loomed over his shoulders. "Losing focus in your old age?"

"Sharper and younger than you still." I studied the crest on the ring. Running and robbery went hand in hand, and I could outrun Rath with my eyes closed. "Mind yourself."

"Always do."

He smacked into the tree.

Rath was a terrible thief. He wanted a real licensed shop with customers and as little fencing as possible, but he'd never make enough to buy his way into the merchant class running under Grell. He'd never make enough without me either, and he couldn't double-cross me because of it. Grell let us keep enough to get by and took enough to keep us crawling back to him. I'd set my sights on cheaper dreams.

Buying my way into the military.

I hefted the purse from my belt, tugged Rath out of his tangle with the tree, and slowed our pace. Rath peered over my shoulder into the purse.

Igna's shiny new silver coins and Erlend's useless old gold clinked around next to a piece of paper. After Our Queen Ignasi ended the civil war between Erlend and Alona, she combined the two nations into Igna and created a new set of currencies. It was meant to unite us or some such nonsense, but I kept finding Erlend gold in Erlend pockets. They couldn't let go of the past.

"Skimming?" Rath elbowed me. "Not like you."

"I'm not reckless." I held up the piece of paper, hiding my fingers behind it as I lifted the ring and squeezed it over an old broken knuckle. "And I like my fingers intact."

"Excuse you." Rath touched the last three fingers of his uninjured hand to his lips, thumb and forefinger curled against his palm. "I'm recklessly ambitious, and who needs fingers?"

"An ambitious ass." I unfolded the paper and grinned. "Praying to the Triad won't grow that finger back."

Rath scowled and made the motion again, exaggerating the move. "What's that?"

"Poster." Emblazoned across the top were branches of lightning striking the green tree of Erlend over the blue waves of

Alona. The Alonian words beneath were repeated in Erlenian, and both were useless to me. "What's it say?"

I could read a handful of words—names and numbers mostly—but Grell preferred to have us totally at his mercy.

"Auditions." Rath traced the Alonian and squinted. He was from the southern coast of Alona, and it showed in the bronze hues of his dark skin and the gray flecks in his black eyes—salted eyes, he called them. "Our Queen of the Eastern Spires and Lady of Lightning requires a new Opal for her Left Hand. Auditions are open to those who receive an invitation or individuals displaying appropriate skill and determination."

Opal was dead then. I picked up our pace. Our Queen's Left Hand was her collection of assassins and personal guards named for the rings she wore—Ruby, Emerald, Opal, and Amethyst.

They belonged to her and did as she pleased, killing those who threatened her rule. Like the Erlend holdouts, the ones holed away up north who'd started the civil war with Alona. They'd used their territory, Nacea, as a distraction to save themselves when the war went rotten. Now Nacea—my country and my people—was dead and gone. It would take me years to get into the military so I could hunt down the Erlend lords responsible, but if I auditioned, I'd have a way into the palace. They'd be mine *now*.

They'd no right to live while Nacea stood razed and empty. Rodolfo da Abreu, the mage who'd done what we'd all dreamed of and murdered the Erlends who'd created the shadows, had the right idea: kill them and make sure they couldn't stir up trouble again.

Of course, he'd ended up dead but so had the Erlend mages fueling the war. I could finish what he'd started and avenge Nacea in one fell swoop.

Six days till the audition. I smacked Rath's shoulder. "Read it to me again—the invitation part."

"Auditions for those with an invitation or appropriately displayed skills." Rath stuffed the poster into my chest pocket. "Who you think got invitations?"

"Young nobles and their friends," I said without hesitation. "Keeps it fair if they think one of theirs is part of the Left Hand and will be for years to come."

I'd never killed anyone, but if Our Queen asked, how could I take issue? She ended the war and corralled the nobles. She was the only person keeping us safe from noble greed, and they courted assassination when they betrayed her—just like Rath and I knew we could hang for thieving.

But I'd have to win to get close to nobles, and I'd never fought trained opponents in a straight bout.

Surely, assassins didn't fight fair.

"There's got to be more to it," I said. The auditions were a closed event, and I'd never heard about what was involved. "If there wasn't, any ass who wanted a title could audition. They must make you kill someone or something."

"The gentle way you say that sets my soul on edge."

I knocked him with my shoulder. "If you can feel your soul, then you need a physician."

"So do you." Rath ripped through a tangle of vines and stumbled onto the path back to town. He'd have been the perfect fighter with broad shoulders and big muscles, but he winced at blood and took to numbers more than punches even after years of robbing coaches. "What would you even do? Rob them on your way to audition?"

"Shows determination, doesn't it?"

"Determination to die." He shuddered. "You never killed anyone, right? None of those soldiers out there rotting?"

I sucked on my teeth. That was a bounty I didn't need. I'd dreamed about killing nobles—kicking faceless Erlend lords till they knew deep in their bones why I'd come for them, till Nacea's final screams were seared into their souls. But those were dreams.

"What would it matter if I had?" I scraped my nail across the silver ring. Plenty of Erlend lords had made fortunes from the razing. Lords like Horatio del Seve, whose name I'd burned into my memory as soon as I'd heard he was selling off Nacean land. "Soldiers would kill us just as quick."

"But it would've been a fair fight—we're thieves. It's their job."

I scowled. "Nothing fair about fighting armored soldiers."

"You're the sort for auditions." He stomped after me, loud and breathy and full of useless opinions. He'd talked about the folks he'd like to have a shot at often enough. "Smashing people's faces in for money."

"I already get paid to fight." I rounded on him, grabbed his collar, and shoved him against a tree. "They know what they're getting into. They sign up to fight—just like me. Don't act like you don't depend on me winning."

"I'm not killing people." The spears rattled on his back.

"Neither am I. You're rigging bets while I'm winning fights."

"Fine." He jabbed me in the ribs and darted around me. "Grell's waiting. Come on."

We hit Tulen a while later, sweaty and shaky. The guards in Grell's pocket let us into the city. I twisted the lady's ring around my finger, glanced down the alley, and pulled it off. Rath was my only companion in the dark, and he was doubled over his knees trying to catch his breath. Our Queen had touched this ring, had pressed her seal into the silver. I'd only ever seen her from afar.

I'd make a deal with The Lady. If I got the ring past Grell, I was clever enough to audition and serve Our Queen. If I didn't, I wouldn't recover in time to audition.

I slipped my knife out of my sheath, slipped my shirt off my shoulder, and drew the tip across my upper arm. Blood welled over the blade, pain burning up my shoulder, and I wiped my knife clean on my sleeve. I pressed the ring against the skin above the cut and wrapped a stolen handkerchief around it. The ring stayed in place.

A little pain, a pretty payoff.

My blood to seal The Lady's prayer.

I wrapped it a few more times, enough to disguise the bulge but let the blood seep through and make it look real. No sign of the ring, a lot of blood, and Rath was still gasping over his boots. Perfect.

The door to the Starved Hatter swung open and Grell shouted, "Check Rath twice."

Rath groaned and struggled to stand. Lorne, one of Grell's chattier guards, lumbered out into the light. I leaned against the door.

Even better—people trusted you if you remembered their name and their problems.

"You're working late." I sucked on my waterskin while Lorne patted his way up Rath's legs. "Thought you'd be suffering through another night with your kid."

"Cayet got the day shift." Lorne unlaced Rath's boots and

yanked up his pants legs, knocking his way around Rath's calves and hips for a while before sliding up to his chest and fluffing out his shirt. "Don't think it matters—kid never wants to sleep when we do."

I rubbed my arm. Pins and needles crawled over my shoulder, but I nodded along like I understood. I couldn't imagine a two-year-old being reasonable about sleeping.

"What happened to you?" Lorne slapped Rath on the shoulder and pushed him out of the way.

"Got stabbed." I held out my bleeding arm and spread my legs, keeping my face neutral. Rath's head jerked to me. I ignored him. He couldn't lie to save his life. Blood kept guards away, and I knew Grell was listening. Drawing attention to a hiding spot wasn't the brightest, but if I named it up front, he'd never think I had anything to hide. "Landed on some fancy, pointy hatpin in the coach."

"You keep it?" Lorne checked my pockets and shoes.

"No. It was wood."

Lorne snorted. "Mouth open."

I stuck out my tongue and turned my head side to side. Lorne collected our purses and walked back to the Hatter, clapping Rath on the shoulder again and patting my uninjured arm. Rath and I glanced at each other. He hooked an arm around my shoulders.

"Hatpin, was it?"

I gritted my teeth. He was smart-mouthed as that noble lady. "Shut it."

Great. Now I needed dirt on him to keep us even.

CHAPTER

THREE

G et up." Rath, his breath reeking of day-old tea, shook me
awake. "Breakfast."

I buried my face in my arms. A flickering, sweaty fire burned
up my arm, and I cracked my eyes open. Rath, backlit and clutch-
ing a cup, elbowed me out of bed. I'd dreamed of storms.

Better than my usual nightmares of creeping darkness, dripping with teeth and blood, but dread still clung to me like it did
on those terrible nights.

I snatched my good shirt from the floor, groping around the
hem, and rubbed the ring with my thumb. It was safely out of
my makeshift bandage and out of sight from prying eyes. Rath
had cleaned my arm while I'd sewn the ring into my hidden shirt
pocket. He'd laughed the whole time.

"You still on about auditioning for Opal?"

"I am, and I know how I'll show my skill." Bounties were plen-
tiful, and I'd the perfect one to turn over as an invitation. Assassins
dealt in death, didn't they? "I need you to distract Grell's guards."

"No. Lords, Sal." He plopped down on the bed next to me, raking a hand through his dark hair. "He kills for looking at him wrong. Whatever you're planning, he'll kill you for it."

Not if I killed him first.

"Might kill us all if the mood strikes him," I said. Grell was responsible for a list of corpses longer than I was tall, and it grew as fast as the children who never had a chance. He killed for skimming, skipping, lying, or anything else that tickled his fancy. He was the one who started kidnapping nobles—I'd found out by accident, and he'd kill me if he knew. Grell and his partners would get us all dragged to the noose eventually.

"He's been running kidnappings on rich folks."

Rath tensed. "Nothing new."

"He cut a deal with some crew down south, but they're killing their marks." Rath would've run if he'd already heard. Hanging for thievery was one thing, but no one decent wanted to be associated with greedy killers. "Moment the wrong rich person dies, Grell won't be able to pay off the guards. They'll come for him, and he'll turn us over to save himself."

Just like the old Erlend lords had. The Erlends had led the shadows through Nacea to slow them down and let the Erlend army escape while Nacea was slaughtered. My people were left as nothing more than stains on the earth where sharp, shapeless claws had flayed them apart. Grell would use us to slow the soldiers so he could escape. We'd all be dead and gone like Nacea.

The only way to stop a slaughter was to stop those who started it, the ones who would do it again—like Our Queen had with the shadows, like Rodolfo da Abreu with their creators, and like I would with Grell and the Erlend lords who'd orchestrated Nacea's ruin to save their own skins.

Rath slumped, fingers gripping my hand. "He'll get us all killed."

"No, he won't. I'm turning him in." His hand, at least, but Rath didn't need to know that. Couldn't risk him snitching on me either. "You run this place right—no killing and no ransoms—and I get my shot at Opal. Everybody in town already loves you. You ran circles around Grell when you were ten."

"You've never cared about being anybody but Sal." He shook his head. "Opal has to kill people for no reason other than Our Queen's say-so."

"That's enough for me." I twisted my head away so he wouldn't see my flush. Our Queen was my hero, and rightly so because she'd sucked all the magic from the land. The shadows were nothing without it. Magic bound them to the earth, trapping them here long after their bodies were gone and their minds broken. The moment Our Queen rid this land of magic, the shadows fell apart. I owed her thousands of lives. My life. "She saved me. I'll do anything she asks so long as it keeps her on the throne."

And I'd enjoy a few of the kills if they were the right ones.

Rath had grown up too far south to see the shadows, but he went fidgety whenever we talked about them. Even their rumors bred a lifetime of fear—monsters quick as the wind and sharp as knives desperately trying to rebuild the bodies stolen from them. Their flayed victims still haunted my dreams.

"It'll be justice," I said softly. Anyone who'd killed so many and could live with that, thinking they were fit to lead the people they'd sacrifice so quickly, didn't have a place in this world. "Doesn't mean I'll torture them. Just kill them."

"Just kill them." Rath laughed and made the sign of the Triad, hand lingering over his heart. "You even sleep last night?"

"Napped a bit."

He sighed. "A distraction all you need?"

"Enough for his guards to leave." Grell always barricaded himself in his room and ran the numbers after a job came in. He never let his guards inside, but he stationed them at the door in the hallway. He'd be alone all day. "Long enough for me to get inside."

"Fine, but you owe me." He dragged me off the bed and squeezed my shoulder. "Go. I'll have them gone by the time you get there."

Lady bless him.

The hallway outside Grell's room was empty and silent by the time I got there. I rapped on the door. My chest ached with each deep, steadying breath, and I shifted. Something about what I was about to do writhed in my chest and tightened my throat. Grell had a bounty on his head—dead or alive. He had it coming.

"In." Grell's rumbling voice rolled through the cracks in the door.

Grell lounged at his desk in a haze of smoke. I clicked the door shut and locked it behind me. With his eye pressed to a jeweler's scope and focused on a jasper ring, Grell didn't notice. I edged forward and ducked my head, and he eventually glanced up at me. The bag of knucklebones on his desk rattled when he moved.

Waiting was fine. We were nuisances, and he was gracious enough to see us. Grell loved power plays. Me playing along meant I wasn't here to surprise him.

I was starting to wonder if I should've gone with surprise instead but too late now.

"What's this about?" He hacked into a handkerchief. He'd been like me once—small, underfed, overworked—but he'd used the years of robberies and money to his advantage.

His giant frame was all muscle and show. Street fighting had built his empire and his temper, but it ruined his left shoulder, right knee, and ribs. They'd snap with a good hit if the easy way failed.

"Rath's crossed you." I pinched myself to keep my lies focused. "He's going to try to buy his way out."

Grell lurched to his feet and leaned against his desk, towering over me with all his scars and muscles.

"And you want what for ratting him out?" Grell spread his arms in the least welcoming embrace I'd ever seen. "Doesn't breed confidence keeping you around."

"I don't want to run with him anymore." I fidgeted in fake fear and shuffled forward, pointing to the map of Kursk on the wall. Grell followed. "If he's planning on splitting, he'll muck us up. I'm not getting hanged because he's thinking about leaving."

"One job." Grell leaned over my shoulder, exhaled sweet blue smoke, and tapped the map with a crooked finger. "Then you go back to your lot, and I replace Rath."

"Thanks." I yanked the pin with my name on it from the wall. It was heavy and thick, with a point sharp enough to pierce thin wood.

"No reward for snitching." He tore Rath's pin from the wall and tossed it aside. "Get out."

I buried my pin in Grell's neck. He flailed and clawed at his throat. I spun, my back hitting the wall. He reared, face pulled up in a wild, openmouthed sneer, and swung for my face. I caught it in the forearm and the hit shook my bones. His fingers curled around my arm.

Shit.

He flung me across the room. I skidded over his desk, knocking papers and jewels to the floor and cracking my head on the ink blotter. I blinked away the black and pulled my knees to my chest. Grell gurgled.

Lady bless, I'd messed up. He'd a pin in his neck, wasn't down, and was spitting angry. I yanked the knife from my boot.

Grell threw himself at me. I rammed my heels into his chest.

His ribs snapped.

Grell smacked backward into the wall, blood oozing from under the hand clutched to his neck. I slid off the desk, floor rolling beneath me and pain aching at the back of my head. I gripped the desk and swallowed the bile in my throat. My ears rang.

"I meant to be quick." I slurred, my mind a step behind. "Sorry."

Grell's red-rimmed eyes fluttered open. Spurts of blood painted the wall, and he blinked at me. His breathing was quick and frantic, chest too tight, and I knelt before him. He tightened the hand around his neck.

"Nothing personal." I stepped on his free arm, pinning it to the floor, and flipped my knife around. "But I need a hand."

Grell tried to tug at my bootlaces, fingers weak, and I pressed my palm to his chest. His heart thrummed beneath my hand as it struggled to keep up with the hole in his neck. I slipped my knife between his ribs, slick and easy. Grell gasped.

His heart stopped.

His hand fell.

I eased away, bitterness stuck in the back of my throat. My knife clattered to the ground. Scattered gold and finger bones rolled around my feet as I pried Grell's old sword from the wall behind his desk. My heart tried to beat its way out of my chest.

I'd the appropriate skill.

I took another breath, fingers catching up with my thoughts as I grasped the sword with both hands. I sliced the blade through Grell's wrist. His bones snapped as easily as Rath's, and the scrape of metal against *him* shuddered down my spine. The sword slipped from my trembling hands.

He was only Grell.

He wasn't good, not even a little bit. He'd taken nine-year-old Rath's finger with a laugh and a sharpened knife.

Opal wouldn't be bothered. Grell had to die, and I had to do it, like Opal with one of Our Queen's marks. Wasn't anything wrong with this.

This burning weight writhing in my chest and bubbling up my throat had no place in Opal's life.

I coughed, heaved, and lost my breakfast in the corner. Up and out, no more of that. Nothing left to make me sick over killing Grell. He'd made his choices, and I'd made mine. I would be Opal.

With Grell da Sousa's hand heavy in mine, I fled.

CHAPTER

FOUR

I left town soon as I was done scrubbing the blood from my
tunic. I fit in well enough with the other dust-covered travelers on the wagon heading to Willowknot, the city next to
the new palace, but I ran out of money after three days on
the road. All I could do was pick at the dried blood under
my nails.

I wasn't used to all that happened with Grell. I'd not been
able to stand the sight of blood for years after the war. It was too
wrong, too against everything I'd been taught as a kid. Just had
to get familiar with it again.

My home, Nacea, had been small, wedged between Erlend and
Alona and ruled from afar by Erlend lords. A territory allowed to
keep its queen and god in exchange for tribute.

Then Erlend and Alona went to war and called their mages
to the front lines. Nacea didn't deal in magic. The Lady, our
godly Lady of Nacea, was not to be stolen from. She wasn't
human or flesh but magic in every form. Mages used her up,

forced her into the old handwritten language of runes, and devoured her power.

She devoured them right back—runes rotted their flesh and minds, leaving nothing but mindless souls.

Shadows of the people they'd once been.

The Erlend mages didn't know, of course. They'd never pushed so far, tried so hard for innovation than during the war, but the damage was done. The perfect soldiers they'd tried to make couldn't be called back. The shadows had no bodies and no minds, only broken souls, memories of a face, and an all-consuming need to get back their stolen flesh. They scoured the lands looking for themselves and flayed the skin off any they found.

Erlend's lords realized their mistake too late but not too late to save themselves and ruin Nacea.

I dreamed of a family I couldn't recognize in death, of neighbors' faces stitched into a patchwork of skin. There'd been no help, no aid, and no memorials. We'd been forgotten.

I would make Erlend remember.

"Lady, help me." I tilted my head to the sunny sky, looking to where The Lady's stars would be tonight.

There was no room for gods in a world of monsters and monstrous men, but tradition endured.

"She's helping herself." My neighbor in the carriage waved a freshly calloused hand toward the horizon. He was new to hunger, clinging to the family crest around his neck that would fetch plenty if he sold it. Runes decorated his arms. An old out-of-work mage. "A shadow on Erlend's rising sun."

An Erlend mage who thought I was speaking of Our Queen. I scowled. The wagon I was taking to Willowknot collected people at each turn, and my seat was more knees and elbows than wood. Grell's hand, wrapped in three old sacks and perfumed linen, was wedged under my thighs. I'd no space to stretch and no patience for asses.

"Did you see the shadows?" I asked. Our Queen's palace was built over the ruins of the old mages' keep on the defunct border between Erlend and Alona. They were one nation now and had no reason for the school with magic gone. She'd been Head Priestess of the Mind before the war. The other two head priests had created the shadows. She'd tried them as war criminals after Rodolfo was done with them, but the gallows were a faster death than they'd deserved.

I liked Rodolfo's methods more—a taste of their own treatment and no Erlends left who could spread the knowledge of shadow creation. He'd died to save us all from the threat of shadows ever returning.

"Lies." The old mage spat out of the carriage. "People afraid of their own damned shadows, afraid of going to war, afraid of protecting what we'd built. And look at the trash that rose from our ruin."

I clucked my tongue. Wooden spires loomed over the roofs and battlements, and sunlight sparkled in the stained glass windows circling the towers. Walls of glass dyed blue and gold glinted with each jerk of the wagon. The new Igna flag fluttered over every peak.

"And look at the trash Our Queen hasn't claimed," I said as I lurched to my feet and yanked my bag from the floor, whacking him with Grell's hand. "When will her Left Hand reach for you?"

He paled. As the carriage came to a halt, I rushed away from him and laughed the rest of my walk to Willowknot.

A collection of guards shuffled through travel papers and checked bags at the city gates. I unwound the linen from Grell's hand. Might as well be upfront with it.

The line of people scattered. Grell's hand reeked, flowers and perfume barely clinging to his rotten fingers.

"How do I declare this?" I asked, holding it up.

"Drop it." A guard, pink cheeks fading to pale green, leveled his spear at my chest. "Tell me your name."

"No, it'll splatter. My name's Sal." I held my arms out as far as I could and flipped back my hood, dirty strands of black hair falling across my eyes. Should've sheared it again before I left. "It's my invitation."

"Take a break, Hackett. They're here for the Left Hand auditions." Another guard nudged the spear away from me and prodded Grell's hand with a gloved finger, chuckling the entire time. "You got an actual invitation or just the hand?"

"Just the hand." I shrugged. "Poster said invitation or proof of skill."

Grell's warrant included a handprint taken when he'd been arrested a few years back, all his identifiable scars immortalized in ink on the posters. They even listed the tattoos around his knuckles.

The too-small signet ring on his middle finger wasn't on the posters, but he'd gotten it after the arrest and had never been able to slide it over his knuckle again. If the handprints and posters weren't enough, it was.

"Who's this then?" the guard asked, shoving Hackett aside before he could vomit on our boots. "Most folks bring heads."

"Grell da Sousa from Kursk. I wasn't going to travel for days with a rotting head, and his warrant description includes his hands."

"Gang leaders fetch a pretty pearl, but Ruby's been rough with the uninvited this year. There's more of you than usual, and they already got eight invitees. You got anything else?" He tossed a handkerchief to Hackett and rapped hard on the gate. "Another one for the auditions!"

"Only knives and the hand." I pulled on my old mask and yanked my hood back onto my head.

The guard beckoned me through a short door in the gate, steps leading down into a well-worn tunnel beneath the city. No room for thieves and killers on the public streets of our new capital. "You travel light."

I'd given up everything else. It would've only dragged me down.

CHAPTER

FIVE

R uby's face was a beacon of red among the black-clothed
auditioners. His mask glowed in the sunlight and cast flickers of red across the ground. He'd no visible eyes or nose, only a
single smiling slit that split his cheeks from ear to ear. The gap
was dark with metal mesh.

I knew there were eyeholes—he had to see somehow—but
when his eyeless face turned to me, I shuddered.

"Name?" The metal muffled his voice. He was dressed in pale
off-whites. Thick tan leggings covered his powerful legs, and his
knee-length tunic, slit up to his hips, was sleeveless and fitted.
The muscles in his arms tensed with each gesture.

"Sal." I lowered Grell's hand.

He tipped my hood back with one long scarred finger. No
armor and no weapons. If not for the mask, I'd not have thought
him Ruby. "Aliases?"

"Sal."

"Nicknames?" I swore I heard him laugh behind his mask.

"Sal."

"Grell da Sousa—an interesting bounty." He plucked Grell's hand from my fingertips and held it up. A nail tumbled from the green-veined flesh. "How'd you kill him? You couldn't have gotten his hand without killing the man."

I winced. The crowd behind Ruby tried to catch a glimpse of me, and I shuffled so Ruby blocked their view. "Pin in the neck and knife in the ribs. It was quick."

The crowd was getting fidgety, and I was too with their eyes on me. They were all thick and tall with well-fed muscles and shiny new clothes. A few sported worn leather bracers and empty quivers. I'd nothing but two knives.

"Your knife work was sloppy."

"I used a sword. A dull one. Pulled it off the wall in Grell's office. Didn't want to ruin my knives." I sucked in a breath and steadied my voice when Ruby huffed in response. "I'll get better with practice."

"Lovely." Ruby flung Grell's hand aside and pointed toward the soldier who'd led me here. "Practice on him."

I lunged. The soldier only had time to widen his eyes and raise his fists. I thrust my foot into his crotch. He gasped and crumbled.

Worked on everyone.

I clutched his collar and pulled him to his knees. He was a soldier. He'd signed up to die for Our Queen and this was his service. I slid behind him, one foot on his pants to hold him down, and pinned his shoulders between my knees. I needed to be Opal, and he needed to die. I gripped either side of his head.

"Nothing personal." I blinked away the image of his face.

"Stop." Ruby pressed a hand to the top of the soldier's head. "Let him go."

I dropped him. He scrambled away and vanished into the crowd watching the auditioners. Ruby tilted my chin up, his mockery of a face grinning down at me.

I hadn't heard Ruby move. Hadn't seen him.

"Join the others." He pulled a small black mask from his pocket, the sort one wore to the gallows that went over your head like a hood—thin and black with a sliver of a mouth and wide eyeholes. A pure white "23" as big as the mask was stitched across the face. "You're Twenty-Three now. No more Sal."

"Thank you." I pulled the mask from his hands, fingers shaking.

One step closer to Opal, to the Erlends, to cleansing the hunger for revenge from my blood.

Ruby huffed and waved me away. The auditioners all stared— Five raked me over with pale eyes, Fifteen rolled his massive shoulders back, and Thirteen, hooded gaze focused on my hands, showed off the old jagged runes etched into her arm. I held back a shudder.

No one spoke. We snuck silent, less-than-secret glances at each other while Ruby paced across the gate. Most auditioners were taller than me. Fifteen was the tallest, and Seventeen was the widest. Three was stoop-shouldered and slouching, all wiry muscles, but her belt had worn spots for knife sheaths. Twenty-One's long nose tented his mask.

Auditioners One through Eight must've been the invited— their masks were slightly better, their stances slightly looser, and most of them seemed my age or close enough.

Great.

The tunnel gate creaked open. Hackett, the soldier I'd made sick, peered around the crack. A brawny arm hooked through the opening above his head and forced the gate open. Ruby stilled.

"Name?" Ruby's voice was the perfect mixture of bored and cutting.

"Victor dal Graf," the newcomer said. He was a street fighter—I knew his type—with scarred, swollen knuckles and a crooked nose.

Two and Four snorted, and a few others I couldn't see laughed. Killers with information were dangerous people.

"Aliases?" Ruby circled Victor. "Nicknames?"

"Snap Bone," said Victor. He looked strong enough to snap my thigh. "I fight down in Kursk."

I'd never heard of him.

"Undoubtedly." He waved Hackett forward. "Victor, kill him."

Hackett backtracked.

"Kill him?" Victor's eyebrows bunched together. "What's he done?"

Ruby nodded and held out his hand. "Thank you, Victor, but that will be all."

Ruby waved Victor to the gate. Hackett clapped Victor on the back while another, with one arm and enough height to reach, whispered in Victor's ear. The gate shut behind them in a puff of dust.

"So." Ruby spread his arms wide in welcome, scars from years of sword work and fighting black in the sunlight, and laughed. "It begins with twenty-three."

CHAPTER
SIX

Ruby stalked around us, eyeless mask looking us up and down. "This audition will end with one of you becoming Opal. Either the Left Hand, under the guidance of Our Queen, will select the most promising from the remaining three or the last living auditioner will ascend to the position."

A side door to the building next to us opened and a line of servants filed out. Ruby beckoned them forward.

"There are only three rules while you are here: kill your competition, do not get caught doing so, and do not harm anyone outside of the audition. If any member of the Left Hand has significant evidence of your involvement in a death—enough to secure an arrest and sentencing were you brought before court—you will be disqualified. If we believe your actions caused injury or could have harmed anyone not involved, you will be disqualified or killed. At our discretion. Any questions?" Ruby raised his head, blinding us with flickers of red light, and clapped. "Excellent. A servant will take you to your room. I hope to see fewer of you at breakfast."

Ruby meandered over to the soldiers we'd been asked to kill upon arrival and dismissed us with an offhanded wave.

A free-for-all. I didn't need a servant getting in my way with laundry and cleaning and whatever else they did. They might be great for gossip, but the last thing I needed while auditioning was nosy questions about my clothes.

Or an extra person who could rat me out to the Left Hand.

"Auditioner Twenty-Three?" A servant wearing a plain gray uniform trimmed in blue with no jewelry or weapons bowed her head to me. "If you'd come with me to your room."

She led me through a series of unobtrusive servants' hallways. Patches of rough mortar from recent renovations dotted the walls, and wooden support beams crisscrossed the ceiling above us. Just enough grip to climb and enough space to hide. My servant opened a door in the middle of a hall.

"A bath is prepared—"

"By who?" I asked. The room was small and drafty—the shuttered windows were glassless and the door off-kilter. A washing tub rested in one corner and a ratty straw mattress in the other. Rath's orphanage horror stories at least had raised beds for the kids to share.

Of course, we'd probably ruin everything with blood. I'd not waste the good bedding on us either.

She inhaled sharply. "I prepared a bath, for bathing, for you."

"I know what bathing is." I checked the lock on the door—weak and easy to pick—and the window shutters. "You clean it too?"

"I did."

I prodded the pile of fresh black clothes on the bed and ran a finger along the tub's rim. Curls of salted, mineralized steam dampened my sleeves. "Where'd you get the water?"

"The well. I am a servant, and as such, I answer to Dimas, not the Left Hand. If you take offense with how I draw your bath, you may take it up with him."

I leaned against the tub. "Not taking offense. I just don't fancy dying before the competition even starts."

"I will endeavor to keep poison out of your baths and meals then," she said dryly. "You've never worked with servants?"

I gestured for her to shut the door. I didn't need everyone knowing my whole life story. I'd robbed a few servants and known folks who'd taken scullery maid jobs, but that was it.

"You'll know me only as Maud." She settled against the door, hands clasped behind her. "I'll cook your meals, except break-fast, do all your cleaning, washing, and other such chores. But I've no obligation to help you win. I report any suspicions, or I lose my job."

I nodded. "I'll keep the suspicious bloodstains to a minimum then."

"That would be preferable." Her mouth twitched into a tight-lipped smile. "But the black should hide most of the blood, and I can remove any stains that aren't."

"Keep my clothes clean and the other auditioners far from my things. No questions or gossiping about me. Not about my scars, my clothes, or my measurements. I dress how I like to be addressed—he, she, or they. It's simple enough." I ticked each point off on my fingers for emphasis. Even when I spelled it out for nosy people clear as I could, they couldn't grasp why.

I'd settled for hand-me-down clothes and shit lodgings for life.

I wasn't compromising me. Our Queen preached acceptance and peace. They'd accept me.

They had to.

"If I make a mistake addressing you, you may correct me." She swept past me to the bath, touched the water, and tapped her damp finger to her tongue. "If it helps you to know, Opal's servant is paid five pearls per month. I take pride in my job, and I need it to survive. I will not err in serving you."

I whistled. Enough to keep four people well and fed for a long while. I'd never heard of serving jobs paying in pearls. My savings were in plain, old copper halves, and sixty-four made a silver.

"Nothing wrong with being in it for the money," I said. If she wanted it that badly, she'd be more open to helping me. With nothing but three loose rules and a broken door between me and the others, I'd be dead by morning. "Do I get any money while I'm here? I'm going to need some things to stay alive."

"The Left Hand set aside a small amount for the auditioners assuming some wouldn't have the appropriate funds." She pulled out a purse no bigger than her hand.

"Twine, wire, mice—"

"What?"

I sighed. "For testing my food. Mice, bells, ax, hammer, nails, and a better blanket." The door was useless, and I'd have to nail it shut and string the entryway with wire. That'd at least slow attackers down. "You get that, I'll bathe, and knock twice when you get back. Bring me breakfast tomorrow too. Something small."

She came back as I was getting dressed. Her sleeves were rolled up, bruises from cleaning dotting her arms in fading shades of blue and yellow, and a large basket dangled on her arm. She locked the door behind her.

Smart.

"I've got what you wanted." She set down the basket and rubbed one of the callouses on her palm. "I will not deal with the mice. They are yours to care for."

"Deal." Mice were better poison testers than Maud anyway. I nodded to the door and held out my hand—might as well make working together official. "You don't get in my way or get me killed, we'll get on fine. And you'll get your five pearls."

Maud smiled, more bared teeth than grin, and bowed instead of taking my hand. "You won't even know I'm here."

Doubtful.

I nailed the door shut behind her. She was serious, and money was a good motivator. If the Left Hand said she wasn't part of the audition, she wasn't. I'd have to trust her not to poison me. The moment she got nosy about my clothes, she was gone. Wasn't like laundry was a necessity.

Sliding the lady's ill-fitting silver ring on for luck, I lined the window with nails and laced the shutters with wire and bells. Least I'd have time to wake up before they broke in, and if they did, there was no dodging an ax in this small room.

"First night," I said to the mice. I tipped the dirty bath water down the drain in the corner, made a person-shaped bump in the bed, and leaned against the drying tub. The ax was heavy in my hands. "Think they'll come?"

Let them. They'd get an ax in the face and a handful of pain.

CHAPTER
SEVEN

T he bells rang once that night, soft and chiming beneath the screams echoing down the halls. Someone's hand plucked the wire, but the bells sent them back into the night. I spent the morning removing nails from the door.

"There's blood," Maud said when she entered, shuddering with each word. "You're expected at breakfast if you can walk."

I snatched up a roll from her small—thankfully covered—tray and squished the thick yellow butter between the two halves. "You get sick at the sight of blood, we'll have problems."

"Breakfast will be served every morning, and you're to attend so the Left Hand can do a head count." She frowned, ignoring my comment about blood. "I won't bring you anything again unless you ask for it."

I nodded. "Where's it at?"

Maud led me down the hallway, servants bowing out of the way.

Food, a room, and no fear of getting robbed the moment I turned my back—I could get used to this. Should get used to this.

It would be this way till I died, no matter if that was tonight or twenty years from now.

Might get stabbed to death at any moment, but that could happen anywhere.

Maud had slipped a long black dress with thick leggings into the basket for me this morning. With a quick twirl, flaring the dress out around me, I nicked a plum from a wide-eyed servant's tray and slipped it under my mask. If we were eating with the Left Hand, we were eating well. I needed to take full advantage of it, gain some weight so I could stand against the others. Maud wrinkled her nose.

"Breakfast." She opened a door at the end of the hall and opened her mouth again, but a soft voice cut her off.

"Can't imagine you sleeping in with those bells."

I spun, plum flying out of my hand. Four, a boy about my age with curly black hair peeking out from the back of his mask, leapt down from a hallway rafter. He was stout and muscular and barely made a sound walking next to me. His hands were a map of pitted scars.

"Don't worry—loved those bells." He followed me into the breakfast hall and held up a freshly stitched arm, the catgut neat and white against his dark skin. He was handsome and he knew it, flashing me a smile when I only glared at him. "Told everyone where I was. Clever, clever."

I rolled my shoulders back and tried to take up as much space as possible next to this firm powerhouse. "I figured I'd get one night of sleep before the real competition started."

"You'd a better night than Twenty-One." Four winked and wandered to the far side of the table, sitting next to Two and Three.

The tall long-nosed auditioner was out then. Of course, the

ones I couldn't tell apart didn't have the decency to die first and make it easy on me.

I dropped into a chair near Two, Three, and Four. They had come to breakfast together and Four kept calling Two "Lady Luck." She waved him off each time with a bandaged hand.

Most of us were young, no wrinkles around the eyes or spotted hands. All the easier to mold us into the assassin The Left Hand wanted. If we lived.

Nine auditioners were missing. The only invited auditioner not at the table was One, and I'd no idea if Ruby would be impressed or disappointed.

Didn't matter much either way. I was here and nine of the others weren't. Only fourteen left.

Five snapped at a passing server. His hands—the blistered pink of sun-seared white skin—cut through the air, fingers pointed and straight as knives, and jabbed at the servant as he whispered. He rudely pointed at what he wanted and where he wanted it. No one else paid him any mind.

Five definitely grew up with servants.

Four too. At least he spoke to his servant like they were a person and thanked them for the little mug of fruity red tea steaming up our end of the table. I clasped my hands.

No use eating unless I knew it was safe for sure. I'd no knowledge of poisons.

The main doors burst open. Ruby swirled into the room in a storm of colored silk with his sword belt bound around his narrow hips and arms thrown wide. His sword hung in a silver-plated sheath, and the melon-shaped pommel slapped his upper thigh. The blade was curved and long as my arm.

"Nine dead. Lovely. If you keep taking my advice, we'll be out of here by dinner." Ruby meandered around the table, trailing his fingers along the back of our chairs, and sat at the far end. He tilted his head to the side in mock consideration. "You're doing so much better than my year."

His invisible gaze raised the hair on my arms. His audition was seven years ago, and I'd been running my first jobs for Grell. Amethyst was the newest member, winning her mask three years back, and gossip about her hadn't spread far either. Emerald was the only original left—handpicked by the Queen at the end of the Mage War as a personal guard. The dead Opal had joined right after her.

"Hardly anything to be proud of—your audition was full of pissants," said a lilting voice behind me. "I bet only auditioners Two through Eight did anything last night other than cower."

I ground my teeth together and twisted round in a huff.

My retort rushed out of me.

Emerald, a vision of steel and green silk, glided through the doorway. She was lithe and muscled, arms bare and flexed, streaked in scars with a pale silver dust shining over her skin like white-capped waves on the cool, deep black of distant ocean. She walked past me in a breeze of perfume and peppermint, the apothecary scents clinging to her like the old black ink of the dead runes scrawled across her. The silk layered and draped over her shoulders matched her high-cheeked, mouthless emerald mask perfectly. Beetle wings stitched into the train of her dress glittered in the light.

Emerald was the only person to ever face a mage's shadow alone and survive—the scar slicing through her hairline and peeking out from behind her mask proof enough of that—and she was only a few strides away from me.

"Killing is simple," Emerald said as she folded herself into a chair and plucked up a teakettle, pouring a small measure in her glass. She added a splash of milk. "Secrets are hard."

Ruby rested his chin on his laced fingers. "Who was seen?"

"Thirteen is disqualified and dismissed." Emerald handed Ruby her cup. "Your servant will gather your belongings and a guard will escort you out. Thank you for trying."

"Who?" Thirteen cracked her hands against the table, upending mugs and sending her plate flying. "You have to tell us who—give us an appeal. There wasn't anyone there."

Emerald picked up a spoon, holding it like a knife, and Thirteen stilled. "Four people reported your blunder. You're dismissed."

Thirteen kicked her chair, heel snapping a leg in half.

"Lady Emerald gave you an order," a rough voice said. Heavy footsteps muffled by the sound of shifting leather armor crept behind me. A pale purple mask—eyes missing, mouth one severe line—glinted in the corner of my sight. "Take it."

Thirteen scrambled out of the hall.

"Unless anyone else would like to disobey, we'll go over the nuances of your new, brief lives." Emerald tilted her chin up, looking for questions in the absence of us seeing her face. We kept quiet. "Whoever you were yesterday is dead. Your lives are ours now, until you are either dead or dismissed. Since we are selecting a new member of the court, there are additional rules you must follow. If you break them, I will kill you."

"We eat breakfast together." Ruby poured a cup of tea and held it out to Amethyst. "We do not attempt to kill each other or anyone else during this time. Breakfast is our time. You finish your business before or after. We always dine together in the mornings, and we'd like for you to learn how to be sociable morning people."

Emerald slid a thick pat of butter into the center of a dark roll, stuffed shaved ham in after it, and stood. A southerner's breakfast. Interesting thing to pick when your mask had no opening for the mouth. "We will hold physical training sessions all day, every day. You need not attend if you feel adequately masterful, but do remember we are watching. One of you will be Our Queen's new Opal, and we cannot afford mediocrity."

"So eat well and relax." Amethyst gestured to the spread of food across the table.

"This morning, we will evaluate you separately. Every other morning until we say otherwise, you are expected to play nicely until training starts." Ruby stood, beckoning a servant with a bloodred collar, and waved halfheartedly to the table. "You will do best if you remember this is a test and we are the overseers."

Emerald picked up her plate and vanished through a side door. Amethyst followed and Ruby's servant slipped through the door ahead of him. Ruby spared us one last glance over his shoulder.

"A word of advice—don't be predictable. From this day on, predictability will kill you," Ruby said. "We'll start with Two."

Two rose to her feet as graceful as any dancer and took a deep breath. Three and Four watched her go.

How were we supposed to stay unpredictable if they had us in timed lessons all day?

"A long night, a longer morning." Four eyed the rest of the table over his cup of tea. "Testing our patience perhaps."

I poured myself a cup—flowery and light, much softer on my tongue than I was used to—and ignored his questioning gaze. Observations, studying your mark, knowing when to make your move. Only difference between robbery and murder was what you stole.

"Tea's too gentle," Three muttered to Four. "You'd think if anyone deserved a pick-me-up, it'd be us."

I grinned. The southwestern coast of Alona was famous for its stronger teas, and it was Rath's one true indulgence.

Four shrugged. "Not enough of us here to warrant it."

I pulled my plate toward me. The table was spread with enough food for an army troop. They'd laid it out to appeal to anyone, and everyone was taking advantage. Five drizzled oil over a piece of toast layered with tomatoes and minced garlic, and seven others followed his lead, reaching for the common breakfast of northerners. I'd never gotten a taste for tomatoes before noon.

But they had, and now I knew where they were from.

"Didn't realize there was an *us*," I said in Erlenian. The languages were so close they might as well have been the same except for a dozen handfuls of odd words and phrases. They had been the same once, but politics had pushed them apart. I dropped a piece of thin bread on my plate, drowned it in oil and garlic, and slid a tomato slice on top. Least I could save myself from the tasteless muck of tomatoes by adding garlic. "You're awful chatty for someone in a competition to the death."

I'd give them no hints about who I was or where I was from, not like the hints they were giving me. I'd no runes and no striking features, only warm umber skin and a handful of scars. I'd nothing left for them to take, no friends and no family, other than my place as Opal.

And it was mine.

Four offered me another tomato. "While the bells were a lovely touch, you're too short to put any fear in me. Nothing personal."

I speared the tomato with my knife.

"Three!"

We all turned to the door. Two glided into the room with her fists clenched and mask askew. She whispered to Three as they passed.

We sat in silence after that. Only the scrape of knives against plates and the rattle of spoons in cups broke the quiet. Five crunched his way through his toast, half-listening to Eight and Seven whispering back and forth. The split between Erlend and Alona had changed more than the languages. Five was the image of an arrogant northern lord, all splayed limbs and cocked head, taking up a good hand's width of Two's spot at the table.

Three returned, and Two knocked Five out of her space in her haste to pull out Three's chair. Four left, returned, and then Five, Six, another and another. Each private meeting lasted long enough to let me settle before the red-collared servant shouted the next number. I twisted the ring round and round my finger, rubbing the sigil with my thumb, and breakfast rebelled in my stomach. Five had sword work callouses and a fancy gold necklace shoved under his collar. An apothecary sigil covered Eleven's slender shoulder. Eight walked with the telltale gait of someone with a knife in his boot. But I was skilled and worrying wouldn't help.

"Twenty-Three!"

I rose, rolling my shoulders back, and took long, steady strides to the door.

Let the audition begin.

CHAPTER
EIGHT

Amethyst's mask was lopsided when I entered, the dusky ribbons loose around her head and barely knotted. Emerald flicked her fingers to get my attention. I sat in the lone chair.

"I can see your first problem." Emerald leaned across the couch and rested her chin on long crooked fingers. "You're far too underfed."

"Not uncommon for uninvited auditioners." Ruby peered at me through his eyeless mask, and the sting of it burned the tips of my ears. Up close, I could tell there was a thin mesh—soft metal or cloth—painted to match the red covering where his eyes would be. He tilted his head to the side. "Twenty-Three, Sal, Sal, Sal, brought the hand of Grell da Sousa. Knife work was sloppy but willing to practice."

Amethyst chuckled. "Grell da Sousa? The old street fighter in Kursk?"

"One and only." I nodded, spreading out the hem of my dress so I was sitting like Emerald—taking up space and showing off what muscles I had but not splayed out like Five had been.

"What do you do?" Emerald studied my feet and worked her way up to my face. She corrected my posture till my spine was straight as hers. "You look like a runner."

"Thief." I stiffened. "Highway jobs, housebreaking, and some street fighting on the side."

"I take it you're one of those haunting the highways, terrorizing poor coaches, and stealing all our things." Ruby crossed his legs and let out a soft laugh that made me think it wasn't a question at all. He turned to the others. "They killed Grell with a pin."

Emerald scoffed. "You killed him with a pin?"

"He marked his routes on wall maps and held them up with old hat pins. It was safer to get him near a map. He expected knives." I shifted, the "they" hot in my ears. "And you can call me 'she' when I dress like this. I dress how I am."

Which was fine by me. I wore a dress, and people treated me like a girl. I wore trousers and one of those floppy-collared men's shirts, and they treated me like a boy. No annoying questions or fights over it.

"And if you dress like neither?" Emerald asked.

"They," I said. Rath had asked once, a while after we'd met and been living together, and I'd not known how to explain it yet. I didn't have the words. He always felt like Rath, and I always felt like Sal, except it was like watching a river flow past. The river was always the same, but you never glimpsed the same water. I ebbed and flowed, and that was my always. Rath not understanding that had hurt the most, but at least he accepted it. "I'm not always 'they' though."

"Understood."

The moment passed, and the tilt of Emerald's chin and nod of Ruby's head made me think it would never happen again.

"What else can you do?" Amethyst beckoned me and pried off my gloves. "Don't be humble."

"I'm quick, good at climbing, sleight of hand." I flexed my arm while Amethyst tested my muscle. "I was the best fighter in Tulen and most of Kursk."

"Any real training in anything?" Emerald tugged Amethyst away and studied the pads of my fingers. "Trade? Carnival? Apothecary?"

I shook my head. "Just street fighting."

"She was about to snap our dear Roland's neck," Ruby said to Emerald. "Not standard street fighting."

I shrugged. "I have many skills."

"Doesn't everyone?" Ruby laughed. "Now, what don't you know?"

"Poisons." I didn't miss a beat and sighed to myself when Emerald shook her head. "I can use knives but not swords. Never used a spear. I shot a bow once and missed, and I don't know a thing about court life. Can't read Erlenian—bit better at Alonian—and never learned how to write either."

The three of them all shifted at that.

"And I need to practice my knife work."

"All fixable ailments if you so desire." Ruby leaned forward, collar flopping open and scars peeking out from under his shirt. White scars on dark skin. They must've been carved by magic. He'd been a mage. "Alona had public schools. Why didn't you attend?"

"I was only five," I said with another shrug. "And you still have to buy supplies and a uniform."

Ruby hummed. "Who are you, Sal, Sal, Sal?"

"What does it matter?"

Sal was gone. That was the point, wasn't it? I wasn't tied to anything, no one knew my face, and I'd no friends or family that could be held against me, no allies to betray me. I had inherited ghosts, and I would become one.

"It matters to us." Emerald tapped her mask. She didn't wear jewelry, didn't drape herself in the silver chains commonly found in the carriages we raided, but her fingers were jewelry themselves. She'd glued ovals of a brassy metal over the nails. "The new Opal will be our partner, our business consultant, and our friend. They will be the only person outside of Our Queen to know our faces, and we will know theirs. They will be one of us."

"We have to select someone we can live with." Amethyst nodded to me. "We have to know who all of you are, so we may know whom we are inviting into our safe haven. And we will find out who you are regardless of how honest you are."

"So who are you?" asked Ruby.

"Sallot Leon."

The trio stilled. My full name gave away too much. Only Naceans kept their mother's first name as part of their own, a holdover from the old days when there were more countries, more traditions. My grandmother had been Margot, my mother Leon Margot, and I was Sallot Leon. It was all I remembered and all I had left.

All I had that was truly mine.

"Why bother learning Erlenian or Alonian when you're not from either country?" Emerald flexed her fingers. "Few Naceans escaped the shadows."

History said we'd been massacred by errant magic. An accident. A casualty of war.

But I knew our murder was orchestrated. I remembered the soldiers reading letters the day before they left. I remembered them fleeing in a panic. I remembered their whispers about "orders."

"One," I said softly. "I have never met another."

Ruby let out a long sigh. "There was no Leon in the Nacean royal line."

My parents had been farmers. Sending off our best sheep as tribute to the queen was as royal as they'd gotten.

"No, the Last Star of Nacea was named Namrantha. No political tangles." Emerald evened her head with mine. "In a few moments, you will head to strength training, archery, and sword work. The nights are for personal reflection and competition, and we may offer personalized training. You will attend all three training sessions every day until we say otherwise. If you're still alive by then."

"I will be."

"Lovely." Ruby unfurled from his chair, rising in a swirl of black and white silk. He opened the door. "Now get out."

He shut the door behind me.

"The Left Hand will grant you time to collect your thoughts." The servant with the red collar smiled, the crook of his lips more consoling than happy. "And would like me to remind you that competing is forbidden in this room."

They were avoiding calling it "murder." I lingered by the door and pulled my gloves on again. I bet they didn't let disqualified competitors talk about the auditions, and if no one else lived, only the servants would know we'd been killing each other. The next auditioners for whatever mask fell first wouldn't know it was a fight to the death till they got here. No one would.

CHAPTER

NINE

The Left Hand made us wait. I stewed in my seat, listening to the drone of conversations around me. Twenty-Two was one of the oldest here—an archer and swordswoman by the look of it—and she asked her servant to bring her wrist guards after the first session. Seven and Eight were twitchy northerners, with Seven keeping his eyes on everyone else while Eight whispered in hushed Erlenian. Twenty devoured plate after plate of food and chewed with his mouth open the whole time. I poured myself another cup of tea.

Eating before running always made me sick. Best not risk it—strength training could mean anything.

The door to the nook creaked open. Amethyst stepped out first and whispered to Ruby's servant. The Left Hand filed out.

"Lady Amethyst will oversee your first session. She suggests you all take a moment to drink a glass of water." The servant looked at us in turn till everyone had downed a glass. Another little test to see how fast we obeyed? "If you'll follow me."

We all rose at once and stopped.

None of us wanted to walk out first. Or last. Two and Fifteen did an awkward dance to see would go first with their backs to everyone else till Two squared her shoulders and strolled through before we could react. Four and Three followed, guarding her back. I'd not thought much on making friends, but they'd be good people to know.

Till they turned on me and each other.

Familiarity bred trust, and trust got you killed, made you think someone was there to catch you when they weren't. The trio would find that out soon enough.

I slipped into the middle of the crowd. Five's massive shoulder brushed mine, and he glanced at me with his dead eyes. The sun might have sapped all color from them if not for the dark ring of gray around the blue.

He knocked me aside. A knife hidden under his shirt hit my arm. *Odd*. I'd figured him for a fencer with his noble airs.

"Anyone they trap in training won't last the day if we're smart," Five said to Eight in a low whisper. "Any archer worth their salt would be Opal by sundown."

Eight stared at Five.

"Any archer who doesn't get caught," Seven said dryly.

"They're looking for initiative." Five clapped Eight on the back, and I caught sight of his bored, crooked smile through the mouth of his mask. He wasn't making friends or keeping them. "Spend your time wisely and they won't care if you skip training."

Seven kissed his last three fingers and sent a prayer off to the Triad while Eight walked on, none the wiser. Five was playing a whole different game.

I stumbled forward into Five, gripping his arm to steady myself and cursing to distract him. My other hand dipped under his coat and grabbed his knife. He elbowed me off without even looking at my number. I sunk back into the crowd.

Five touched his chest and stopped. I ducked behind Twenty.

Five could play his game, and I could play mine. One less thing for him to kill me with.

Later, sweat-drenched and trembling under the weight of my clothes, I just wanted to fling my belt and knives and all extra weight away from me. Amethyst stalked over us, mask blinding in the sunlight. Only seven of us were on the ground, noses close to the dirt and bellies pulled tight to our spines so we looked like planks as we balanced on our forearms and toes. I was sure only four of us needed it. Four and Two were across from each other in our circle and keeping an eye on each other's backs. I could barely keep my eyes open.

"Ten, nine, eight." Amethyst walked past me, legs barely trembling even though she'd run laps around the courtyard for ages with us. "Seven, six, five."

I sucked in a long drowning gasp through my nose and counted her footsteps. The cloth stuck to my face in an itchy, sweaty clump. "Two, one."

I collapsed. Amethyst clucked her tongue.

"Up. Straighter. Another ten." She stuck her foot under Eleven's stomach and toed her off the ground. "I do not care how untrained you are—your back should be straight. Controlling the muscles at your center will widen your range of motion and abilities. People without control have no place here."

I clenched my jaw and straightened my back. Again.

"Chin up." Amethyst toed my nose off the ground. "You should only stare at the ground if you're giving up."

On a shaded wall way across from me, Five watched us. He'd not been one of the weaklings included in strength training, and he hadn't moved since he'd climbed up there. Waiting.

Eight was nowhere to be seen. Emerald and Ruby must've been evaluating those not in training. Judging what the auditioners did in their downtime.

But why was Five auditioning? If he was a noble, he'd all the wealth and forestland he needed to live on. Unless he got greedy, but still.

"Down." Amethyst tapped her foot.

I lowered myself to the ground, hands next to my shoulders and elbows up like she'd shown us. Eleven collapsed into a panting heap and curled into herself. Under her new clothes, she was all bones and dead runes. The deep, aching burn in my own stomach begged me to roll up into a ball and never move again.

Showing weakness like that would get me killed.

"Being able to support yourself is a must as Opal." Amethyst, still in armor despite the sun and not showing a single sign of feeling it, grabbed one of the bars standing head-height and horizontal in the center of our ring. With two hands shoulder-width apart, she lifted her feet from the ground. Her arms didn't shake, her back didn't bend, and she pulled her chest over the bar with her legs straight out in front of her. "While our positions consist of public displays and protecting Our Queen, there are also a number of jobs that require discretion. Escape routes are subject to chance. I have hung by my fingertips in winter from a windowsill waiting for a room to clear—from sunrise to midmorning.

Letting go would've killed me. Gripping the sill with my hands fully would have gotten me killed. You must be able to support yourself and your gear, or you will fail."

And she repeated that lift exercise ten times. While speaking. I could maybe do it once. Without armor. Shaking.

Amethyst was spectacular.

"I do not care how strong you think you are. You must be stronger." Amethyst lowered herself to the ground and got into the straight-backed, stomach-sucking position we'd been in earlier. "On your stomach, hands slightly wider than your shoulders, and back straight. Push yourself up and lower yourself down—not touching the ground—and push up again. Don't stop until I say so."

A chill shuddered up my spine and a pool of sweat collected in the small of my back. I pushed myself up.

The rush of air awakened another shiver. My breath left me on the way down, stomach scraping the ground, and I curled my nails into the dust. I had to be Opal. I was strong enough. I would be Opal—noble and deadly.

I shoved myself up, and my elbows creaked. Amethyst shook her head at me. I hadn't even thought beyond claiming the mask, claiming those Erlends who owed me Nacea, but I'd be noble. I'd have an equal rank to all those old nobles sitting on the high court.

I'd be equal to that lady from the carriage—in rank, if not in brazenness.

My nose smacked the ground. I winced, pain flaring behind my eyes, and rolled my head up till the ache faded. Five was gone from his perch. The hair on the back of my neck stood up.

Eleven huffed beside me. I glanced to my other side as Twenty dropped to the ground, elbows going everywhere. Three, Five, Seven, and Eight were nowhere to be seen, and I paused. Amethyst cleared her throat.

I looked up. Light sparked in the window beyond her head.

Arrow tip.

I pushed up, flying backward, and fell on my ass. Twenty laughed.

An arrow tore through his neck. It clattered against the ground where my chest had been, splattering blood across the stones. Twenty collapsed, grasping his throat with both hands and sucking in wet, drowning breaths. I twisted back to the spark of light.

Nothing.

Amethyst turned Twenty onto his back. His chest didn't rise again.

She glanced around at all of us. "Anyone see who did it?"

No one answered. I'd options but only one good guess—either Five was doing his own work or Eight had taken his suggestion. Neither was comforting.

"Abel?" Amethyst waved her servant forward. "Have them clean this up. The rest of you shift to your left and keep going. Stay out of their way."

We all crawled out of the servants' way and back into position, gazes darting to the windows and roofs. I half-followed Amethyst's directions after that, pushing myself as far as I could while listening to the people around me. Two was diagonal from me, and I made sure to watch her reaction whenever she looked my way. No one saw anything and no one else died.

I was one step closer to Opal but so was everyone else.

Well, except Twenty.

CHAPTER
TEN

An eternity later, I rose on shaky legs. Two and Four looked for archers, and I slid into step behind them and in front of trembling Eleven. Four grabbed a waterskin from his servant, and Two accepted a mug of crunchy nuts from hers. Eleven pulled a canteen from a hidden pocket.

Knives, sure, but water had never been a weapon. Now it could kill me or save me. I'd not told Maud to—

"Auditioner?" Maud appeared at my other side, a leather canteen in one hand and half a sweet potato in her other. She leaned in closer. "I was the only one to handle these."

I downed half the canteen in one go. "Thanks."

"Of course." Maud looked away as my exhausted, shaky hands splattered water everywhere. "Would you like anything else?"

"No." I plucked up the potato and sniffed. Smelled safe. I'd have to take her word for it now. I bit into it, flesh melting over my tongue, and groaned. Running all night hadn't been this hard, hadn't left my stomach clawing at my ribs like this. Hunger, sure, but this was *need*. How did anyone do this?

How would I do this again tomorrow?

"Can you bring me more water next break?" I glanced toward the group. "Or whenever you can."

Maud pursed her lips. "Keep the canteen. I cannot interrupt your sessions, and you will have no more breaks."

"Great." I hooked the canteen to my belt and shoved the rest of the potato into my mouth.

She fell behind and vanished with the rest of the servants. She was useful.

So far.

This new courtyard was large and airy. Steep-roofed build-ings overhung the path and towered behind us. Windows dotted the walls, dark and empty with plenty of notches for handholds, and a tall wall encircled the rest of the land in a long semicir-cle. Beyond the head-high bricks, evergreens and browning oaks blocked our view of the eastern spires. A decorative forest between us and the real palace.

A few trees between me and the Erlend lords.

"Wipe your hands before you touch my bows." Emerald squeezed my arm and breezed past me to a rack of longbows and quivers.

"You'll be shooting toward the wall." Emerald handpicked a bow for each of us based on height and appearance. She pointed to the forest. "But first, I want to see how you stand."

Emerald demonstrated how to hold the bow. Fingers weak, I nearly dropped mine. The open, shaded air chilled the sweat coating my skin, and I tightened my grip on the bow. Five stood next to me, back from wherever he'd been, and glanced at my hands. I forced myself to be steady till he looked away.

Emerald marched to the other end of the line so they could see what she was doing.

With her gone, I dropped my stance and rested the bow on my foot. Eleven hooked hers across a shoulder and doubled over her knees, still trying to catch her breath. I slid a hand along the bow. It was finer than anything I'd ever handled and certainly better than the ones Grell let us carry for dangerous runs.

"Absolutely not." Emerald smacked my shoulder with an arrow. "Bow off the ground, or you'll spend the night eating dirt."

I jerked up, one hand gripping the bow and the other on the string. Emerald shook her head.

"Shoulders perpendicular to your target." She glided past, nudging my feet wider and tapping my stomach. "You should think of your body in angles. Your angle to the target, the angle of your arm from the ground, your bow from your body."

She raised her voice and walked to Five.

"Your eyes will not lead you to your target. Your body is in control, and you must be in control of your body." She shoved his shoulders down from his ears and adjusted Eleven. Pleased—or as pleased as she ever was—with all of us, she picked up her bow. "Now don't move."

My shoulders ached. A slow, seeping pain dripped down my spine, tightening every muscle and burrowing under my shoulder blades. A needling pressure burned in my lower back. The ache trembled down my arms till my elbows locked.

"Your target," said Emerald, arms not shaking at all, "will not always be in an easily accessible position. You will have to wait for them to move within range where you can kill them, harm no one else, and escape unnoticed. Or you will adjust accordingly."

She drew back her right arm as though to shoot, and we all followed. My right hand tensed, and I wasn't sure I'd be able to uncurl my fingers if I tried. The ache was bone deep and gnawed at my joints. She held us there till sweat dripped down my forehead, nose, chin, and neck. The canteen was heavy on my hip.

"If you are Opal, the day will come when your duty will demand patience, and you must be ready for that day. Or else you have no business being Opal."

Emerald moved to lower her bow. Eleven dropped her arms with a loud sigh, and I cracked my shoulders out of position. Finally.

Emerald froze again and clucked her tongue. "You cannot rush things—impatience courts failure."

She lifted her bow back into place.

No one moved. My shadow grew longer with each agonizing shake of my arms, my fingers stretching into misshapen claws around the bow. I let out a raspy breath into my shoulder and bent my knees to ease the stone-jointed weight that had settled in my legs. Emerald lowered her stance and shook out her arms. I collapsed over my knees.

"Stand up straight." Emerald collected my bow with the others. "You're not done yet."

I rose, holding back a groan at my pins-and-needles arms. Five crossed his arms over his head, hands dangling over his shoulders. His fingers were calloused.

Four did stretches down the way, hooking one arm behind his back. My shoulder popped when I tried it.

I downed the rest of my canteen instead of copying the rest.

Ruby swapped places with Emerald. Three vanished into the small copse of trees growing near the wall, leaping into the branches. Five meandered back into the building, arms not shaking at all.

Ruby passed out too-heavy swords with blunted ends. My hand could barely hold the hilt, and I stumbled my way into the shade. Any archer would have to lean out to hit me there, catching Ruby's gaze, and I hadn't seen anyone in the other building. At least I'd be able to dodge.

If my body did what I asked it. Ruby slowly led us through the motions of fighting—one parry and lunge, another parry, another lunge, a block. A stitch clawed at my sides with every twist, exhaustion scoured my calves clean off the bone with each step, and my head threatened to drift away on the breeze with every wavering thought. I couldn't focus.

"Weight off your front foot." Ruby bowed over my feet, impossibly limber for a person his height, and he jerked me into the right position. "The lines from your heels should form a corner. Back leg and chest sideways, front foot forward."

There was no hiding my trembling with him so close. He tapped my right arm up.

"What did you normally do during the day?" He slid a palm down my arm and forced my elbow to move. "Don't lock up. You'll drop your sword."

"Slept a lot. Worked the crowd when the market was busy." I pushed myself through the first motion he'd shown us, body so light I'd float away if not for the heaviness in my stomach. Last time I'd felt this chilled in the warmth of autumn, I'd been sick and passed out on Rath's feet. "If I was fighting or running, I'd sleep more and skip the crowds."

"You didn't mention eating."

"Gets expensive." I shifted back into the start position. "Real jobs go to kids with parents or all those old mages. They can afford to work for less. Could be a laborer, sure, but you can't start that till you're ten. Most get pulled into thieving young. They don't let you leave. I got enough to keep me alive and stole enough to keep me strong. If I looked too well, Grell'd have felt threatened."

Grell only let me get away with being so good at fighting because my bouts brought in plenty of profit.

Ruby made an odd sound in the back of his throat and smacked the sword out of my hands. It clattered to the ground between us.

"Mediocre."

He moved to Eleven. Her stance was shaky as mine, and I yanked my sword off the ground. At least no one could see me flushing, heat racing up my cheeks at his words. I swallowed it down and watched him tear Eleven's stance to pieces.

What did it matter what I'd done? There weren't jobs—with magic gone, a whole generation of mages lost their empire and flooded the world with jobless adults. The mages were adults who could afford to do whatever people wanted and already knew things, and they had all the right manners and money saved. Kids couldn't compete with that. We scrounged for the fringe jobs no one wanted.

I didn't do much else because there wasn't much else to do, and moving was the last thing I wanted to do after a night of fighting.

I jabbed the air in front of me in time with Ruby's call and scowled, fingers gripping the hilt so hard my knuckles strained against my gloves. Ruby hit my elbow.

I didn't drop my sword.

Nearly disemboweled myself with recoil but small steps.

"It is day one, I suppose." Ruby waved us to the rack in the corner closet, barely-there runes lining the undersides of his fingers. "Dinner is served in the dining hall, but it is entirely up to you how it goes. There will be food and servants, and you may continue to compete, granted you are not caught and you do not harm anyone else. I'll see you at breakfast. Or not."

Four and Two glanced at each other. Three lingered in the doorway, dirt under her nails and bark clinging to her mask. They disappeared down the pathway, and Ten, Eleven, and Fifteen followed them one by one, not going together but not willing to take their eyes off each other. I eyed the forest.

"The quarters for our honorable court members are beyond that little forest. Lovely cherry trees in spring." Ruby paused in the doorway, wiggling his fingers toward the wall. "If you're caught beyond the wall, they'll arrest you for trespassing and we'll disqualify you."

I nodded. Ruby glided away, humming.

Good thieves didn't get caught.

And I was the best.

CHAPTER
ELEVEN

The forest beyond the wall was overgrowing with deep green pines and towering oaks. A small stream trickled softly under the hum of insects and birds, and I pulled myself onto the edge of the wall. The windows behind me were dark and blank, shadows flickering in the holes when I stared too long. I shook out my arms.

Nothing but the fuzzy haze of darkness.

An arrow ripped over my head. I dropped to the wall, stomach to the bricks. Another tore over my shoulder, missing by a hairbreadth, and I rolled forward into the forest. A line of decorative shrubs broke my fall. An arrow burrowed into the tree across from me.

No footsteps followed. They must've been shooting from a window.

I tossed my glove above the wall. Another arrow slammed into the tree as I caught my glove. They were either on the roof or in one of those windows, but the rooms would be safer. They were out of the way, and I'd no idea how to get to them—I doubted anyone else did. How'd they find that perch in such a short time?

A guard wandered down a winding path nearby, sword slapping his thigh and empty left sleeve fluttering in the breeze. I waited for him to walk out of sight. Thick curtains of green needles and fading red-gold leaves filtered out the evening sun and forest sounds. It was a miracle the guard hadn't heard and come running. I dragged myself to my feet.

"Still there?" I wiggled my fingers over the edge of the wall. Nothing.

I peeked over it. The courtyard was empty and the windows dark. I'd not seen them last time I'd looked though. Black gloves, black sleeves, black bow would do it. And arrows arced, didn't they? I traced a line from the arrow embedded in the tree.

A large empty window at the top of the left building, sill a solid block of wood. It was perfect—high ground, only window on its level, and probably only one entrance. They'd think they were safe.

I followed the wall till it was flush against the left building, leapt to the top, and slowly scaled the roof, arms and legs burning. No one there but me.

And the bloodstains from last night.

The roof outside my window was speckled with red. I peered sideways through the shutter and spied Maud pacing round the room on the other side. I tapped the sill. She tripped.

"Bless!" Maud pried apart the bells and helped me inside. "There is a door."

"And a dozen people waiting for me to walk down that hall." I flopped onto the bed, pain shooting up my arms. "Can you make me dinner?"

"That is precisely why I'm here." Maud fluttered around me, tugging the clean blanket from under my dirty boots. "They didn't tell us you'd miss lunch, but I have compensated with a meal we usually reserve for floundering new recruits."

I glared at her. "Floundering, am I?"

"Thin." She set a tray of food next to the bed. "There are clothes in the corner, clean bandages, and a physician's basic care bag. Change. I'll set up your food."

I rolled out of bed. Maud turned her back to me and busied herself with the food. I peeled off my dress and pulled on a loose tunic. She'd filled the tub, but I'd have to bathe after. Least I was dry.

"Do any foods make you sick?" Maud stared idly at the opposite wall, kneeling before the tray, and poured a cup of dark chicory. She added a large dollop of honey. "I'm assuming you won't be sleeping anytime soon."

"No foods make me sick, and I won't be sleeping unless I'm dead." I fell back onto the bed in time to catch her wrinkling her nose. So she had a sense of humor after all. "You know anything about the last auditions?"

She pulled a lid from a bowl. Mutton drowned in thick red paste spotted with peas, green chilies, and garlic slivers gave off curls of peppery steam, and I fished out a piece of meat. The mice devoured it before it hit the cage bottom.

"Only that they happened," she said dryly. She tossed the mice a pinch of bread. "Dimas was here for Amethyst's year, and he said we should stay away at night."

"Probably best." I glanced at the mice—still alive. "If you wanted to slip something into an auditioner's food, how would you do it?"

"No." She pushed the tray toward me. "We keep the food covered while we walk. With all the construction, there's too much dust in the air. You couldn't do it. Not to my food."

I sighed. "It never leaves your sight? Not for a wick?"

"Vin doesn't let strangers in his kitchen, and none of us are going to poison you. Each servant cooks each meal, and all of us are in charge of breakfast." Maud shuffled to my discarded clothes and gathered up the dress. She froze. "The lids sit out overnight. I'll start washing mine."

And no one would guard drying tray lids. I ran a finger down the inside of the lid and came away with nothing but water. I tasted it.

Warm water.

I dunked the bread into the egg and took a bite. Lady bless, Maud could cook, and she was clever knowing that the lids sitting out could mean trouble. "Why'd you pick me? What did they tell you about us?"

Servants had the best gossip, and if Maud wrinkled her nose when laughing, I bet she'd a similar tell when lying.

"I didn't, and I wouldn't have." She folded my shirt over her arm and leaned against the full tub. "We drew lots, and I selected twenty-three. I am pleased you showed up. One horse in the race is better than none, and I'd have been ruined if they'd stopped at twenty-two."

I snorted into my bowl.

"Why would I pick the scrawniest auditioner?" She shrugged. "I'm not going to lie to or for you."

I'd have picked me, but I liked me.

"We've more rules than you," Maud said after a long moment. "Typical ones—no relationships, no stealing—and specific ones. Nothing important, as far as you're concerned."

"And if your auditioner wins, you're five pearls richer and sporting a fancy collar." I tucked into the meal—mice weren't dead and I was starving—and brandished my spoon at her. "You supposed to stay away so you don't get hurt? I'm not going to hurt you."

"No, it would get you disqualified." Maud grinned, lips taut over gritted teeth. "Auditioners in the past have not always accepted the appropriate moral code, and the Left Hand holds a romantic spot within the court."

I winced. No wonder the rules about hurting those outside the audition were so strict. A physical hit wasn't the worst way to hurt someone, and we'd command over servants. "I won't touch you."

"Good."

"What do you mean romantic?"

"Desired. Adored." Maud gestured to the napkin folded next to the tray. "They are Our Queen's chosen, and the only ones who have her ear. The court members think that if the Left Hand likes them, they are safe. It's fake—flirtation, adoration. The last Opal loved it, but it means that some auditioners come here looking for a taste of that. Dimas told us to limit our time with you. He says people who kill for money or standing are the worst sort."

He wasn't wrong. Lord Horatio del Seve had made a fortune selling off Nacean goods to Shan de Pau and his questionably legal traders. They would sooner kill a person and strip the corpse than simply pick a few pockets. Loyalty to riches far beyond necessity and no sense of proper responsibility had gotten us into war in the first place. They served themselves and no one else.

But the Left Hand dispensed justice.

"Smart." I wiped my mouth. Eating in a mask was about as easy as breathing in one. "Attempted murder I can handle. Don't think I can handle you romancing me."

"You're not my type. You're very short." Maud stared down her nose at me, blinking slowly. "Plus, it's completely against the rules. I can't get promoted if I'm fired."

"You're shorter than me, you know."

"Doesn't change your height, does it?" She pushed herself off the tub. "Leave your dirty clothes by the door, and I'll pick them up in the morning. The water's clean. This shirt fits you best, so I'll wash it tonight. The others were the only ones I could find that looked like they'd fit—I guessed your measurements. Do you need anything else?"

"No." I glanced at the folded clothes in the corner, a chill crawling up my throat. She'd brought me clothes—a long dress and a tailored shirt with a floppy collar, thick leggings, fitted pants, and even a pair of wool socks. No questions, and she'd done as I asked. "Not a word about me to anyone. They know what I look like, I lose my shot at surprise."

And that was when folks usually started asking a bunch of questions I didn't want to answer.

"The tailor who sells secondhand clothes had to take in some of them, but I had him leave the dresses. He always makes them too short. I can tailor anything that doesn't fit well enough."

Maud smiled, really smiled, showing her teeth and dimpling her round cheeks. "Your measurements aren't anyone else's business, and they won't find out anything from me."

I sucked in a breath, any words of thanks I might've had buried under years of explanations and tears, and all that came out was "Thank you."

"Of course, Auditioner." Maud nodded and left me speechless.

I dove for the pile of clothes. They weren't made for me, but they were clean and dry and the nicest, newest things I'd owned in ages. I laid aside a long flowing tunic—more dress than shirt— and dug through the pants and leggings. The black pair I found was thicker than I was used to wearing but would still fit under my boots. I'd be prepared for the chilly nights at least.

Maybe Maud was more than all right.

CHAPTER
TWELVE

I bathed fast as I could, the cold water cleansing the ache from
my bones, and dumped the dirty bath water down the drain.
My bells were still in place, and it didn't take long to nail the
door shut, just a dozen shoulder cracks and groans of pain. I
rubbed my thighs.

I was stronger in my legs than in my arms, and it showed.
Might've been what tipped Emerald off. But why did my calves
still hurt so much then?

I curled up in the still-damp tub. Dinner settled heavy in
my stomach, dragging my eyelids down and hunching me in on
myself, and I slid low enough to keep the Twenty-Three–shaped
lump in the bed in sight. The darkness closed around me, shadows flickering through the shutters. Light glinted off the bells
and gave the pile of blankets in my bed the illusion of breathing.
I rolled the ring around my finger.

Maybe the others would be as tired as me and drop off to
sleep first chance they got.

Stillness fed the darkness, fuzzy shapes creeping under the door. I blinked, and they reeled. The shadows were gone. They were phantoms of my mind come to keep me awake and on edge. There was nothing there. No matter how trained my competition was, they couldn't move through locked doors and shuttered windows. I laid my knives in my lap. The ax rested at my side.

I slipped the silver ring up and down my finger. I should give it back. Opal or no, she wouldn't be hard to find if I ever had time to myself, and seeing her again wouldn't be all bad. She was an Erlend, but she was pretty and clever. Talking to her had been fun.

Made me feel listened to.

I tucked my fingers under my chin, ring against my throat, and watched the window. Darkness crept through the shutters, moonlight cutting through the slats, and I sighed. Listening would do me just as well. I closed my eyes.

The bells chimed. I leapt up, four soft rings echoing in my head, and tripped over my ax. The bells threw silver light across the room, giving life to the shadows twining around the walls. I grabbed my knives and crawled out of the tub. The ringing stopped.

The back of my neck itched. A breeze rustled the wire, whistling between the bells, but they didn't sound. The wind rolled over my skin, but I couldn't hear it. Gooseflesh prickled up my arms. I peeked outside.

Nothing.

The darkness in the corner of my eyes shifted. I froze, breath trapped in my chest. A shadow unfolded itself from the wall, blackness curling and twisting between the bricks, spilling onto the floor. It was shadows come to play tricks. Nightmares while awake.

It wasn't real.

They were never real.

Darkness rustled over the floor, reaching across the stones and reeling up, writhing in the air, a flicker of a shadow rising to my height and wavering in the breeze behind my shoulder. The sweet, cloying scent of rot crawled into my nose. I squeezed my lips shut.

Not real, not real, not real.

Blood dripped on my shoulder—drop after drop seeping beneath my skin and pushing me to my knees. Trails of red leaked down my arm, curling around my wrist and pooling in my palm. Breath whispered against my ear.

"Is this me?"

I twisted in the darkness. My sister stared back at me.

Blood clung to the edges of Shae's face. The braids I'd twisted around her crown were matted with blood and dirt.

I dropped my knife. The blade clattered between me and the thing wearing my sister's face. It tilted its head to the side. Blades were useless, and fighting was worthless. I couldn't fight my way out of this. I was nothing next to it.

This was what Erlend had done to us—stolen us, torn us away from what we were, ripped children from their homes and souls from their bodies. Broken bodies, broken memories, broken souls. They'd made us nothing.

"Is this me?"

My trembling hands splattered blood across my legs—warm and wet and seeping. "Take her off."

"Is this me?"

"Take her off." I reached for her face, fingers slipping over the clammy damp of her skin, and gagged. Bile clogged my throat and burned in my nose. "She's not you. Take her off!"

"Is this you?" The shadow rolled its head, and Shae's face slid off. Tendrils of shadow looped around her, stretching the skin into some warped memory of her face. It held it up to me. "Is this you?"

"Shae." I pushed her away. "She was Shae Leon."

The darkness surged over me, heavy and hot, reeking of flesh and blood and dirt, blowflies scurrying over my skin and maggots roiling under my feet. My heart pounded between us, the only reminder I was alive, and I turned away, desperate to leave, run, wake up, keep my skin away from this thing slipping under my clothes as if they weren't there. Warmth sliced through my mask and brushed my cheek.

"Is this me?" it whispered.

I flung my arms out, second knife ripping through the darkness. My body fell forward, nothing to keep me up, no flesh to hold my blade, and I crashed into the wall. My ears rang, and my arms locked up, fingers clenched around the hilt. The darkness in the room receded.

No shadow.

Only real shadows flickering on the walls. I slid my hands along the floor, searching for Shae and found nothing. No blood, no skin.

The heaviness in my chest wouldn't lift. The chill on my skin wouldn't leave.

I was wet.

The bells chimed again. Drizzle drifted through the window shutters, striking the bells and setting them off. Water misted my arms. I smelled my shoulder.

Rainwater. Nothing but rain and nighttime.

It wasn't real.

I unclenched my fingers and tossed the knife away, cold weight spreading to my arms. No more sister, no more shadows.

Only a trick of my mind in the dark.

I'd thought I was over these nightmares. I dragged myself back to the tub and tumbled inside. My shoulders rammed into the rim, knees uncomfortably folded against my chest, and I tightened my mask over the back of my neck.

"Only a trick," I whispered to my hands. I rubbed my fingers over my shirt, erasing the clammy touch of Shae's long-dead skin. I pressed the ring to my lips. Real—Our Queen was real and warm and alive. Shae was dead, and Our Queen had banished the shadows. I was alone.

I drifted in and out of sleep, shadows flickering in the corner of my sight all night, peering and writhing over the edge of the tub with browned, rotting eyes and gaping mouths. The rain stopped at dawn.

I'd gotten no rest and had no strength left. I wanted to sleep but needed to run and never stop, flee from the memories and shadows lingering in this room. The window beckoned.

I took off over the roof. The shutters were drawn and bare, rainwater dripping down the sills and echoing in my ears. I half-ran, half-slid down the rows of windows rising out of the roof. A pair of bleary eyes that looked like Eleven's glanced back at me through the slats of one. I raced away from her.

On the other side of the building, the trio of invited had holed up together in a large room. Two, Three, and Four paced about, getting dressed and stretching. I scaled a defunct chimney nearby, slipping on the wet tiles, and dangled my legs over the chimney's edge. The tiles laid out beneath me were all loose and slick. Even acrobats wouldn't risk it.

I needed to feel them out. If they were to be a trio till they died, they were an issue. I couldn't fight them all at once.

"If you're only in this for the money, there's a troupe missing tumblers you could join," Four said before waving to me as he crawled out the window set into the sloping roof.

"That how you all know each other?" I yawned.

"Wouldn't you like to know," Two muttered. She stretched and tugged her arms behind her back.

"That's why I'm asking." I copied her. Cool, burning relief slid down my shoulders and spine, and I sighed. "An odd place to take friends, is all. Keep secrets all you like."

"Says Sal, Sal, Sal who knows nothing about secrets." Three— who must've overheard Ruby the first day of auditions—crossed her left arm across her chest and pulled it close. "Do this one."

I did and my shoulder cracked, but, Lady, was it worth it. Wasn't fair them being my age and having all this training. Circuses traveled all around picking up kids to train and offering up a bit of joy in the aftermath of the war, but they didn't pay you till you were in the show and had earned your keep. I'd no time for that growing up.

"Should do your legs too." Three grabbed her foot and pulled it over her head.

"I'm not doing that."

Two leaned into Three, using her shoulder to balance, and whispered in her ear. I cocked my head to the side—couldn't hear them.

"Any particular reason you're here?" Four stuffed his hands in his pockets.

"Sunrise was nice." I shifted backward, ready to jump and run, and covered the motion by waving to the fiery clouds spilling over the eastern spires. "Wanted to know where everyone sleeps."

"Don't worry," said Two. "We'll switch it up."

"Keep you on your toes." Four frowned.

I grinned. "Sounds fun."

He ripped his hand from his pocket, and I tumbled backward, landing crouched on the roof behind the chimney. His thin throwing knife sliced through the air above me and clattered to the tiles. I darted away from them.

"Less fun," I shouted over my shoulder.

Four's booming laugh followed me across the roof. I glanced back, but they weren't chasing. Four clapped Two on the back, and Three waved. I raced along the tiles and inhaled, head clearing with each breath.

CHAPTER
THIRTEEN

I entered the dining hall from the strength training courtyard just as Four, Two, and Three walked in from the dorms. Three shook her head at me. She nudged Four.

They'd have been good friends to have. They were good friends.

And they'd have to kill each other eventually.

I took the seat next to Four and fanned my dress over my knees. There wasn't much use for pretty things with Grell, but if our coming days were all push-ups and stances, I'd take my chances. I could move just as easily in this dress.

And it made me feel better. I'd not been able to wear a real one for ages.

"If I were, hypothetically, to talk about you behind your back," Four said, pouring a cup of tea and swirling a spoonful of sweet orange blossom honey into it, "how should I refer to you?"

I grabbed the honey—of course the palace had fancy honey to waste on people doomed to die—and spooned it into my cup.

"I've got a giant number stitched to my mask." This was easier with people I only met once and who only knew how I was that day. Most everyone else wanted me to pick one, make addressing me easier on them by denying myself. I was already dressing so they could get it right. The least they could do was try. I didn't see why I had to choose. "Who do I look like?"

"Someone who's going to regret the sweetness of her tea after we start training."

Two laughed into her stuffed roll.

"Address me however I look." I was both. I was neither. I was everything, but that wasn't exactly a friendly conversation between strangers trying to kill each other. Least he asked nicely. "Why are you talking about me?"

"Either way, eat some real food." He smeared half-melted butter over a thick slice of bread and took a bite. "I said it was hypothetical. It means I theorized—"

"Means you guessed, but no one asks that if they're not really talking." I glanced at him over the rim of my cup, honey already too sweet for me. I'd never heard the word before now, but I'd no desire for everyone in the room to know that. "You really want to play teacher in a fight to the death?"

Two snorted. "He does it to everyone."

"The eternal older brother," Three said, popping a handful of berries into her mouth.

Four scowled, finally looking more seventeen than thirty.

"Stop pouting." I took another sip of tea and grinned. "You'll wrinkle faster."

Four's mouth snapped into a straight, unwrinkled line.

Abel, Amethyst's servant, led Fifteen into the breakfast nook with the Left Hand. They'd skipped over most of the other auditioners.

I took another sip of tea. The trio hadn't been invited to speak with the Left Hand today. "Why haven't you tried to kill me?"

"Rude saying Four didn't try," Two said. "He's been throwing knives since he started walking."

He'd not been trying to hit me. I'd seen knife throwers often enough to know what aiming looked like.

"I like you." Four brushed the crumbs from his mask and wiped his hands clean. "And I don't enjoy killing people I like."

"I'm not leaving. Have the decency to do it quick, as quickly as you'll do it for each other when the time comes."

Two squeezed her eyes shut and Three winced.

Four glanced over my shoulder. "I heard you that day. *Nothing personal.*"

"Twenty-Three?" Abel leaned over my shoulder, purple collar bright in the corner of my eyes. "The Left Hand would like to see you."

I downed the last of my too-sweet tea and marched to the nook, trying to keep the exhausted shaking from my knees. Emerald wore green again—she lived up to her name. Ruby turned to me when I entered, red mask at odds with his sun-yellow clothes and black stitching.

"Don't bother sitting." Ruby held up his hand. "One question."

"Do you want to start learning how to read and write now?" Emerald leaned forward, brass nails tapping her mask. "If you progress further in the competition, you must attend tutoring, but you may start now if you wish."

"Yes." I'd never had a chance, but if they were offering and it made me more likely to be Opal, I'd do it. It hadn't been useful before. "When?"

Emerald glanced at Ruby. "Come here after sword work. Your tutor is a lady of the court, and you will treat her as such. You will be safe during these lessons, but we will be watching. Any attempts on your life are allowed the moment your time ends. Any actions that put her in danger are not. Understand?"

"I won't get her hurt." I bowed to Emerald. "Thank you."

She flicked her hands to the door. I joined the others eyeing the doors to the courtyard. Were the others they'd called in getting tutoring too or something else? I'd have to find out.

But how?

I was trapped in training. Amethyst ran us into the ground with stances that burned through my legs and raged in my center. I made it through slightly stronger and sweatier than the day before, but I couldn't talk to anyone or sneak away without Amethyst knowing. Five watched from his perch the whole time.

The downside of all this training was that I'd barely be able to stay awake tonight and survive tomorrow. The ones who weren't training had all day to scout us and all night to kill us while they were well rested and ready. They weren't exhausted to the bone.

Tutoring would be a rest—time to gather my thoughts and learn what all the fuss was about with the nobles.

I tried to think during archery, mapping out the buildings and paths between me and my room, but with each shift of my feet and draw of the bow, my thoughts and fingers shuddered away from my control. Emerald clucked her tongue at me.

"You won't hit anything shaking like that." She slid a finger down my bow, steadying my aim and moving it toward where she'd pointed. "You can't even fully draw it."

I pulled my elbow back. "Not yet."

"Not soon," she said as she wandered away, already uninterested and focused on Five's form.

His feet were wrong today. His arms were perfect.

He was definitely an archer and definitely faking.

By the time we got to sword work, I could barely grip the hilt and Ruby was having none of it.

"Harder! Tighter grip." He beckoned me forward and blocked my lunge. "You're locking your wrist. Your arm is too tight. You won't be able to move fast enough."

He attacked before I could move. He ripped the sword from my hands and twisted around, sending Eleven's sword flying. Two, Four, Five, and Fifteen—who'd shown up sporting a black eye and a limp—shifted around us in a circle. Ruby brandished his sword at Eleven and me.

"Pick them up." Ruby pinched what would've been the bridge of his nose if his mask had one. "Face each other. Eleven attacks first and Twenty-Three blocks. If either of you drops your sword before we're done, you're disqualified. Don't be predictable, but be consistent."

Eleven picked up her sword. I knelt, tearing off my glove and coating my hand in dust to help my grip. We stepped across from each other.

"Raise."

Eleven lifted her sword. She couldn't kill me, not outright while everyone watched, but training was wearing me down. After archery, my arms were all lead joints and shaky muscles.

The end-of-day bells had to chime soon. Ruby couldn't keep us forever.

"One."

I whipped my sword to my right thigh, point down with the back of my hand bared to Eleven. Her blade smacked mine near the hilt.

The shock rattled up my arm.

"Two."

Eleven pulled her arm back—too far, too slow—and I held my position. Her blade swung for my lower left side, and I rammed mine into hers as she nicked my leggings. Her arm ricocheted back.

But she held.

Ruby's third call never came. Eleven looked first—Ruby had the other auditioners paired off and was lazily circling them. I lunged for Eleven.

She backtracked. I lunged again. She blocked, blades scraping down each other. I couldn't kill her and she couldn't kill me, but there were a dozen ways to make life terrible without killing someone. I drew my knife with my other hand, darting forward one last time.

I ran my knife down her sword arm.

Eleven shrieked. Her fingers loosened, and Ruby turned, red light blinding in the evening sun. The bells rang.

Eleven's sword clattered to the ground between us.

"Acceptable." Ruby collected the swords from the others, pausing before Eleven and me. "But slow."

Eleven exhaled. "I'm still in?"

"Yes." Ruby shook his head. "Hardly. You two are awful."

I sheathed my knife. "Working on it."

"Of course you are but so is everyone else. And the ones who don't have to work on it? I love people I don't even have to talk to." Ruby cocked his head toward the fading bells. "Love dinner even more, and you two are keeping me from it."

Eleven and I walked side by side to the dining hall with Ruby's red gaze on our backs. Eleven fidgeted with each step—nails picking at the shallow gash. I steered clear of her.

She turned toward the dorms, and Ruby vanished down some side hall. I slipped into the dining hall with the willowy servant, Dimas, and smoothed a hand down my dress, leaving a trail of grime behind me. If they were testing me to see how well I did with nobles, they should've let me bathe first. I opened the door to the nook.

"Hello," a soft voice said. "I suppose enough propriety to knock is too much to ask?"

I dropped into a bow, words failing and my gaze stuck on the pretty, stormy girl I'd robbed seven days ago.

CHAPTER
FOURTEEN

A t least the bow was low and long enough to be proper. Probably. I'd lost all ability to move.

"You may sit." She smiled, dark gaze settling on the mask covering my face. The face she didn't know, couldn't know. "Etiquette tutoring comes later, and we don't have time to waste if you're to learn anything today."

I swallowed. There were days and masks between us, and she didn't recognize me.

"Thank you." I cleared my throat. She was only some lady I'd robbed, and there were plenty of them in the world. Couldn't get disqualified for that. "For agreeing to this."

She laughed softly. "I was asked by Our Queen to share my knowledge. No need to thank me."

Of course she didn't agree to it. Erlends always thought they were smarter and better read than anyone else—kept enough records to drown the nation in paper—and hoarded all their knowledge.

"Let's not disappoint Our Queen," I said, watching the noble's face to see how she handled the phrase. Most old lords flinched enough that I could see it from afar. "How would you like to start?"

She only smiled and leaned forward, copper rose locket tumbling out of her dress. "Introductions—I'm Elise de Farone."

Elise de Farone. Unmarried. Daughter to the lord who ruled over the northeastern stretch of Erlend—Igna now—flush against the mountains and bordering the lands outside of Our Queen's control. I'd heard nothing about her parents being involved in the massacre, but most of them used secret names.

All except two: Lord Horatio del Seve and his backstabbing merchant, Shan de Pau. Seve ruled the lands that had neighbored Nacea and begrudgingly served Our Queen, paying just enough taxes that she let him be. Pau had nothing to do with the massacre, but he jacked up the prices of everything after the war, fenced stolen Nacean property, and ran half of Igna into debt. Everyone wanted him dead.

No one had managed it yet.

"Nice to meet you, Lady Farone." I nodded. Might as well play nice for now. "I'm Twenty-Three."

She sniffed, glasses rising in distaste, and swept a curl behind her ear. "You really go by numbers?"

"We really do." I twisted my gloved hands in my lap—I was still wearing her ring—and fought the heat curling in the pit of my stomach. She better not have noticed it. "Least you'll be able to tell us apart."

"I doubt I'd confuse you with anyone, Twenty-Three." She fiddled with her papers, staring at me over the rim of her glasses. "You're comfortable speaking Erlenian and Alonian?"

"Since I was a kid."

"Let's start with Alonian." Elise pulled a thin book from her stack, hands only marred by smudges of charcoal and thin paper cuts, and laid it out before me. "It was the first language of Our Queen and has fewer conjugations. You'll pick up Erlenian quickly after that."

I grinned. "If I'm still alive."

Elise dropped her brush pen. Soft-skinned nobles weren't used to gallows humor, and Lady de Farone was soft all over— except for her tongue. Teasing her was the most fun I could have without risking death.

"Just joking." I picked up the pen and set it near her hand. The chubby doodles of a smaller, younger hand decorated the pages. I'd fought more people than five times my age, yet I was learning out of a children's book. I recognized the letters, but I couldn't make sense of them jumbled together. "So how does reading work?"

"Letters," she said without missing a beat. "Which ones do you recognize?"

I studied the alphabet. The pages were old, yellowed, and crinkled at the ears. I traced the curves of a cat, the left half a sideways arch.

"Cat." The letters were twisted to form the animal, but I rec- ognized the word. The Cat and The Fiddle was the most popular music hall in Kursk, and I walked under that sign near every month. "The ears give it away."

"They do that." Elise grinned. She made the hard sound at the start of "cat," her fingers drawing the first pointy letter in the air before I could respond. "We'll go over what sound each letter makes, and you'll write them down in charcoal. Messier, but if you never learned to write, probably easier than starting off with a pen. You'll learn the sounds and the shapes at the same time."

I narrowed my eyes at her. "All right."

"It has two more letters that make the last two sounds."

"The triangle and the corner." I leaned across the table. "You're being awfully nice to an assassin."

"Would-be assassin." She licked her lips and leaned back, tilting her chin up. "The triangle is the middle sound. Say it."

I did, stumbling over where the sound ended, and plucked up the charcoal. "And the corner is last."

"Good." Elise wrote on my paper. The letters flowed and peaked in beautiful lines. "Hold it like a pen, not a knife. Glide, don't stab."

Hilarious.

I stared at the letters on the page and drew a terrible copy of her script.

"Your turn." Elise clucked her tongue and repeated the sound. "Cat—like a burglar."

I dropped the charcoal and narrowed my eyes.

"I'm surprised to see you here." She grinned, only one side of her mouth lifting up in a twisted smirk, before tossing her hair over her shoulder. Neck bared and completely unafraid. "You couldn't even rob me properly."

I froze. The words I'd meant to say fell back down my throat.

"How?" I'd worn a mask. I wore one now. I'd new clothes, new dirt, and a new name. How did she know me?

Lady, don't let her be turning me over to warrant officers.

"The mask." She gestured to my face and lounged back in her

chair. "I've only ever seen your eyes and mouth, a little bit of your cheeks, and your voice is the same."

How was some noble girl from Erlend better at finding out secrets than me?

Elise reached across the table and picked up my hand, fingertips walking along my palm till they reached the ring.

"And I doubt you're a member of Our Queen's high court," she said. "I'll take my ring back, thank you."

"Right." I tugged off my glove—useless anyway, if she could see the sigil through the thin fabric—and offered her the ring. One thing from Our Queen and of course I couldn't keep it. "Here. I washed it."

She took it from me and slid it back onto her finger, grinning the entire time. "Why'd you wash it?"

I bit my cheek, fighting down my exasperation. Because I'd wrapped it in bloodied bandages and wanted to own something pretty for the first time in my life.

"Dirt." I rubbed my left arm. "Filthy business, thieving."

She looked me over—eyes going from muddy boots tucked under my chair to the dust clinging to the ends of my dress. "Undoubtedly."

The ring fit her finger perfectly—a striking silver against her skin.

"Of the two of us, I'd say I know the most about the Left Hand and what they do." Elise handed me the charcoal and wrote "cat," waiting for me to copy her. "I grew up around Emerald and the previous Opal. I've known Ruby since I started studying under Lady dal Abreu. I know exactly what you and the other auditioners are doing here. What I don't know is *why* you're here."

She did know everyone—everyone I needed to know. Maybe

she was more useful for information, but she'd not tell me anything if I was an ass. I palmed the piece of charcoal, flipping it from my palm to the back of my hand and down my sleeve, and spread my empty hands out before her. She laughed softly.

Good.

"Auditioning's better than getting arrested." I dropped the charcoal back into my hand. "And tutoring, of course."

Elise's smile fell. "Then let's get to it."

Elise ran through the alphabet, and I followed her lead, leaving everything as it was and using the silence between writing to sneak glances at her. Smudges of charcoal darkened her delicate hands, wisps of curls at the base of her neck escaped from gold pins with every twist of her neck, and her pulse fluttered beneath the blue lace collar of her dress. She was clever and so caught up in actually trying to teach me that she didn't notice she'd scrawled lines along her cheeks as well as the parchment when she brushed back her hair. She was nothing like any Erlend noble I'd ever met.

A knock rattled the door.

"Time's up." Elise dropped her charcoal back into the tin. "Same time every night. We're supposed to be through the basics in a few days in case you make it through round one."

Optimistic of them.

So there were rounds. That was more than I knew about the auditions this morning.

"Thank you." I pulled out my one handkerchief, an old robbery relic embroidered with a word I didn't recognize, and handed it to her. Time to get on her good side. "You've got black on your cheek."

Elise accepted the cloth, dotting her cheek. "The entire time?"

"You kept adding to it, so I figured I might as well wait till you were done." I grinned at her blush and nodded. It was going to be doubly easy to draw information from her if she liked me. A little flirting was nothing, even if she was an Erlend. "Looks charming too."

Elise opened her mouth, nose crinkling, and didn't say anything. I stood and bowed.

"Tomorrow night."

"If you're still alive." Elise stilled, like the dark humor gave her a chill she had to stifle, and pulled out a fresh booklet of paper.

I nodded. "Hope so."

"Me too."

This would be too easy.

CHAPTER
FIFTEEN

I peeked out of the nook before leaving. The one-armed soldier who'd knocked was a glaring giant who didn't take his rune-scrawled gaze off me. The back of my neck itched with these tight stone walls and low ceilings, and I dug my fingers into the wall. Quickly built and sturdy but still rough around the edges. I climbed into the rafters.

A colony of sleepy spiders and dust motes greeted me. At least I knew no one had been up here in ages. I could stop cracking my neck to glance up every time I was in the hallway. The soldier chuckled.

I'd have the advantage in a knife fight up here no matter how much he laughed. Even Fifteen, for all his muscle, would pull back a punch and smack his elbow on the wall. I leapt down and shoved up my sleeves, scrawling my new letters along my arm in charcoal. They weren't near as nice as Elise's.

Of course, she'd had a childhood of practice. I brushed the charcoal off with my dress—black on black, not like anyone would notice—and peered down the hall to my room. I wasn't going to be good at getting information from her if I spent the whole time thinking about her. I'd have to think of some leading questions.

Darting around the corner, I froze.

The door to my room was open.

I crept toward it, fingers drifting to my knife. Light footsteps paced back and forth in my room, and I toed the cracked door all the way open. Maud jumped.

"Finally." She beckoned me into the room, fingers shaking, and raked a hand through her hair. It was a mess with the normal plait falling apart from constant worrying. "There were hands."

"What?" I locked the door behind me and pressed my back into the far corner, well out of sight from the window. A crossbow bolt could've taken the shutters and me out easy. "What hands?"

"Hands at the window." She sucked in a breath and shook her head. "I didn't think it'd frighten me, but I looked up and they were there."

She shuddered. I leaned off the wall far enough to pour her the tea she'd set out for my dinner and retreated to my safe place.

The least dangerous place. Safety didn't exist anymore.

"The rules matter. A lot. The Left Hand harps on them enough, none of us would think about breaking them." They'd never want us to be Opal if we couldn't be trusted to keep our weapons to ourselves in the palace. I slid down the wall. "And you don't look like me."

Where I was all angles, Maud was soft with round hips and dimples. Her light-brown, hooded eyes were nothing like my black ones, and she'd a waist-long plait of shiny black hair that must've been a trial to braid in the morning. Her button nose had never been broken like mine.

We shared the same rough hands though. Years of work and blisters.

Not that I couldn't look like her with a little help.

"You're prettier," I said after a long moment. Maud was unsettled and needed the compliment. "And much shorter. They could turn around and not even see you, unless they ducked."

She laughed. "They set off the bells. You'd have heard them."

"You could've left. I wouldn't have minded. Whoever owned those hands is someone I'll have to fight eventually." I pulled the tray of food toward me.

"I need you to be Opal." She let out a low, long breath and cupped the mug in her hands. "I need the promotion, and I can't help you, not really, but..."

She twirled her free hand in the air like she was gathering cobwebs, eyebrows rising to her hairline, and her gaze drifted to the mice fighting over the last of the sausage. She smiled as tight-lipped as she had when we first met.

"You're being awfully nice." I chewed, mulling over my words. I trusted her about as far as I could throw her—soon as our wants didn't line up, she'd have no reason to help me beyond her duties as servant—but she was all right. Cooked better than anyone I'd ever known and picked out my clothes better than me. "I've never had a servant before."

"I know." She patted down her hair. "You're not subtle."

"Might've been a bit hasty."

"Not all competitors are as nice as you." She fixed me with a narrow-eyed stare, all seriousness and in a tone I was sure no servant ever used with an employer. "We talk about you—we have favorites—and we can't help you, but hurting someone without anyone noticing is an art in Our Queen's court. She can't stand it, but no one can risk outright warfare. You're an etiquette travesty, but you're polite about it, and that goes a long way."

"And the folks who've had servants before aren't nice?" The invited were nobles or rich. They ignored the servants, pointed and took them for granted. They were the ones who needed to be told we couldn't hurt servants. "The invited?"

Maud hummed. She gathered up her skirts and rose, mostly back to sorts. "Would you like a bath?"

"No, thank you." I raised my voice so it carried out the window. Let the other auditioners come. "I'm exhausted. Going straight to sleep."

She arched an eyebrow but didn't say anything.

Rath and Maud were cut from the same cloth—too quick to be lied to and too clever to not pick up on signals. I'd bet my mask she was as clever with numbers as him. In a different life, she might've been more like him.

I shut one eye, finished eating, and nailed the door shut again. By the time I snuffed out my lone candle, my eye was ready for the dark.

Silence settled over my room. Curls of smoke from chimneys drifted through the shutters. I crept behind the bathtub, eyeing the makeshift dummy in my bed, and waited. The dark closed in, bleeding into the corners of my eyes. I shook my head.

No shadows here.

The window creaked, bells chiming softly in the wind. I let

out a slow, quiet breath and slid my knives into my palms. I was faster with them than the ax, and I needed to be fast. A hand with pale white fingertips peeking out of a black glove curled around the bells. Silence returned.

I could deal with people. I gripped my knives tighter, breathing in the smoke, and shifted to my toes. I had dealt with people.

And would.

I flattened myself between the bathtub and wall. The auditioner who'd come to kill me paused, staring at my bed from the window. Anyone would've caught my trickery by candlelight, but with clouds filtering unsteady moonlight through the shutters and shadows playing across the walls, they'd assume the lump of blankets was breathing. Hopefully.

The auditioner unhooked the bells. Another arm slithered between the wires and unhooked the broken shutters. The white ribbon stitched across Eight's mask glowed in the darkness. Halfway through the window, hands flat on the floor and feet still dangling outside, he stopped and stared at my bed. I leaned forward.

Lady, guard me.

I lunged. Eight raised his head in time to catch my knee in his teeth. His head snapped back, and his arms collapsed, dropping to the floor. I buried my knife into the back of his neck. He gurgled.

"Sorry that hurt." I twisted the knife.

His last few breaths left him in a rush.

I stripped Eight of his weapons. He'd a few vials in his pockets, unlabeled and useless to me either way. The daggers in his boots were nicer than mine—expensive and well cared for—and I took his ankle sheaths too. He'd nothing else of note except an archery brace and callouses like Emerald's. He could've killed Twenty easy.

He'd crawled in here on the half-thought notion I'd be sleeping peacefully though. He wasn't clever enough to have his own nest above the archery yard.

And I wasn't clever enough to realize that killing him in my own room would leave me with a body. I had to get rid of him.

At least he was small—light on his feet and all lean muscle.

I worked the nails out of my door. No one was in the hallway or up in the rafters. The roof was equally empty, with only the hushed whispers of servants and guards circling the paths below breaking the silence. I dragged Eight as fast as I could into the unoccupied room across the hall from mine. The thin blood trail left behind I mopped up with a spare shirt.

I shut the door, and the dead eyes of my first competition kill stared back at me.

"You prayed to the Triad the first day." I smeared a bloody triangle across his forehead. "I'll send you back to them."

I didn't put any faith in the three divisions of magic—mind, body, and soul. Nacea hadn't worshipped the Triad, hadn't handled magic at all for fear of The Lady taking offense at us using blood to bind magic to our wills. She was magic, and it was her. You didn't use someone to do your bidding. I remembered that much from my childhood.

Remembered how much magic and its shadows had taken from me.

But magic was gone, and the Triad and their power went with it. Only prayers and empty motions lingered to comfort the believers.

I drew the marks for mind and body over Eight's heart and heels, with the final mark of his last rites dripping down his boots.

I dragged Eight's corpse through the window and onto the roof, leaving him tucked between chimneys where anyone could've killed him. There were no auditioners in sight. I slunk back into the empty room, then to my room across the hall and collapsed into the tub.

I slept well till dawn. My rumbling stomach woke me, and I stumbled out of the tub, body weak and aching. The sun reached over the eastern spires and cast long shadows across the windows. The sooner I got to the safety of breakfast, the sooner last night was behind me.

The dining room was quiet, only a handful of servants setting up for the meal, and Maud's superior, Dimas, watched over everything. I sat in a spare chair off to the side.

"Twenty-Three?" Dimas stopped two strides away from me and bowed—just as Maud had done when we'd first met. "Do you need something? Breakfast doesn't begin until the Left Hand arrives."

A reminder that I wasn't safe here till then. I sighed. "There enough time for me to find the kitchen and get some tea before they get here?"

"I'll let Maud know." He straightened and gestured to a servant's door across the room. "You may follow the servers to the kitchen, but please let us know if you need anything so we can retrieve it for you without causing any issues."

Without me messing up their habits, more like. I nodded and took off after a twitchy server. The gall of it—I was an assassin, in theory, and bloodthirsty for all they knew. The auditions before this one must have set the tone. Assassins followed the rules and respected the servants. Maybe I was in the right place.

I might've cheated my way through near everything, but there was no point in hurting servants or putting them in danger.

No wonder Maud wanted to work here forever—Our Queen took good care of her people, even if there were snakes in her gardens. I had to take care of them for her.

Magic and its shadows hadn't ended the war in favor of Erlend, The Lady hadn't saved Nacea, and praying hadn't spared Eight.

I had to place my faith in me.

CHAPTER
SIXTEEN

I watched the servant who'd brought me tea return to the kitchen with an empty tray. Young, new—they were training just like us.

"You cleaned your room."

I turned and found Maud staring at me.

"I got restless this morning." I gestured toward the dining hall. "Dimas said he'd tell you."

"He did." She fell into step beside me but still slightly behind. "Did you think I wouldn't notice blood spots under the bed?"

I winced. "One of the auditioners snuck in and tried to kill me. I broke their nose, they ran off, and I was left to clean up the mess. Must've missed a spot."

We stared at each other for a long moment. It was obvious Maud was weighing her options. She could turn me in if that was suspicious, but then she'd be out her promotion.

"That's not too far-fetched." She shrugged. "I suppose you could win a fight."

"I've won hundreds," I said, trying to keep my voice even. "It used to be my job."

She raised an eyebrow. "But do remember—if you bleed to death, I don't get promoted *and* I have to clean it up."

"Your priorities are spectacular." I checked the knives at my waist and tapped my heels against the ones at my ankles. With Eight dead, the others would start feeling the pressure. Maybe I'd luck out, they'd get paranoid, and they'd kill each other for me. "Thank you."

"Don't mention it." She smiled and opened the door for me, ushering me into the dining hall. "I won't see you again today. Good luck."

Eight and Twenty-Two were missing. Dimas's long gray tunic swirled around his knees as he paced the length of the table and directed servers, making sure all of us had what we wanted. There was twice the number of water pitchers there usually were. I waved him over.

"Twenty-Three?" He bowed, the silver cuff that curled around the scarred, holey edge of his right ear sparkling. He was barely older than Maud and me, and the scents of silver polish and cleaning chemicals clung to him. Another orphaned war kid.

"What's with the pitchers?" I poured myself a glass and spooned grits into my bowl. The food was as varied as it had been, but there were more ground foods—speckled oats, grits, cornmeal cooked with milk. Things I'd eat if I knew we'd be running all night from guards. "And food."

His lips twitched. "We're simply providing what is necessary."

"Thank you." For nothing.

I ate light and drank as much water as I could while he walked away.

"Servants?" Four asked.

I peeled a boiled egg and nibbled on the whites. "I knew you lot had servants. You treat them like nobles would."

They'd come from one of those big carnivals then. The sort that trained you from birth and only let you go when you died—or got invited to Left Hand auditions.

Three sipped her tea, grinning. "At least we know she's never had servants."

"From Kursk, fights, and never had servants." Two smiled. "Narrows it down."

"Up!" Amethyst threw open the door to the nook.

We all shot to our feet. A shiver ran down my spine—they'd done this when they caught Thirteen. They'd caught me. They knew what I'd done, and I was out.

"Eight and Twenty-Two are dead—poorly." Emerald slid into the room, light cotton tunic the color of dandelion stems and leggings dark as damp earth. "That leaves ten of you."

Ruby laughed behind his mask and applauded. "Congratulations to our final ten auditioners. Welcome to your first real test."

I sighed. I could survive a test.

Ruby held up ten pairs of thick iron shackles.

I'd gotten out of those before—three times with picks and once with a hatpin.

"Stop." Amethyst shooed Ruby out the door and turned to us. "Follow me."

She took off running. Emerald vanished up a servants' staircase. Running I could handle, and the others could try to keep up with me. Five was at my heels, faster than I thought he'd be, and Amethyst spun around, a plume of dust engulfing us. I sucked in a breath of dirt.

It was sharp and thick, but then we were outside and running and my heart pounded against my chest in the sheer joy of knowing I could run. No nudging and no corrections.

"Our Queen, despite her power and mercy, has not persuaded all the nobles clinging to their Erlend roots." Amethyst's voice didn't waver despite the dust and footfalls. I hated running with a mask, and she managed to yell midsprint. I sped up, gaze stuck on her, and pushed myself to run faster. I wanted to do that. "We are her last resort in such cases. Those against us are not kind or merciful. They do not care who gets in their way."

My answer of dressing in their colors and avoiding them completely probably didn't help.

"We do not kill if it can be helped. We serve Our Queen, and she serves her people. It is our job, then, to make sure they are safe, even when the machinations of their traitorous masters put them in our path." Amethyst slid to a stop at the gate leading into Willowknot.

"Two and Eleven," Emerald shouted from her perch on top of the gate. "Three and Fifteen, Four and Twenty-Three, Five and Seven, and Six and Ten."

I spun around. Eleven, Fifteen, Four, Seven, and Ten were the last to arrive at the gate. Ruby stepped forward with his shackles.

They wouldn't. We couldn't run or fight or do anything chained to another person.

"The forest has been cleared for the occasion, and the dal Abreu and del Contes families have loaned us their guards. They will attempt to stop you. You may disarm and stun but cause no lasting damage." Amethyst grabbed half the shackles from Ruby and starting chaining us—hands shackled behind our backs and chains linked through the shackles of our partner. "Our last Opal died because he could not escape while shackled to another prisoner in Lord del Weylin's cells. We will not make that mistake again. You escape, you follow me, you keep up, and you don't kill anyone. Except each other, of course."

At least Four and I were roughly the same height.

I snuck my lock picks from my pocket into my sleeve, trying not to attract attention. Ruby eyed me. Maybe. Why'd they even bother? His mouth was little more than a mesh slit, and they weren't putting me at ease pretending they could look at us. He leaned in close enough that I should've felt his breath on my ear, but there was nothing.

"About tutoring." He locked the shackles in place and looped me back-to-back with Four. "Lady de Farone said you were acceptable."

I doubted Elise had used the phrase "acceptable." She seemed more flowery. Maybe an "adequate," but that would've stung.

"She's an excellent tutor," I whispered back to him.

He laughed.

"You may kill your partner." Emerald loomed over us, carrying a bow and hunting arrows—the blunt kind with a hooked end meant to capture game alive. "We will immediately suspect you though."

"And you may escape the shackles," Ruby said, ushering us to the gate. "If you can. How you finish this race is entirely up to you."

"We only care that you finish it." Amethyst looked at each of us in turn, purple mask turning to Four and me last. "Keep up."

And she was gone.

CHAPTER
SEVENTEEN

T he lot of us stared at her fleeing back. I slipped the lock
picks out of my sleeve and tugged on the shackles. Four
smacked into my back.

"We will be duly impressed if you and your partner survive."
Ruby took a spear from one of the soldiers and righted Two and
Eleven, who'd fallen over as soon they'd tried to move.

Emerald leapt from the wall to the gate to the ground quickly
as could be. "But it's not a must, so long as we don't think you
killed your partner."

"All right." Four steadied himself, his shoulders popping. "We
stay calm and you do what I say, and we can get out of this easily."

"Speak for yourself." The cuff around my right wrist clicked
open and I untangled myself from Four. I held up my picks. "You
need help, or you good?"

He jumped, swept the chain under his feet, and pulled his
arms in front of him. A similar set of picks appeared in his fingers. "I'm good."

Five and Seven, still stuck together, took off into the forest with Five shouting orders. Either he didn't want us to see him escape or Seven was about to lose a hand.

I ran through the gate. The creak of leather armor sounded to my left, and I ducked right, tumbling off the path. I rolled over my shoulder and launched myself to my feet without stopping.

Amethyst was far ahead, a purple glint among the pine needles, and I was the only auditioner in the trees. I glanced over my shoulder and grinned, sprinting farther away from the pack of auditioners stuck at the gate. Four fought off a soldier while Two dragged Eleven toward him. The soldiers were good at slowing us down.

And I was good at outrunning soldiers. All I had to do was finish the race, and Four had enough skills to take care of himself. I didn't need him slowing me down or finding some clever way to kill me without arousing suspicion.

But Amethyst was long gone. She had to be heading west or we'd be too close to Willowknot proper. I'd only been running for a little while, and I could already hear the far-off sounds of the town behind the grunts of the fights. I sprinted west through the trees.

"Found you!" A leg shot out from the underbrush and ripped me from my feet. The soldier who'd led me to auditions, who I'd been so willing to kill, rose up from the forest floor. He grinned. "Nothing personal."

He loomed over me. I crawled backward, putting as much distance as I could between us. I couldn't kill him, and he'd not drawn any weapons either. I stood.

"It wasn't personal." I slid my right foot back and raised my fists, balance shifting to the balls of my feet.

He laughed. "I know, but that didn't make it hurt less."

Fair enough.

I darted forward, slapping my palms over his ears. He hooked a foot behind my ankle and shoved me. I grabbed his collar, falling back and bracing myself, and jammed my foot into his stomach as I hit the ground. I kicked up, and he went tumbling over my shoulder.

"That's not personal either," I said.

He pulled himself to his knees and opened his mouth.

The blunt end of a spear rammed into the side of his head. He fell with a sickening crack. I drew my knives.

That wasn't a disarming hit.

"Do you know how much time I wasted dealing with Eight?" Five tossed the spear aside and drew his short sword. He moved perfectly into the guard position Ruby had been trying to teach me. "Come on then."

Five waited. I shifted back and forth, flipping one of my knives down. I could dodge a sword, block a few weak hits, but he'd planned this. He must've run nonstop to catch up with me.

I lunged, faking left. He slid his feet aside and drew the sword across his right. I twisted away from him and dove for the soldier, ripping his sword from his belt. Five stared at me, eyes drooping and bored, and straightened his mask. I tightened my grip on the hilt.

Five huffed. "Easy."

He swung at my left. I blocked, the hit shaking my arm, and faster than I could follow, his blade cut across my chest and slipped into my right side. Pain, white-hot and blinding, bur-rowed into my chest, and the slick pull of his sword leaving my skin shivered down my spine. Blood seeped down my ribs, and he flicked his blade against mine. The sword flew out of my hand.

"Amateur," he muttered, pulling back for a final strike.

He had the noblest, northernest accent I'd ever heard. Panic and rage washed over me, fluttering in my veins till my fingers shook against my side and sharpened my thoughts. I curled my fingers into the dirt. He leaned closer.

He wasn't better than me.

I flung dust in his eyes. He stumbled, sword arm falling. I thrust my knife through his shoulder, twisting the blade till he screamed, and ripped it out. He smacked my side, fingers digging into the cut.

I couldn't beat him in a fair fight, but life wasn't fair—and neither was I.

I kicked his sword aside. My wound was agony with each twist of my torso, and the soldier—my soldier who Five could've killed—was stumbling to his feet. I punched Five in the nose. It snapped.

"Amateur," I said.

He could be better than me at all the noble things he pleased, but I would be Opal, and he would be dead eventually. Even better if he panicked and dug his own grave. Let him tremble.

"Every night when you're holed away in your little nest"—I stepped on his hands and grabbed his collar, pulling him up so I could stare into his eyes—"think about how the only reason you're still breathing is because that guard woke up, how the only thing keeping me from climbing up there and putting a knife in your neck is how little I care about your face, and dream of me. Dream of me coming for you."

I shoved him back into the dirt. He twisted and coughed up a glob of spit and blood. The soldier blinked up at me.

I took off. Again. At this rate, Amethyst would be seventy by the time I finished the race.

Blood oozed between my fingers, making my grip on my knives slick and impossible. I'd need stitches.

Tomorrow would be the worst.

I kept quiet and low. I couldn't afford any more fights unless I struck first, fast, and hard. Screams and hurried footfalls echoed through the woods. Maybe I should've stayed with Four—he couldn't kill me without being blamed, and Five wouldn't have taken on both of us. I needed soldiers and all the helpful supplies they carried with them.

And they were easy to find, breathing too hard and alone. I snuck up behind one, creeping onto a stump so I could match his gangly height, and trapped him in a choke hold. He fought and flailed, right arm getting a few good hits before he passed out.

"Thank you." He'd bandages in his pocket. I washed off my cut and wrapped it, shuddering with each brush of cloth against my torn skin. It wasn't too deep, not too deep at all.

Heavy footsteps pounded up the path. I picked up the soldier's bow and slid behind a tree. Memories of Emerald's hands ghosted over my skin—back straight, stomach in, and arm bent back till the string brushed my cheek. I sucked in a thin breath.

Seven stopped in front of me, dodging an arrow from the other side of the path. He was worse for wear with a new black eye and shackle-shaped bruises around his wrists. He leapt to disarm the other archer as I fired, and he didn't notice my too-wide, wobbly shot. I practiced a few shots into the trees next to me. My aim was spotty at best, but Seven was broad. A body fell across the path.

Seven emerged from the bushes, nose bloodied.

I fired. My arrow tore through his shoulder, taking a strip of his shirt. He clapped a hand to his arm, and I drew back for another shot. It flew over his head.

Shit. I tossed the bow aside and grabbed a spear, clawing my way up into the branches of a needle-heavy pine. Seven crashed through the curtain of thick leaves and toed the soldier. I hooked my knees around a branch.

Nothing personal.

He spun, wits catching up too late, and I swung out of the tree. The spear ripped through his chest, pinning him to the trunk, and he took a bubbling breath. His last breath burst from his lips in a spray of pink.

"Sorry." I gripped the branch and unfurled myself from around it, dropping unsteadily to the forest floor. "That probably hurt."

I couldn't work the spear from the tree. Staring at him itched at me, a prickling at the back of my neck that wouldn't let up. If I'd been a little slower, a little weaker, he'd have killed me as easily and left me out here to rot. If his death at my hands was justice, what would that have been?

I walked away, the imaginary weight of his dangling arms heavy on my shoulders.

A long ways after, a rough voice grunted on the path and metal clashed against metal. I crept forward slowly.

Four flipped a soldier over his shoulder and hissed as one of the blunted arrows hit his thigh. The shot came from near me, and the soldier looped an arm around Four's ankles. I moved through my side of the woods as quiet as I could.

Four sent the soldier running with a quick jab and a threat. The archer rose from their hiding spot, and I kicked the back of their knees. Collapsing into the path, they dropped their bow and scrambled away from me. Four stepped on their sleeve.

"Stop." He glanced at me, mask twitching with his smile. "Fancy meeting you here."

"Thought a stroll would be nice." I knelt over the soldier, hooked an arm around their throat, and squeezed till they went limp. "It's been refreshing."

"Refreshing?" Four nodded to the cut on my side. "You good?"

"Great." I pressed harder on my wound and gritted my teeth. "Real good. How're you?"

"Better than you." He leaned around me, eyes focused over my shoulder. A throwing knife slid into his palm. "Duck."

I sat down hard. An arrow tore through the leaves where I'd been, and Four threw his knife across the path.

The patter of fleeing feet sounded behind me.

"How long it take you to learn that?" I nodded to the knife in his hand. It wasn't at all like one of mine, too long and thin to be of much use up close.

He helped me to my feet. "How long it take you to learn how to fight?"

"Not long." I grinned at Four's snort. "The moment between me getting punched and them trying to hit me again."

"My aunt threw knives and taught all the kids. Kept us too

busy to get in trouble," Four said. "I'm ready to be done with this if you are—side by side, run straight through with no stopping?"

Only carnival folks would think knife throwing wasn't trouble.

"Sounds good." I nodded and drew a knife. Better safe than sorry. "Let's—"

A scream drowned me out, the sound bone-shatteringly loud and drawn out, raising the hairs on the back of my neck and gooseflesh on my arms. Four shuddered.

"Myr—Three?" He turned to where it had come from, but no second shout came. "Three!"

I grabbed his arm. "Hush! You'll draw everyone here."

"That was Three." He shook me off and started running, his wide eyes and panicked breaths finally showing his age. "We know better than to scream."

He vanished into the trees. Lady bless. I stomped after him, one hand holding my side and the other grasping a knife. If she knew not to scream, whatever had happened to her was enough to break that training. I squished through the mud, pushing branches aside. Red smeared across the wood.

If I was bleeding that much, I was done for. I touched my side—no fresh blood.

Sweat rolled down the back of my neck. Four's frantic calls faded in the distance, and I took a step back. A steady drip splattered against the ground.

I looked up.

CHAPTER
EIGHTEEN

A n empty face stared back at me, skin gone and bones bare.
"You're not real," I whispered, hands flying to my neck.
The damp was sweat. There was no blood. There was no body.
My nails scraped down the back of my neck. "You're a dream.
A memory."

Red stained my fingers.

I stumbled in the mud. Mud—water. There must be water
nearby. That was it, had to be it. I was simply too thirsty to think
straight, had lost too much blood, and my dreams were creeping
into the day. I fell to my knees, sinking into the earth, and the
farther I reached, the drier it got. There had to be water, a river,
a pond. There had to be.

It wasn't real. It was never real.

The *drip* rang in my ears, loud and clear as bells. I took a
breath, hoping for the damp scent of earth and springs, but the
metallic, salty taste of blood invaded my mouth. I tore my hands
away from the underbrush and cloth came with them.

Three's mask, torn as her flesh, hung from my hands. Strands of hair fluttered in the breeze.

I screamed.

The sound ripped from my throat, rattling out of my mouth, and a rushing filled my ears. Three was real, had been real, and this was real. The drops of blood crashed loud enough to deafen, and I dragged my gaze up. The mask fell from my hands.

Three hung from the branch like laundry left to dry, a stiletto knife sticking from the back of her neck.

I clawed my way up a tree. They were back, they were back. The shadows had found me, the only Nacean face they'd missed. Twigs ripped through my arms, bark splintered under my nails, and I clung to the sturdiest branch I could find, trembling among the leaves. They couldn't climb. They never looked up. They wouldn't find me.

A muffled, breathy word broke the shrill whine in my mind.

"Who?"

Three! Three, Three. Lady, I didn't know her name, but she wasn't theirs to take and tear and play at. She'd such brown eyes.

Staring.

"Who is that?"

I tried to breathe and couldn't, air catching in my throat. My hands shook till they blurred. I pressed my palms into my eyes.

My tree trembled. The shadow moved beneath me, nothing rasping over bark, clawing for my skin.

"Who are you?" the blackness muttered.

They couldn't have me.

A shriek cut through the haze—overpowering the rushing in my ears and dripping burned into my mind.

The others. I'd forgotten the others. They didn't know what the shadows were like, what they really were, how to stay clear of them. No one deserved this death.

Four sobbed, one hand fluttering around Three's face and the other clenching her mask. He screamed and screamed and screamed, and I was sure the sound would never stop.

"Climb." The word died in my throat, buried under breaths I couldn't take and the taste of blood. I sucked in a deep gulp of air and shimmied down the trunk. "You have to climb."

Four looked up. My feet hit the ground, slipping in the mud.

Black claws curled around his shoulders and dragged him back. He howled, the sound filling my head. Three's mask hit the ground.

The noise died.

I ran.

The others, all the others—Ruby and Emerald and Amethyst. The auditioners, the soldiers, Our Queen. The shadows would kill everyone.

They'd kill Elise.

I pumped my arms and legs harder, toes flying across the dirt. Darkness rushed past the corners of my eyes as I ran—rustling in the deadfall, twisting behind trunks, shifting from real shadow to real shadow. I forced each breath through my nose till it burned and ached, and, Lady, no one deserved this.

I'd not been strong enough to outrun them then, but I could now.

I skidded round a bend in the path. Ruby stood in the center of it, expressionless mask staring down at me. I rammed into him, running too fast to stop, and we went tumbling. His hands closed around my shoulders, trying to keep us upright. My elbow cracked against his metal face.

"Shadows!" I crawled to my feet.

Ruby groaned, adjusting his mask.

"Shadows," I said, my breath catching. "They're back."

Soldiers screamed for Ruby behind me. I sprinted away, his red face blurring with the other images of the damned I fled past. A stitch in my side ate at my ribs and stole my breath. I chanced a look back.

Ruby raced back toward Three, toward the shadows, toward death.

"Twenty-Three!" Emerald, mask a bright spot at the edge of the woods, drew her bow.

It would do no good.

I slowed enough to shout, "Shadows."

She grabbed me. "What?"

"No, no." I tugged her back toward the palace with me, heels failing to find hold in the dust. "Shadows. There are shadows. They got Three. They—"

I gagged, the weight of my running and her staring eyes bubbling up the back of my throat. Emerald's fingers tightened around my wrist.

"There are no shadows," she said. "And there never will be again."

"No, no, no." I stumbled and collapsed. I stared at each of them in turn. They had to believe me. "Three's gone, and a shadow got Four. I saw it."

Ruby, panting behind his mask and dragging Two by the arm, appeared behind Emerald. "Three's flayed."

"See!" I tried to stand, and my knees betrayed me.

"Hush." Emerald knelt next to me and grabbed my face in her hands. "You saw Three flayed and your mind did the rest. You saw them in Nacea, didn't you?"

I nodded. "It was morning. I climbed up to get a better look at The Lady's constellation."

I'd climbed up. My siblings had played below, too young to do much but stumble. Shadows had ripped through them like thorns through flesh.

"Who am I?" Emerald asked as she gripped me so tight I couldn't look around.

"Emerald." I shook my head. "You're Lady Emerald."

"The first of the Left Hand and the only one known throughout Igna," she said softly. "You know I survived them."

"You tore it in half with runes, but magic's gone."

"I tore apart the runes holding it together. Without magic, they cannot exist. Trust me, I am one of only four left living who knows how to create and destroy the shadows." She let me go and leaned aside. "Look."

Four stood with Two, eyes rimmed with red and hands dripping blood. He clutched Three's mask with shaking hands.

"What?" I glanced around. "How?"

"Like I said, you saw Three and your mind did the rest. Three was an auditioner kill. A cruel one but one nonetheless." Emerald stood. "Lady dal Abreu is a royal physician. Let her look at you, and be polite while she does."

I nodded, heart still hammering away at what was left of my ribs.

"I do love being right though," Emerald said as she patted my shoulder. "You are quite the runner."

I'd thought death was at my heels. "I don't like being chased."

"No one does."

She moved away, and Four took her spot. He gestured to me.

"Two grabbed me." He shook his head like a mourner trying to keep tears at bay. "Not a shadow."

"Whoever killed Three was a butcher." Lady dal Abreu kneeled next to me, her evergreen dress stitched with thick, black thread like a turtle's shell fanning out around her. She pointed to the strands of hair clinging to Three's mask. "Not a shadow."

I took the flask of water from her. Of course everyone here had seen them, been to war against them. She was Rodolfo da Abreu's twin and knew the shadows just as well as he had. All the stories said she'd offered a fortune to anyone willing to return his corpse for funeral rites—illegal since his vengeance had meant killing folks who'd surrendered. She knew the shadows as well as Emerald—knew how to create and destroy them.

Knew better than me how to tell fears from reality.

Face drawn and gray eyes narrowed, Lady dal Abreu peeled back my soaked shirt and hasty bandage with rune-scrawled hands. The turtle designs inked into her skin—the ones that had granted her healing powers and would've severed her arms at the wrists had she misused them—were the only runes I'd ever liked. Now, in the filtered forest light, they were white and dead and useless, drained of everything that had given them life. Just like Three.

Elise's face, dimpled cheeks smeared with charcoal and blood, flashed through my mind.

I winced.

"Stop it." She pressed a rag soaked with witch hazel against my side. "Any one of us would've been afraid." She dropped her voice to whispered Alonian. "Most of us can't even sleep in the dark anymore. Ruby's hopeless without a lamp."

I let out my breath in a low, long hiss and scratched at a cut on my hand. "I can't either. Not back up here."

How could she stand to stitch me up when I stood for everything she swore an oath to stop—injuries and death?

"Scratch it again and I'll stitch your fingers to your dress." The threat of violence assuredly not to come was southern enough. "Scratching will make it worse."

I nodded. She smiled, thin lips twisting up into a crooked grin so wide it crinkled the corners of her eyes and stretched the runes lining her lids.

Only Our Queen's most trusted peers—Emerald, Nicolas del Contes, Isidora dal Abreu, and Rodolfo da Abreu—had those runes, the ones that let them see the shadows' magic.

Rodolfo had been Isidora's twin, the same hair and eyes, same freckles, all the rumors said, and I'd enough pain simply remembering my dead siblings. Looking in a mirror for her must've been torture.

I'd grown up listening to the stories of Rodolfo da Abreu as fondly as most kids listened to bedtime tales. He'd killed the Erlend mages responsible for the shadows to prevent the knowledge of their creation from ever being spread, but I'd never considered the pain his life might've left behind. The shadows left nothing but pain in their wake.

Four plopped onto the ground next to me.

"I never saw the shadows," Four said as he tucked Three's mask into his pocket. His eyes were glazed, and he was out of it, completely in his own world. He didn't even notice Two's worried stare. "I never knew."

He trailed off. I handed him the flask I'd stolen. If it wasn't shadows, we'd nothing to worry about. Monstrous people were old news.

Still, seeing your friends like that never got easier.

"I'm sorry you know now."

CHAPTER
NINETEEN

I sidora dal Abreu fixed me up with evenly spaced stitches that puckered my skin around the edges. She covered the rest of my hurts in sweetly scented salves, and she slipped me a jar of it with a pat on the hand. I sat with Four and Two in silence, trying to erase the memory of that *drip* from my mind, and watched the other auditioners race through the gate. Five showed up while I was still getting bandaged, his shoulder already taken care of and his face sporting a black eye I hadn't given him. Six and Ten stumbled over the line together, their shackles unhooked from each other but still dangling from their wrists. Eleven and Fifteen raced for second-to-last place.

Fifteen won.

Ruby ran circles around Eleven as she finished, tapping her heels with a spear. The familiar, shaky panic of the shadows hadn't left me, and grim-faced guards filtered in from the forest. Three's death hung heavy over all of us.

Too heavy for Two and Four to even speak.

"With eight left alive, your physical training is now over." Emerald's soft voice drew our attention. "Your training is not however."

Elise had been right: there were rounds, and I'd survived the first one.

"You will cease your attempts on each other's lives tonight." Ruby tightened the knots of his mask. "Your servants will help you relocate, and you will be on your best behavior."

"Your new rooms are as much a test as this run," Amethyst said. "You will be housed within the true grounds of the palace, beyond the River Caracol, and you will be expected to behave as guests of Our Queen. We will be watching."

They were letting us into the palace proper? With all the lords and ladies and honorable court members who balked at dirt? They couldn't let everyone beyond the river and wall, and they'd have to trust Opal to behave properly at court. Which meant our next lessons were—

"Poisons, etiquette, and basic medicine training will begin tomorrow after breakfast." Emerald had to be grinning like a fiend behind her mask because her voice was laughing at us. "At which point, you may resume the competition."

"We expect you to kill in ways to reflect your growth." Ruby gestured for us all to stand. "Those of you taking other lessons will still attend tonight. We'll explain everything else tomorrow."

Amethyst nodded. "You've all done well. We were trying to break you physically. The next part may let you rest your body but not your mind. Rest well. You'll need it."

The Left Hand turned away from us to address a crowd of

soldiers all sporting various bruises and scrapes. Isidora and Ruby turned to each other, whispering back and forth.

We were dismissed.

Maud walked me back to my room. She offered me her arm once, after catching sight of the bandage around my side and the dried blood dotting my clothes, but I shook her off. I'd already nearly died and made a fool of myself. The other auditioners didn't need to see how weak I was.

But Isidora said Ruby slept with a lamp, and the rest of the Left Hand had seen the shadows. Surely they'd understand my panic.

When we reached the room, Maud peeled my shirt away without disturbing the stitches. My room was spotless—the tub tipped in the corner, the mice gone, and all my clever contraptions for keeping people out taken apart. She set a washbasin next to me.

"Isidora gave me salve—in my pocket."

"Lady Isidora dal Abreu?" Maud rifled through my ruined clothes and pulled out a tiny jar.

"Suppose I should get used to using their titles." I leaned back, eyes too heavy to stay open. "She was nice. Emerald said she treats the Left Hand."

"She certainly does." Maud hummed and checked my stitches. "She and Ruby have been inseparable since he won his mask. Can't blame her—he's terrifying but polite and protective if he likes you."

I snorted. "What else you know about her?"

"Only gossip—married Nicolas del Contes five years ago when she was eighteen, sticks close to Our Queen and the Left Hand, and keeps a laboratory scarier than anything I want to do with.

Her husband's a sneaky one, dressing up like soldiers and servants to keep an eye on things." Maud pushed a tray of food toward me—a small slice of bread slathered in butter and a smaller bowl of berries. "She's nice though. She doesn't charge you anything if you're sick and can't afford the medicine."

I knew of Nicolas del Contes—an Erlend who'd sided with Our Queen—but nothing useful. I'd have to worm some information out of Elise.

Elise. Tutoring. I still had to go to tutoring. How had it only been one day?

"Maud?" I waved my arm, too tired to sit up. "I have to go to tutoring tonight. Can you wake me up when it's time?"

I'd not really, truly slept in days. Thank The Lady we were safe tonight because there was no way I could stay awake through it.

"Of course," Maud said. "I'll take you to your new quarters after."

The door clicked shut. I meant to say "thank you," but the words didn't come. I stared at the closed door from my slumped seat on the bed, cheek pressed to the wall, and closed my burning eyes. Only a moment, one small break while the sun still shone and nightmares couldn't come.

"Up, Twenty-Three." Maud touched my arm. "Time to move."

I jerked awake and swung. Maud lurched backward. At least she wasn't calling me "Auditioner" anymore.

"Don't do that." My mouth was cotton and my tongue stuck to my teeth. I downed a cup of too-hot tea. "Don't touch me before I'm awake. I might hit you."

A lifelong habit wouldn't distinguish between Maud and enemies.

She exhaled loudly through her nose. "Good to know."

"Good." I waited for her to pour me a second cup of tea, curling my fingers around the mug. Last thing I needed was to get disqualified for hitting someone I didn't even want to hit. Maud didn't deserve a bloody nose and no promotion. "Where's the new room?"

"The Left Hand have quarters near Our Queen, but each keeps residences in the outer circle for visitors. You'll be housed on Amethyst's grounds."

The River Caracol spiraled out from under the palace, natural springs older than Erlend and Alona combined that had been twisted into shape ages ago. Each loop of the spiral served as an extra level of defense for the main palace walls at its center. I'd only now gotten used to the layout of this place.

That was probably the point.

"And I don't get to know where everyone else is staying?"

Maud dropped a spoon into the bowl and didn't answer.

I cracked my sore back and muttered, "Fun."

She smiled.

I stretched my sore limbs and shoveled as much food as I could into my mouth. If our next test was all poisons and healing, I'd be hard-pressed to find safe food, especially with Eleven—her apothecary sigil and fast fingers were a terrifying combination. We'd be learning etiquette too. I didn't even know where to start with that.

"I look all right?" I fiddled with my sleeves, the well-tailored lines heavy and unfamiliar. Might as well start being proper now. If I was going to work my way into Elise's good graces for noble information, I'd have to look good. "Good enough for all those honorable court members I'm going to be meeting?"

"Your hair's a mess," Maud said without missing a beat. Fair enough—I'd shaved it last winter and it was growing in wild. "Your bottom lip is split, and there's a hole in your mask. You don't hold a candle to anyone at court clothes-wise either."

I touched my mask. A thin slit gaped under my fingers, and the scratch across my cheek underneath was rough and new. I sighed.

Elise had already seen me at my worst. I could only improve.

"Can you fix my mask without me taking it off?" I snaked my fingers under the mask and held it out. "No stitching it to me."

"I think I can manage that." Maud sat down next to me, pulling a needle and thread from her pocket. Buttons, ribbons, rags, and an old thimble tumbled out of her pockets. She threaded the needle and pried wax from the point. "Hold still."

She stitched it up neat as my side. I could stitch flesh well enough to leave a small scar, but my hands shook too much on normal days to be good at anything other than sloppy darning. I rubbed the thread.

"Sewing part of being a servant?" I asked as I sniffed my tunic.

At least I smelled all right. Bet Elise had a dozen different fancy perfumes. And a dozen different flirts.

Hopefully she liked dangerous people.

"I'm an attendant." Maud stuffed her collection of sewing tools back in her pocket. "I was a housekeeper, but attendants have a higher rank and better pay, and this was the fastest way to become one."

I nodded. There was a story there, but she didn't trust me with her truths, and I didn't trust her with mine.

"Personal attendants take care of schedules, clothes, makeup, accountants, and such needs," said Maud. "Everyone at court has one, and if they can't afford one, they make another servant take the place of one. Appearances matter as much as anything else."

Great. Another thing I could fail at. I didn't like depending on Maud for so much.

I walked to the nook alone, smoothing down my hair as best as I could under my mask. Elise was the daughter of one of the old lords who'd bowed to Our Queen—couldn't be happy about it—and she'd embraced the new court. She'd know all the noble things I didn't, like which Erlends were unhappy, who knew what about Nacea, and where all of them lived beyond the Caracol.

Where Lord Horatio del Seve was.

Where the lords who'd withdrawn their soldiers from Nacea and left us to die were.

Who all owed me the blood of thousands and had yet to pay up.

Lady, guide me. With the right push, Elise de Farone could tell me everything I needed.

CHAPTER

TWENTY

E lise set down her pen when I entered. Her hair was loose today and the window behind her open. Tight curls bounced over her shoulders, strands as dark as a midnight pansy, and two pearl combs shaped like Our Queen's jagged lightning bolts kept her hair from falling into her eyes. She rested her chin on a fist.

Flirting with her would be easy.

I bowed. "Lady de Farone."

"Twenty-Three." She nodded to me, the azurite powder lining her eyes tilting up like ocean waves. Silver dotted the tips like salt. "You're still alive."

"I'd hate to miss studying with you." I took my seat and shifted my shoulders back, chest slightly out and tunic falling off my shoulders till the base of my neck was bare. I needed to know if she was truly interested in me or even could be. "You look lovely."

"Thank you," she said, "but we're here for you, not me."

"And I continue to wonder what kind act I performed to grant me time to see you."

She laughed, covering her mouth with her hand. I let myself relax.

She opened her mouth to speak, shook her head, and laughed again. I picked up the piece of charcoal.

"My apologies." I pulled the little booklet of phrases toward me, ignoring the scribbles of another auditioner—another person Elise was probably as kind to—and tapped a section near the end. "We left off here."

"We did." Elise reached across the table and gently pulled the charcoal from my fingers.

I glanced up. Her glasses slid down her nose, revealing the dusting of dark-red freckles dotting her face from round cheek to round cheek. A small scar clipped her upper lip.

"Why are you flirting with me?" she asked. "I loathe politics, and I've no time to get tangled up in some Left Hand auditioner game."

"No game. I like you." It wasn't a complete lie. I took the charcoal back, carefully brushing my fingers against her hand. The ring I'd stolen rested comfortably on her right forefinger. "And you're the prettiest person I get to talk to these days."

"Please, I've met Lady Emerald." She narrowed her eyes at me. "You're terrible at this. You'll need to get better before you can survive court."

Good—now I knew Elise's likes. And they were good. Lady Emerald was a jewel among mortals and dangerous as death itself.

"You could teach me," I said, leaning forward and running my tongue along the cut on my lips.

Her gaze dropped to my mouth and darted back up to my

eyes. "I'll teach you to read and write. I don't flirt with people who could kill me as easily as they could kiss me."

Fine, but she was as attracted to me as I was to her at least.

"Fair enough." I traced the lines of the words I was supposed to be learning. "But I wouldn't dream of killing you."

She caught on and glanced away, brown skin warming along her cheeks. "Write down the alphabet, and we'll see what you remember."

I did. My letters were a little shaky, but they were correct. She watched me, head angled high enough that I couldn't see her eyes through the glare on her glasses. I doodled "Ignasi" on the paper while she looked over the alphabet and words I'd learned to write last time. "Good." Elise set aside the paper, shivering when our hands touched. "I suppose we can work on penmanship later."

"How do you write 'Erlend?'" I asked, tapping my scrawled "Ignasi" and pursing my lips in the image of feigned confusion. "And your name? What do the titles look like?"

She hummed and nodded. "That would be more useful for you. Let's start with Our Queen and the Left Hand, and then we'll move through the ranks of people you'll probably meet."

She pulled out a blank sheet of paper and began scrawling names. I recognized Our Queen Marianna da Ignasi. I'd prayed for her as a kid, writing her name in blood and burning the pages so The Lady would get them. The rest I could guess at—Ruby was short, Emerald was longer than I thought it would be based on how it sounded, and Amethyst looked ridiculous even in Elise's pretty handwriting.

"Will you write Opal too?" I asked. Best to know what it

looked like now since it would be my name if I lived. "And all those Erlend nobles? I know the Alonian ones."

"Igna nobles." Elise continued writing, making the letters separate and clear. A handful of the names were harsher, the tip of the charcoal digging into the paper with each jagged flourish. Someone had pissed off Elise. "We're all members of Igna now."

Political and polite even when they'd angered her. I copied her as she wrote down more names, only recognizing some—del Contes, del Farone, del Seve. Horatio del Seve was among Elise's collection of names that were more stab wounds than words. I pulled the paper toward me.

"Not so fast." She grabbed the edge of it. "I'll say a name and you point to it. Let's see if you can sight-read them."

I touched the name below Seve's. "Sure, but what did this paper do to you?"

She winced. Good, feel a little bad and offer up an explanation. Information I could use.

"They are perfectly fine people," she said, and I could practically hear the "but" her politeness stifled. "Lord del Seve's land borders my father's land Hinter, and I am attempting to standardize education between the free schools and private tutors. He found my proposal too costly." She eyed me over her glasses, guarded and passionate. Passionate people loved talking about their passions. "Valid but unfortunate. You're learning much what the public schools cover. So show me what you've learned."

Of course, no matter what else I wanted out of our meetings, she was still teaching me to read and write. She said a random name, and I pointed to it, running down the list with only a few mistakes.

And now I knew what Seve's name looked like. Least Elise was a good judge of character—of course he didn't want everyone taught the same. Couldn't have the folks you ruled smart enough to overthrow you. I brushed a smear of charcoal from her hand.

"That's good." Elise leaned away from me, tapping her fingers against the table. "Let's try something new. Say 'march.'"

"March." I copied her, leaning back in my chair and resting my chin on my fingers like Emerald. I knew she liked Emerald, and I had to get her to like me well enough to talk to me about more than words and letters and sounds.

"If you remove the first letter, what word does it make?" she asked.

I opened my mouth and stopped. "What?"

"You already know the languages," she said in Erlenian, waiting for me to nod. She switched to Alonian. "We need to connect what you know to what you don't. So I'll say a word and you write it down. Queen?"

That was easy. I'd been writing it down for prayers since I could remember.

Elise grinned. "Good. Lady?"

And it went on like that, Elise saying a word and me writing it down. I'd a good memory, always had, but sounds didn't always match the letters, and combining them was a pain. I got more wrong than right.

And snapped a piece of charcoal by accident after the third mistake.

"It's all right. Stop frowning. I'll see you tomorrow in the new quarters." She gathered up our papers and tucked them aside as a knock sounded on the door. "I'll actually have all my things then."

"Where exactly are the new quarters?" I helped her collect the stray pieces of charcoal and a wayward pen.

She glanced up at me, and the silver dust clinging to her lashes softened her gaze. "I don't know where everything else will be, but I will be tutoring my charges in Emerald's guest parlor. Her residence is the most spacious."

Well, more than I knew before.

"Till tomorrow then." I took her hand as I'd seen courtiers do and bowed over it, but I didn't kiss her knuckles—too much, she already didn't trust me.

She let out a breathy laugh. "I told you I don't flirt with people who could kill me."

"Course not. You just humor the ones robbing you."

"You could hardly rob me," she said, shooing me out of the door.

Fifteen was in the dining hall when I left. I nodded to him, uncomfortable with his glaring presence even with the Left Hand's demands for us to stop killing each other, and darted around him. Maud was waiting for me outside.

"Time to move?" I asked.

She nodded. "The only thing left is you."

Maud led me through the buildings flush against the training yard. Dimas waited for us at a locked door—one with a brand-new lock. He pulled a collection of keys from his pocket—none of them bearing any identifying mark I could pair with the door—and selected the right key on his first try. Maud adjusted the new black ribbon adorning her collar. He sniffed.

"What's with the collar?" I asked once the door had shut.

We picked our way over the neatly groomed path of clipped grass spotted with wildflowers. The forest was quiet, a few lanterns bobbing on guards' hips in the distance, and shadows rippled in the trees. I fixed my eyes on Maud.

She glanced at me. "If you can't figure it out, I'm not allowed to answer it."

"Great." It was obviously a quick way to signify who was allowed where, but still. "Where are we?"

"The palace grounds are a circle," she said softly. "We were on the outer edge of it near the wall, and now we're moving closer to the center. Everything circles the palace at the center."

The thrum of the River Caracol grew.

She led me through a maze of paths I couldn't keep track of to a broad footbridge guarded by two soldiers holding lanterns and spears. The Caracol rolled beneath, slow and steady, waters warming the air with the scents of salt and brimstone. Maud nodded to the taller soldier with silver-streaked hair. The hilt at his hip had no blade.

"So," I said once we were past them, "soldiers and servants get their own secret entrance."

"The front gate's for visitors. We're not to be seen until called." Maud pulled me down a path, and a breeze ripe with the tang of oranges whipped over us. "Emerald oversees the orangery. Amethyst's residence is next door to it and the other greenhouses."

"Where do all the nobles live?" The paths were more forest than road and the skyline a canopy of thick leaves and hanging gardens. With such stringent rules about who could enter the two gates, they could afford such indefensible grounds. "The ones I need to bow and scrape and defer to?"

"Bowing is enough." Maud exhaled slowly. "You couldn't care less about that, and I'm not helping with whatever plot you've got going."

"So when I trip over some high court member, you'll look the other way?"

"The nobles live deeper in the spiral and closer to the palace proper, past Ruby's residences," Maud said. "Emerald keeps rooms close to the orangery, then Amethyst, then Ruby, and the people next—merchant heads, ambassadors, court members. Everything's in a spiral, and the closer you get to the center, the nobler they are."

With Our Queen at their center.

I nodded. "I'll try not to trip on them."

The windows of the eastern spires glittered like stars above me, and I wandered after Maud with my eyes to the sky. Towers and arches split the expanse like lightning, glass windows lit by chandeliers cast rainbows across the grounds, and trees twisted together to block patches of sky. Maud stopped outside of a building framed with twining honeysuckle. Amethyst's dour mask was burned into the door.

No mistaking whose residence this was.

"You're here." Maud pulled two keys from her pocket and handed one to me. I turned it over in my hand. The lock was a tumbler and easy enough to pick. "I drew a bath before I came to get you—extra hot, should be all right now—and laid your clothes out. I'll come get you in the morning."

She unlocked the door. I peered inside and whistled. The

room was simple but nice. A real bed with pillows and quilts stitched like the night sky sat in one corner, and a thin screen painted like a spring woodland split the small room in half. The bath steamed behind it.

"Much nicer than the last one." I traced a finger along the wooden wall, carvings of bears and deer smooth under my nails.

"With the understood obligation you'll leave it as you found it." Maud smiled softly. "I'm betting even nicer than wherever you were before this. My room's much better than the orphanage."

"What would you know?" I said, dismissal coming in an instant, but I snapped my teeth together to stop the rest from coming out. Orphanage—that explained a lot. Rath carried everything in his pockets too. "I was never quite sure if I was better or worse off than the orphanage kids."

"Up to chance—mine wasn't the worst. Taught me to clean and sew." She nodded toward the bath. "I'll wake you up in the morning. Two knocks. You've no windows—just the slats in the ceiling—so you only need to worry about the door."

I hadn't even noticed, but the roof was open to the night sky, thin pieces of wood missing every few spaces so that slivers of moonlight shone through. A finely woven mesh covered the gaps.

"Thank you." I held open the door for her, intent on locking it soon as she left, and offered her my own small smile.

Maud stepped outside. Without looking back, she said, "And thank you for not dying."

"Your continued approval keeps me going." I closed the door behind her. Definitely a quality tumbler lock but still a tumbler. I paced the room from corner to corner and checked for any hidden passages she might've missed. Nothing.

Staring at the dark ceiling later, wrapped in the finest blankets I'd ever touched and cleaner than I'd ever been, I traced the map of scars my lifetime of running and fighting, thieving and fear, had carved into me and smiled.

They'd welcomed me into their house, and I was going to tear it down.

CHAPTER
TWENTY-ONE

I dreamed of bells and blood. It was harder to wake up than it was to fall asleep, and I battled with my body for control while staring at the ceiling. The tense, muscle-taut pain of waking before I was ready eased away slowly. The unsettling darkness of the room, broken only by the finger-thin slats in the ceiling, pressed down on me. I rolled out of bed.

Maud's double knock broke through my hazy dreams.

"Twenty-Three?" She knocked twice again, and the tumbler lock clicked open. "I'm coming in."

"Sounds good." I crawled back onto the bed, pulling on my mask, and shuffled around till the shirt I'd slept in was turned right side out. "Light's weird with no windows."

Maud held up her tapered candle. "The Left Hand prefer it."

She lit the lamps while I straightened myself up for breakfast. She waited at the door, lighter smoking in her hands, and shook her head when I stepped forward. I stopped.

"You're learning etiquette and palace life." Maud pulled a

longer tunic from the pile. "You won't be in the dirt all day now. You have to impress."

"All my clothes look the same." I grabbed the tunic, gesturing for her to turn around. "Black and cheap."

"I bought the nicest ones," she said loudly. "They know you don't have much to work with, but you should at least try."

Not much to work with, my ass. I yanked the old shirt off and pulled on the tunic. It was nicer with a back hem sweeping to my knees and the hemline edged in dark-gray swirls. The black buttons at my throat were as shiny as my leggings. I definitely looked better.

"I don't see how this is an improvement," I said to Maud, gliding past her and out the door. No need for her to get cocky and think I needed her.

She locked the door behind me. "Of course you don't. You don't know any better yet."

I stopped.

"Breakfast is this way." Smug smile in place, Maud led me down a winding dirt road shaded by a canopy of wire, ivy, and climbing bittersweet. Five entered from a path to the west a ways ahead of us.

"Whose residence is down there?" I rolled my eyes west so Five wouldn't catch me snooping.

"Ruby's." Maud made a sharp, dismissive sound with her tongue.

"Don't like Five?" If I was going to get back at him for the forest run, I needed to know every little secret and rumor about him. And where he was sleeping.

Maud glanced at me, lips pursed, and whispered, "He's very

demanding, and that is certainly nothing new. It's our job to do what is asked and take care of what isn't, but he's—"

"The very definition of arrogant Erlend?"

"You're insulting me too, you know?" Maud walked with me the last few steps to the door. "He's cruel when he doesn't need to be."

"Entitled to things always going his way?"

She nodded. I'd be taking care of him soon enough and his servant would be free.

"I'll have a server bring you a canteen during breakfast, and you can fill it yourself," she said. "I'll be busy with other things."

Two and Four sat together at the table. The others who'd died hadn't filled as much space in my mind as Three. She'd told me how to stretch, liked strong tea, and now she was dead, gone in a spray of blood and pain no one had the right to suffer. I took my seat across from them and next to Fifteen. Four nodded to me.

"And again." Four raised his tea to me, the sharp sting of liquor in the air, and downed it in one go. "No more running at least."

"Here we are, eight of twenty-three." Ruby swept into the room, holding the door open for Amethyst and Emerald, and took his seat at the head of the table. "I'm sure each of you is dying to know the new rules."

"They're the exact same." Emerald poured herself a cup of dark chicory. "But be polite about it—no mess, no fuss."

Easy enough. I finished off my plate and accepted the canteen from the server.

"And if you do make a mess, clean it up," Amethyst said. "Breakfast is still safe. Eat up."

I poured water into the canteen. Fifteen reached for another plate of food while Five leaned back in his chair, gaze on Ruby.

"You'll head to poisons first." Ruby twirled a spoon between his fingers. "You may, of course, skip anything you feel adequately prepared for, but we will be watching."

"We are always watching." Amethyst laid a hand on Ruby's shoulder. "Ruby will teach you etiquette after poisons, and your final training session will be healing. Lady Isidora dal Abreu and I will lead you through basic exercises. Other necessary tutoring will still take place after that. The moment you step outside this room, the competition begins again."

Good. I still had Elise to tell me where Seve was and what he was up to. Maybe I could even find Shan de Pau.

"Up." Emerald beckoned us to a far door. "We might not be running, but I won't abide slowness."

She led us to a greenhouse with a fancy combination lock, glass walls, and pointed ceilings taller than most of the surrounding trees shining in the early morning sun. Trellises crawling with twining orange sunrise roses lined the inside walls; hanging gardens dripped with dark-green, leafy vines and midnight-blue flowers; and a curtain of soft green thyme spilled over the planter above the door. Emerald held the vines aside for us before pulling on a pair of thick leather gloves. I slipped through the door after Four. Eleven slunk away from us.

No surprise that she knew her poisons.

Water settled over my skin. The air was thick with it—drops of it beading on my arms and the damp scent of dirt filling my nose. My shoes clicked softly against the boards laid over the ground, designed to keep us off the plants, and a bee flitted through the purple bittersweet over my right shoulder. Ten leaned over a cluster of snowbells.

"Do not touch anything while you are in here unless I tell you to do so." Emerald circled behind a worktable in the center of the floor. Her green cotton tunic and brown trousers were well made but comfortable looking, and mud streaked her gloves. A tiny butter-yellow flower clung to her sleeve. "If you do and it's poisonous, I cannot guarantee I can save you. Or that I'll try. I've more important things to do than fuss over you. Among other things, we're looking for a certain intelligent drive in all of you to stay alive. Touching plants in a greenhouse full of poisons doesn't breed confidence."

I tucked my hands into my pockets. I was fairly comfortable that no one could harm me in here without being caught, and I was rested enough to yank my hands free in time to block a blow. It was only last night, but I already felt worlds better without paranoia and exhaustion hanging over me.

"Anyone in this world could kill you if they tried hard enough, and the same is true of plants." She picked up a small yucca root. "I'm sure most of you have eaten this one way or another. There's a reason yucca is treated before it's eaten.

"As a member of the Left Hand, you'll use poisons that kill quickly with little effort, if you use them at all. You'll encounter all sorts." She beckoned us forward with a finger and pointed behind her to a forest of dangling white flowers and thorny blossoms. "I'm going to show you the most common poisonous plants and describe their symptoms. Odds are that you won't know you've been poisoned until it's too late, unless you're well trained. In the coming days, I will test you on how to detect them in your food and drink. Avoidance is the first key to survival."

"But wouldn't learning how to survive them be more useful?" Fifteen pointed to the yucca on the table, fingers crooked. He was a boxer through and through. "Knowing how not to die?"

"I'm not here to keep you alive. I'm here to make you deadlier than you already are. I am here because whichever of you rises to the top and becomes Opal is going to need to know this, not because the lot of you could be poisoned," Emerald said. "Your survival depends on you, not me."

No one else asked questions. Emerald led us through the room—a silent parade of furrow-browed auditioners. She lingered over a bundle of long green stems crowned with blue flowers and swarming with swan moths. Another bunch of the same plant with yellow flowers was next to it. She plucked a leaf.

"Eating is not the only way to die." She rubbed the leaf between her gloves, crushing it till it was paste. "Touching one of these with your bare skin could kill you."

Great.

Emerald exchanged her gloves for a fresh set and led us to a corner with small flowering shrubs that had dangling orange blooms and a deep pleasant scent. Another plant growing in its shadow had small green leaves with wicked points and bell-like white petals that deepened to dark velvety purple. The contrast was pretty.

"There are certain qualities that give away a plant's defenses." Emerald bent at the waist and plucked up one of the white bells. She held it close to the left eyehole of her mask. "Bright colors where they shouldn't be." Purple stripes lined the stem of the plant. "Thorns and spikes, shiny leaves and white sap—all indicate that a plant is probably poisonous. If you have the misfortune of tasting one, it will be bitter."

She laid the stem next to its mother plant and held a hand over the dangling orange flowers. This shrub displayed none of those characteristics.

This was going to be fun. My mice would be fat and happy so long as no one tried to poison me, and I'd know what flowers to avoid if stranded and starving in a garden.

Emerald led us around the greenhouse, pointing to flowers and berries as she went. I committed them to memory—thorns, three leaves, bright colors—and hung back behind the rest of the group. The glass walls were practically impenetrable with their climbing vines and walkways. Eleven was either plotting or resting.

Five and Six were gone. If I stayed in these sessions, no matter how much I needed them, I'd be dead by morning. I needed time to plan my survival. These lessons were too predictable—same times, same places, every day—and the others had the advantage when I was stuck in these sessions.

Long after the damp dimpled my skin, Emerald removed her gloves and shooed us from the building. The heat outside scoured my lungs and dried me out, and I twisted my head toward the sky. It was well past midday. Maybe we were lucky and Five and Six had killed each other.

At least there were no high spots here for archers to pick us off.

"This way please." Ruby's red-collared servant bowed before us and started walking down a path.

I glanced at the others. Eleven and Five had slipped back into the crowd, and Two and Four followed the servant. I followed them with Eleven shuffling behind me. Five's light, confident strides a few paces behind me echoed in my head. I touched my side.

Lady bless. Was them killing each other too much to ask?

CHAPTER
TWENTY-TWO

A long semicircle table set for a banquet but devoid of food greeted us in Ruby's domain. There were eight chairs around the table and one seat at the head, slightly raised from the rabble. Ruby lounged across it.

"No." He waved a hand at us, head lolling back as though he were rolling his eyes, and held up a finger. "All wrong already."

We all stopped. Five laughed.

Ruby leapt out of his seat and stalked toward us. "I am Lord Ruby of Our Queen's court, the fourth of the Left Hand. You wait to be granted permission before entering a person's room—especially if that member is of the Left Hand."

I backtracked to the door and narrowly avoided bumping into Two.

"You do not approach Our Queen without bowing and waiting for her to approve your approach. Forgo bowing with everyone else—the Left Hand is above them." Ruby herded us all into a straight line and stood at the end, back pin-straight next to

me. I drew back my shoulders to match him. "Once you're welcomed into the room, approach until you're three paces apart
and then bow."

He swept into the perfect bow, his back straight and feet
apart—a holdover from the days when mages wore runes on
their feet and bridging the gap brought the magic to life. I copied
him. Everyone else followed suit.

"A good rule of thumb is to stay horizontal in the time it takes
you to take a breath. Continue bowing. I'm going to check your
form." He straightened and eyed me. "All honorable nobles hold
the same place in Our Queen's heart now, and the only ones
above them are the members of the high court, the Left Hand,
and Our Queen. If you cross their paths while living here, you
will bow to them as they pass and stay bowed until they are out
of your sight. Understand?"

I nodded.

"Don't nod while you're bowing. Just say yes," Ruby muttered to me, checking my spine with a palm. "And straighten
your back."

He moved down the line. I curved my spine toward the floor,
shoulders popping, and lifted my chin. At least bowing was the
same for ladies and lords. Learning two sets of rules under Ruby
would've been unbearable.

Five had perfect posture. Of course.

Ruby corrected everyone and shooed us back to the door.

"What a pleasant happenstance!" He fluttered a hand over his
chest, faking surprise, and gestured to the table. "Do take a seat."

I straightened up and stopped. In the corner of my eye, Five
stopped too. Copying him made my skin crawl even if he did

know his stuff. Ruby *tutted* as Eleven sat down at the table, and he dragged her back to the door to wait for his permission to enter again. Ruby launched into a monologue on proper manners and the traditions of bygone nations joined together, and I studied Five instead of listening. I was here to be Opal, not learn the history of sitting at tables.

Five wasn't paying attention either. He'd a good betting face—gaze steady, nodding at all the right points when Ruby's voice pitched to note an important fact. Five had replaced the knives I'd stolen with a smaller set and a stiletto in his boot, and I feigned peeking around Fifteen's arm to get a better look at the table. A bird's beak paring knife rested against his thigh. Each bore the mark of a raptor with its tail feathers splayed.

Breakfast rolled in my stomach. Paring knives were for taking off skin.

Five glanced at me. "You're not as subtle as you think."

"You're not as frightening as you think," I whispered back, hidden by Fifteen's broad shoulders.

"I don't have to be frightening when you flinch at shadows."

I shifted away from him, anger bubbling up my throat till I thought I'd vomit all over Ruby's dining table. I wouldn't put it past Five to have ripped the flesh from Three's body, leaving her to die. No slit throat or knife in the heart—

No, in the neck.

Like I told Five I'd do to him.

Ruby clapped his hands, his words drowned out by the furious rushing in my ears, and escorted us from the room. I followed the others out, body numb and mind racing. Five had killed Three.

Five had killed Three and used my words against her.

I stared at the back of his neck, fingers itching and fury I'd only known as a child before I knew the words for rage and wrath coursing through my veins. He'd skinned a woman for no reason, and he was walking round normal as could be.

Not a shadow but a monster still.

I slid to a stop to keep from hitting him. The rest of the group followed Amethyst's servant to the next lesson, and after watching every auditioner turn the corner, I dug my palms into my eyes and held in a scream. I'd killed but never tortured. There was no other word for what Five did to Three.

Lady Isidora dal Abreu and Amethyst were addressing everyone when I slid through the door. No one noticed me coming in late—hopefully, they'd not notice me leaving either—and I leaned against the back wall while Lady dal Abreu talked about common injuries the Left Hand suffered. The white runes inked around her wrists, so small and fragile, matched the white stitches of her dove-gray dress. It cinched under her bust and matched Ruby's gray trousers and ivory tunic. He leaned against the wall near the door.

"How're we supposed to practice this?" Fifteen asked. He gestured to the catgut, scalpels, needles, and bandages laying across the table next to him.

Ruby pulled a knife from some secret sheath in his sleeve and sliced open Fifteen's arm. "Practice on that and don't interrupt."

"Since you would most likely be alone if injured, you will learn on yourself." Isidora handed a bandage to Fifteen, who sniffled at the shock of the cut. She then glared at Ruby and he fled the room. "It's not deep. Apply pressure and it'll stop bleeding."

I held back my shudder. I could already stitch myself up and set a broken limb. I was Nacean, and we didn't bleed ourselves unless we could send it back to The Lady.

I'd better things to do.

CHAPTER
TWENTY-THREE

I slunk out the door. Retracing my steps, I walked back to the road that led north and traveled into the woods, avoiding the path. The journey north of the eastern spires didn't last long.

The buildings were squat and stone, laid out like the curving mountain ranges covering the north. Erlend's colors didn't hang in the windows and decorate the doors, but they were scattered throughout, slightly brighter and more vivid than the rest of the paint. Servants, soldiers, and messengers paced the paths.

Hidden behind a thick curtain of pine needles, I crawled into a tree and watched them pass. The messengers were the easiest to spot because their traveling clothes were acceptably nice for the palace grounds but functional. Each carried a letter with the name of the recipient on one side and Our Queen's stamp on the other. Some hid the name. Most didn't.

They must've had to pass through the front gates and be approved by the guards to deliver their letters. No notes or people passed through the gates without the stamp of the guards.

The curvy first letter of Seve's name caught my eye.

Looked like his name. Probably.

I leapt out of the tree and followed the messenger, peeking under his arm at the hidden side of the letter.

Definitely addressed to Lord Horatio del Seve. His seal was even stamped at the end of his name—a double-toothed kite spreading its wings after a storm, ready to strike again.

He'd positioned it so it loomed over Our Queen's seal.

The messenger stopped at a two-story building, roof garden dripping with every flower native to Erlend, and bowed to the guard at the door. Thin paper window shades dyed the soft green of pines lined the upper floors. I slowed to listen.

The guard, a broad-shouldered man with a spear in his hands and a sword on his belt—overarmed for show—grinned at the messenger. "I'll leave it with his attendant."

I journeyed till there were no guards in sight and ducked back into the trees. If he wasn't there, I was safe to snoop around his things and find the best way inside. The only door was guarded, but the windows were large and could be opened, and that garden had to have a door. I climbed an oak rising higher than the roof.

A little courtyard with a pond fed by rainwater barrels occupied one side of the roof, and a small dining area underneath a thick awning took up the other side. Furs and stained glass lanterns nicer than any I'd ever seen surrounded the table. I could picture Seve eating dinner wrapped in furs he'd bought—not hunted—under colorful lights more expensive than most people's breakfast. He'd cleaned out the salvageable goods from the war and sold them to Shan de Pau. People weren't treated as well as what he could sell.

The very idea of him made me sick.

I mapped out Seve's rooms as best I could from the tree branch. A servant's shaky silhouette flitted behind the window screens—back and forth from one side of the building to the next. I memorized the guards' predictable movements.

Timing my jump, I landed on Seve's roof with a soft thud. I stilled—no footsteps or shouts, no opening door or nosy servants. I crept around the little nook, fingers drifting over deer hides and decorative elk antlers that hung with candles. The table was set for tea.

A nightly ritual right before bed if the soft scent of valerian oil was anything to go by.

I moved Seve's bird-covered teacup aside and bowed over the table, taking a deep breath.

My fingers slid over worked wood. An intricately carved puzzle box rested beneath my hands. I tapped one of the hinges and a piece slid down to reveal a lock. Not a puzzle box but a container made to look like one, made to make you look smarter. I picked the lock.

The papers inside were nonsense—all bookkeeping and man-agement and words I didn't know because I'd no need for them yet. "Nacea" wasn't anywhere on the list—just fallow land and beasts of burden getting restless. I set the papers aside.

A small note fluttered to the floor.

"Wait for Winter to move and the Storm will pass."

The writing was as controlled as Elise's, but the ends were sharper and jagged. I tucked it back into the box.

Whatever it meant, it couldn't have been good. The plainness and small size of the paper—just tiny enough to be slipped from palm to palm without being seen—screamed secret correspondence. Seve was still snooping even if the war was over.

Erlend's last holdouts led by Lord del Weylin were tucked away in the impassable mountains, plotting their revenge against Our Queen as sure as I was plotting mine against them. A treacherous crown of ice and fog twisted around the peaks and protected them from Igna's armies. No one from Weylin's lands ever journeyed here.

If not for the occasional threat and raid, we'd have thought them all frozen and dead.

I threw up my hands to stretch and smacked one of the silver lanterns. The filigree caught the light.

Nacean silver.

Nacean silver cuffs he'd no business having.

I tore them from the wire, pried apart the glue holding them together, and stuffed them into my pockets. I'd nothing left of Nacea, and he'd all the things no Erlend should've had.

Mother had worn silver cuffs when she'd married Father and again when the three of us were born. She never stopped talking about feeling good memories in the silver, remembering the weight of the cuffs on her wrists. They were for special occasions.

I'd make him remember us, make us more than stolen relics and open graves.

I paced the roof. The sides dripped in expensive gold paint and landscaped ivy. There were no trellises for me to climb and no windows for me to sneak in through. A tumbler lock protected the only door leading inside.

I hung from the back edge of the roof by my fingertips. When I dropped and my feet hit the ground, I bounced up and rolled.

The shock rattled my knees, but nothing hurt too badly. The small grove of trees behind me didn't erupt in shouts from guards.

Amethyst would've been proud.

I raced back to my room, rage spurring me on, and slammed the door shut behind me. Of course Seve was here. I knew he was here, living well, no harm for what he'd done, but seeing it was a whole different world. And that lace!

Of course he'd kept the nicest things. Of course he'd hoarded the last pieces of Nacea.

But why was he still here? Why hadn't Our Queen done anything about him? Wasn't like he was hiding it with Nacean treasures hanging throughout his home away from home. How many more lived with him year-round up north? I collapsed onto my bed.

Maybe, with Seve so close at hand and so close to dead, my memories of Nacea and shadows wouldn't wake me.

TWENTY-FOUR

M aud woke me up with a sharp rap on the door. Another night, another tutoring session with Elise de Farone.

I rubbed my side. All my jumping about today had awakened the ache in my stitches. I fiddled with the silver cuffs in my pocket. I'd never had something of Nacea to carry with me.

I bathed and got dressed in silence. The quiet was familiar and welcome. No one playing word games or trying to kill me. Nothing to worry about but my own thoughts.

"Where's the parlor for tutoring?" I made an effort to straighten my hair under the mask, stomach uneasy.

"I'll lead you," Maud said over the changing screen. "Don't worry. You have plenty of time to get ready for your tutor."

I frowned. "What do you mean by that?"

"Only that you put an awful lot of care into your looks when you go to tutoring." Maud hummed softly. "More than you do any other time."

"Such a bitter tongue for such a sweet face." I straightened my mask again and shook out the long hem of my dress. Wasn't anything wrong with me caring about what Elise thought.

"Shush." Scowling the whole way, Maud led me out of my room and down a path.

The air was fragrant as an apothecary. Mint leaves ruffled in the breeze and wind fresh from the orangery blew over our shoulders. Little glass lanterns cast wavy, colored lines from their perches in the overhanging branches, and each footstep was muffled by the carpet of well-cared-for grass. A short, long building glowed with light at the end of the path. The palace spared no expenses.

Wherever they came from.

"Through that door." She gestured to the building and stomped away, nose in the air.

I took a breath, shaking out my limbs and holding my sore side. Elise looked up as I entered.

A net of gold fine as fishing line held her curls at the nape of her neck. She wore no cosmetics today, and her tunic was plain—long and black, falling in a flow of shadows around her knees, every shade of night mixed within the threads. Pale gold flecked the high collar, and her tightly laced boots covered her leggings. Each movement drew my eyes to the smooth curves of her arms, her hips, and the lines of her crossed legs.

I bowed, flexing my hands.

"I told you," Elise said with a sigh. "You can stop doing that."

"They're teaching me etiquette for a reason." I stayed bowed, hand out and waiting. Her fingers slid over mine till I could gently grip her wrist the way Erlend nobles did when greeting Erlend ladies. I pressed my lips to her knuckles, shaken by the warmth in her hands and the pleasant brush of her skin against mine. An unfamiliar heat pooled in my stomach. "You smell like lemons today."

The sharp scent of spring fit her so well.

"I use it to remove ink stains." She shifted her hand, fingers brushing my lips, and pulled back. "Today?"

"You wore rosewater perfume when we first met." I took another deep breath, the bite of lemons already fading. "I remember."

"You remember what I smelled like the first time we met?"

"That night changed my life." I flexed my hand, off-balance by the prickling feeling coursing up my arm. The warmth of her skin lingered.

She flushed. "That's a bit of an overstatement."

"No." I'd found the poster in her purse for the auditions that night, but thinking I was talking about her would seal whatever feelings she had for me. I needed the history and rumors she knew, and I'd no better way to get them. Wasn't like lemon was a bad smell either. Pleasant. "It's really not."

"Still." She hid behind a tall book bound in exquisite leather. "We shouldn't waste time—best to show the Left Hand you're learning quickly."

I grinned. "Of course."

We repeated last night's lesson with new words, moving through prewritten lists. Halfway through, Elise stopped. She dropped the last word she'd made me read—pretentious.

"It's odd," Elise said. "You don't speak like you can't read."

There it was.

I rested my chin on my hands like her. "How am I supposed to sound?"

"Common" was the answer. Merchants and higher-ups said it enough without ever saying it. Rath had been turned down for plenty of jobs he could do because he sounded like an orphaned commoner with no education. Reading was well and good, but people didn't believe you unless you sounded how they wanted.

And one could sound the part. Spouting off common slang one moment and throwing out old pretentious words the next was part of living in two different circles.

Reading didn't teach you words like "pretentious" and "hypothetical." People said them all the time. Seeing them on paper didn't magically make you know what they meant. It helped, but it wasn't the only way.

"I'm sorry." Elise's fingers tightened in her lap.

"Why?"

"I feel like I've insulted you."

"You have." I shrugged, pushing the papers we'd been using aside. "The way people talk doesn't mean anything. Only means you had private tutors and a fancy education that taught you how to talk a certain way, and I didn't."

She shook her head. "I'm sorry."

"You keep doing that." I smiled wide enough so she could see it through my mask even though most of me was still fuming. And confused—Erlends never apologized. "I didn't know nobles could do that."

"Could do what?" She narrowed her eyes behind her glasses and tilted her chin up.

"Apologize." I tapped the table with my right hand—drawing her attention away from her collection of supplies—and swiped a handful of paper and charcoal sticks with my left hand. She didn't notice. "Thank you."

"You're welcome." Elise laid her fingers over mine, dark smudges shadowing her skin. "What? You've got the look of someone thinking of what to say."

I hid my laugh with a cough. "All those names you taught me yesterday worked out well."

"Really?" She sat up straighter, resting her chin on her other hand. "Did you write them down, or did you recognize them?"

The push and pull, like scamming a mark. Enough flattery to get her to talk but not enough to get her suspicious.

"Really." I met her eyes and ignored her other hand still on mine. "With all the messengers running around, I recognized a few names. Your handwriting's better though. And I met Lady dal Abreu. Her husband's Lord del Contes?"

Elise nodded. "Do you know how to write her name?"

"No." I pushed the paper toward her, hoping to get her talking about the divide between the nobles.

She pushed it back to me. "I'll spell it. You write it down."

Lady, she must've been an annoying child.

I spelled the name right at least. She set me to copying letters and words after that, working on my writing. I traced the lines of her name onto the side of the paper.

"You always live here?" I asked.

"No." She wrote out new exercises for me. The books stacked next were history and medical books, words I didn't recognize stitched to the fronts. She flipped through one and stopped on a page full of calculations. She must've been teaching another auditioner about numbers. "I lived at home until Our Queen requested my presence. She needed tutors and scribes, and I wanted to see court." She paused, fingers tracing the tear on one page. "I preferred studying with others, and the war left everything…"

She trailed off, the achingly familiar sound of bad memories in her voice.

"Ruined?"

She shook her head. "Damaged. If it were ruined, it wouldn't have been fixable. I was too young to be a proper scribe, but Our Queen wanted people who remembered the war, and Isidora agreed to take me in. I think she just wanted another sibling, something to focus on that wasn't grief. Father didn't think Hinter was a place for me then anyway—a broken land full of broken men back from war. He wants me to go back now, but returning home feels final. I'm still not ready."

"I remember the sounds—catapults and crashing rock, screaming, bodies hitting the ground." She shook her head. "I didn't realize how scared I was until I left. I'm responsible for everyone in Hinter, and I know I could never protect them from that. Not without help, so Our Queen called and I answered."

The chasm in my heart usually reserved for Nacea pitched. Elise wasn't old enough to have damned Nacea. Living off the legacy, sure, but she'd no part in it. She'd lost things too—her mother, her home, her childhood.

I reached across the table and squeezed her hand. She returned the touch.

How easy it was to recognize a pain you knew.

"I'm glad you didn't see the shadows," I said and meant it. No one deserved that but especially not Elise. Especially knowing—actually knowing—the scars of our childhood still lived in her too.

I smiled back at her. "But I'd like to hear about living with Our Queen and Lord del Contes and all. What's life at court like?"

At least prying wouldn't drag up all her bad memories.

"Hectic." She handed me a new list of words. "Most of the high court lives here year-round, and everyone else is constantly coming and going. Lord del Contes likes to wander—I'd swear he knows everyone on the grounds."

And yet I'd never seen him.

"How am I supposed to scare nobles into submission when I'm Opal if they're not here?"

"So humble," she said dryly.

"You don't like me for my humility." She liked me because I was dangerous and new to her. I was a mystery. Safe but dangerous enough to pique her rebellious interests.

"And yet." She paused to correct my writing—too sharp again, a point where there should've been a curve—and held up another new list. It was a miracle she'd not shown me every word in existence already. "I am not fond of arrogance. Perhaps I don't like every aspect of you."

I frowned. "You flirt a lot for not liking me."

"Get used to holding this but no ink yet." She swapped out my charcoal for a brush pen. "I said an aspect of you. Everyone has flaws." Tipping her chin down, she glared at me over her spectacles, somehow looking down at me despite both of us sitting. "Like my mistake earlier."

Only nobles could be helpful and infuriating all at once.

"Flirting to get what you want isn't a court thing. People do that all over." I brandished the brush at her, completely unused to the thin grip.

She laughed. "Of course they do, but they don't remember what perfume I was wearing when we first met."

The memory of rosewater lingered. My memories of her lingered, but no matter how warm they were, they were dangerous. "But talking to you isn't like flirting in court," she said softly. "I like talking to you. And thank you for correcting me earlier."

No one had ever thanked me for that.

"You'd be foolish to do more than flirt." I tried to smile to clear the ache in my chest, the teasing tone in her voice helping. I must've hit my stitches. That had to be why I was feeling so unsteady over her. "I'm dangerous, and I could die at any moment."

"Terrible combination." She glanced at the candle clock in the corner and plucked the pen from my hands. "Wick's out. I suppose we'll have to continue tomorrow."

Elise ran me ragged with words, but talking to her was pleasant.

At least I'd grabbed the charcoal. If Seve had anything useful to say before dying, I'd make him write it down.

I nodded. "If I'm still alive."

I would be. Tonight, I'd watch Horatio del Seve, and tomorrow, he'd be dead.

"You'll be alive." Elise shuffled my papers into a pile and pushed them aside. "I have faith."

From her lips to The Lady's ears. A little extra luck wouldn't hurt. Curling an arm around my side to quiet the ache in my chest, I stepped out of Fifteen's way. He must've been her student studying numbers. A red glare shone through the leaves over his shoulder.

"Evening," I said and bowed my head like Ruby had taught us.

Fifteen returned the gesture and stepped around me. The door slammed shut before I could even catch a word of Elise's greeting for him.

Didn't matter. She'd told me what I'd needed so far.

"You can't make time for training, but you make time for tutoring?" Ruby leaned over till our faces were even. "And I had such high hopes for you."

It took everything within me not to flinch away from his unnatural face. "You said training's optional."

"But highly recommended."

"I went to yours." I turned to face him, no need for any other unearthly creatures looming over me. The man behind Ruby lingered in the shadows. "I only skipped healing."

"Medicine." Ruby dismissed me with a wave. "It's called medicine now. Has been for a hundred years."

"You're being awfully hard on Sal," the other man said. He stepped forward, nearly twice as tall as me and drenched in runes—ink shaded the back of his one remaining arm, dripped down the arches of his bare feet, and lined the lids of his black eyes. Only two men bore those marks, and one was dead.

I bowed to Lord Nicolas del Contes just as Ruby had taught us.

"Don't drop your shoulders. It's rude." Ruby huffed. "You will be in etiquette tomorrow, or I will nail you to a chair until you know all your table manners."

Nails and table manners were the least of my worries if Nicolas del Contes was spying on me, but I nodded anyway. "Of course, Lord Ruby."

"It would be rude to send a Nacean to study under Isidora—so much bloodletting." Nicolas drew a finger across his throat, stopping at the same spot I'd stabbed Grell. "Curious that you'd even audition."

I scowled. So they'd shared who I was, and he knew enough about Nacea to be annoying.

"Fine, fine." Ruby dismissed me with a wave, walking away. "At least make good use of the time you have for skipping medicine. We'll know."

"Why are you spying on nobles?" Nicolas fixed me with a glare so cutting I was sure magic had returned if only to strip all my secrets bare. "Or are you just having some fun?"

"Exactly." I bowed to him again and memorized everything about him as he swept away after Ruby. "Just having some fun."

CHAPTER
TWENTY-FIVE

I wandered after that, half wanting to follow Ruby and half wanting to run back to my room and pretend it hadn't happened. Nicolas del Contes couldn't know what I was up to. And even if he did, he couldn't stop me. I just had to be sneakier than him.

And thieves had been better at skulking about long before nobles even knew the word.

A muffled curse—the sound of words trapped behind a linen mask—broke through my annoyance. An auditioner. I peered around my tree.

Five.

Leaving his room.

He locked his door behind him and fiddled with something I couldn't see. His servant, a nervous-looking girl lacking Maud's straight back—too nervous to keep from mussing up her hair—trembled beside him. He tossed the key at her, and she tucked it into her chest pocket. She flinched with each move of his hands.

"Stay out." Five flipped up the hood of his cloak and stomped away from her. "I'd rather have no servant than a useless one. Wash my clothes, fix my meals, and learn how to do your job."

Bad luck getting Five. He was probably used to a herd of servants doing everything and anything he wanted, exactly as he wanted—not one new servant struggling to keep up.

I waited for Five to leave. His servant stayed, taking deep, calming breaths.

I pulled off my mask, face painfully bare, and fixed my hair. I might've been in black, like every other auditioner, and wearing secondhand clothes, but the tunic was proper and fancy. I pulled the silver cuffs from my pocket and snapped out the hinges, folding open the silver filigree like blossoming petals. They should never have been pried from dead arms. They needed new memories.

Just like I did.

I raced down the trail so I could walk toward the servant. Busying myself with cleaning an imaginary speck from my cuffs, I marched straight toward her. The servant glanced up and started angling away from me. I veered into her path.

I crashed into her. We stumbled into each other, arms tangling in an effort to stay upright, and I slid my right hand over her shoulder. My fingers scooped up the key from her pocket and my other hand gripped her arm, righting us both and keeping her attention away from my fingers. The key fit well between my second and third fingers. She tried to pull away.

"I'm so sorry." She bowed with her arm still in my grip, gaze darting to the silver on my wrist. "My apologies."

"It's fine. Really." I grinned and helped her up. She'd be

starved for kindness after dealing with Five, and she had to think I was some silver merchant come to the palace for business. Best she remember my words and wrists but not my face. I flicked the key down my sleeve. "I wasn't paying attention to where I was going."

I drew out my words like Rath did—the telltale dialect of the Alonian coast and not at all how I normally spoke. Now to show her I'd not lifted the key.

"No harm done." I spread out my arms and splayed my fingers. "I'm not hurt. You're not hurt. No foul."

She nodded, eyes still wide and mouth drawn. "Thank you. Have a good day."

"I will." I smiled one last time and took off to Five's haven.

His room was as bare as mine. A pile of dirty clothes was in one corner, bloody bandages beside them. Scuff marks—the footprints placed like Ruby's sword stances—marred the floor, and a long bow half as tall as me leaned against one wall with a quiver full of arrows. A military-issue sleeping roll was propped against one wall.

It'd been used recently. The cloth was wrinkled, and dust that wouldn't be found here clung to the edges.

I'd found the archer.

Wasn't enough to get Five disqualified, but it was good to know.

I snapped a thread from one of his clean shirts and knotted it around the key, hanging it at eye level on the wall across from his door. To let him know he wasn't safe.

Fear and nervousness would make him twitchy and force him to make bad decisions. I needed him twitchy.

Pulling the charcoal from my pocket, I drew a wide staring eye behind the key.

And a dozen more—small narrowed pairs with pinprick pupils hidden on the wall behind his pillow; large eyes with their lids ripped away all staring at his bed; and a series of handprint-size eyes staring down at him from the ceiling over his bed.

He could wipe the easy ones away in a heartbeat and fret over the hidden ones as soon as he lay down to sleep. He'd rip apart the room trying to find everything I'd touched.

Removing the silver cuffs and tucking them into the clean safety of my pockets, I rolled up my sleeves and shoved his bed out of the way. I covered the floor in charcoal and created a pool of rippling, dusty shadow where the dark under his bed would be. I left two bare slits for eyes in the center and dragged two spindly arms up the wall, jagged fingers reaching for Five's head. Safe behind their walls and armies, Erlend hadn't feared them.

If Five wanted shadows, I'd give him shadows.

He'd no right to invoke their brutality.

I pushed the bed back into place, made sure the shadow drawing was completely hidden, and washed my hands in the washbasin. A wooden memory box sat on a table next to Five's bed—a tradition older than Igna, Alona, and Erlend combined, usually packed with memories of the recently dead. It rattled as I moved past it. They were supposed to be buried a year after death, with the grief of death returned to the earth. But this box was old and well cared for. I pried it open.

Finger bones. I'd seen enough during my time with Grell. Five had enough bones for two hands, and the edges were worn down to smooth polished points from constant touch. Constant prayers. I dropped them and closed the box. My stomach rolled.

I locked the door with my picks and pushed the dismantled hands from my mind. Whatever Five was up to, it didn't involve me and might even get him killed before I had to deal with him again. No one with a box of bones had peaceful intentions, even if they were a treasured memory. I tossed the charcoal into the woods.

What a good day.

CHAPTER
TWENTY-SIX

I made it to breakfast in time to stuff a roll into my pocket and be ushered to Emerald's greenhouse. She vanished through the door, a wavering green blur through the damp glass, while her servant kept us outside. I leaned my back against the wall and glanced around—rooftops and tree branches, any nest for an archer. Four paced, his gaze always landing back on me. I ignored him.

It wouldn't do me any good to think of the others as people with their own lives and desires.

It would only bring more nightmares.

"You'll go in one at a time," Emerald's servant said, holding open the door, "and remain inside for the duration."

"Thanks." I slipped through the door before anyone else. I wasn't staying outside in the open.

Emerald smiled when she saw me, the skin near her ears wrinkling under her mask and giving it away. A table was set up in the middle of the building, and plants—green, prickly, smooth, striped, flowering, and dripping sap—were laid out for us. She gestured to the spread.

"Eat the nonpoisonous ones."

Lady, help me. I wasn't hungry for this. I nudged the hooded blue flowers aside with my sleeve, careful to keep them from brushing my skin. The mottled branch with white flowers went next, and I studied the yucca for a long while. This small piece wouldn't kill me without cooking, but it would be unpleasant. That must count.

I pushed it away. A bright-yellow dandelion was next in line. It looked like a dandelion, smelled like a dandelion, and it didn't sting when I rubbed it against the inside of my wrist. I held it to my lips. Nothing. I set it aside.

A pale purple trumpet flower gave off a foul scent. The leaves were dangerous and teethed, and I pushed it into the pile with the hooded flower and yucca. Anything with that scent wasn't for eating.

The final plant was a creeping, dull-green cactus sprouting violent pink flowers. The baker back in Tulen had one of these in her window box, and I'd never tried to eat it. I plucked one of the flowers, spied a speck of nectar at the base of it, and sniffed. It wasn't much—a little sweetness under the normal scents of dirt and growth. I smeared it on the inside of my arm.

"I'm not eating those." I waved to the ones shoved aside and stared at my arm. I wasn't itching or puffing up. I nibbled on the dandelion. "Tastes like grass."

Emerald nodded. "And the other one?"

"Grass." I chewed on the petal. "Flowery grass."

They could do with sweetening, but I wasn't dying.

"Stand here. Give nothing away." Emerald cleared the table and laid out new pieces of the plants I'd been tested on.

I was being tested on poisons and secret keeping then.

No one died. Ten took forever but lived, and Fifteen nearly ate the hooded flowers. I nibbled on my roll the whole time, going over the layout of Seve's life and roof in my head.

Exhaustion dragged my eyelids down. I slipped away from the group and back to my room. I needed sleep, not manners and more bandages. I fell into bed without even removing my boots.

"You need to wake up."

I jerked up, arms flying out and knife tearing through the air.

Maud sighed across the room with my dinner in hand. "You have tutoring."

I dropped my knife. Little silver flecks spotted my sight, and I steadied myself. Blurry, fading memories of silver and blood, eyes in the darkness, prickled over my skin. I wrapped my arms around myself.

I was finally going to get answers.

I was finally going to make Seve beg. Blood owed and blood paid.

"You look peaky." Maud leaned in front of me, staying an arm's length away, and narrowed her eyes. "How are your stitches?"

I reared back. "Fine. I look how I always look."

"Malnourished and unkempt, yes," Maud said with the air of superiority that reminded me more of an older sister scolding her sibling than a servant. Not like I'd been holding her to normal servant standards. I liked this bluntness. Kept us both mostly honest. "But you look exceptionally tired today."

"Least I'm exceptional at something." I shrugged. "You ever met Nicolas del Contes?"

He'd the rune-scrawled face of a hawk and the legs of a stork, easy to spot and easier to recognize, and I needed to know as much about him as he knew about me.

Maud frowned. "He's always skulking about, knowing things he shouldn't. He's nice, but it makes me jittery to think he's watching even if it's for Our Queen. Asked me how my siblings were once. I nearly died."

So he was a spy. And a bad one if everyone knew it, which meant he probably hired out folks to research us while he followed us around as a distraction from the real spies. I'd nothing to worry about long as I kept on as I'd been doing. He'd have stopped me if he knew what I'd truly been up to.

And if I didn't talk to him anymore, he couldn't drag any other secrets from me.

"He's interesting," I said.

"That's one way to describe him." She pursed her lips and smoothed out the wrinkles in my slept-in dress. "Regardless, I'm glad you're not dead."

"Me too."

Getting ready was a rushed affair. Maud tossing clean clothes at me over the screen while I sucked down a bowl of soup. She sniffed as I walked out the door.

"You smell like sweat and dust." She pulled a small vial from her pocket and unstopped it. The watered-down, clean scent of peonies washed over me. "Completely unfit for seeing your lady."

I froze as she tapped her fingertips to either side of my neck, smearing the scent of spring against my skin. I swallowed. "She's not my lady."

"Of course not." She tucked the perfume back into her pocket.

It must've been hers—a treat she'd bought after working hard. She'd not poison me with so much on the line. "But best not suffocate her."

I'd write "Maud did it" on my arm soon as I was out the door.

Wouldn't hurt looking nice. Elise was always pretty, and she'd expect nothing less from me.

Maud hummed. "You could pass for Honorable Opal if you'd better clothes."

I took off before Maud could say anything else. Honorable. Such a better title than Lady or Lord.

I didn't bow to Elise this time. Flirting was over. I'd be equal to her as Opal, and I owed her nothing. She'd surely lose interest in me soon as I stopped flattering her.

But then I'd have to live with her glowering at me in court day in and day out.

"You're scowling," Elise said softly. "And you've not spoken a word except 'yes.'"

I startled, guilt gnawing at my ribs. "Big scowling road agents with dual knives and masks ugly as their manners?"

"I was embellishing that night." She set down her pen, lips set in a severe line. "I know our interactions are largely exaggeration, but it's obvious you're upset."

"I'm not upset—only thinking, and I don't want to talk about it." I shrugged off my anxiety. I wanted to move, climb, watch Seve sip his evening tea and shake all the well-kept secrets from his bones.

"You don't have to tell me anything." She sighed, picking up the paper again and turning it over so she could write down a new series of words. "Read these."

Of course I didn't have to tell her anything. I read the words aloud, mind on Seve, and by the time tutoring was over, we'd said nothing to each other except the words I was learning.

I shook away the aching worry rising up in my chest as Elise's hollow goodbye rang in my ears and rose from the table.

A hand on my shoulder held me back. The scent of lemons filled my nose.

"Erlend's traditions remain. It's unseemly for me to flirt with anyone not a nobleman, but men are not the only people I am attracted to, and I'm tired of keeping quiet about it." Her fingers tightened, barely there but burning through my dress and searing her fingerprints into my skin. Her voice dropped. "You flirted back."

I shuddered. "I can't have been the first one."

"Of course not, but my father would have less cause to complain if I were flirting with Opal," she said. "It would be politically savvy."

Of course her father would be so set in his ways he'd not accept Elise as she was.

"What's his name?" So I could avoid him forever.

She sighed, half smile grim. "Nevierno—it's old Erlenian. He's exceptionally traditional and spectacularly furious right now because he has a cold and can't stand to let Isidora anywhere near him."

An Erlend named after ice and cold would hate depending on an Alonian.

"You hate politics." I locked my knees, refusing to turn even though I knew what she meant. "And even when I'm Opal, no guarantee we'll still like each other."

"I like you," she said. "And I only want you to know that."

I opened the door. "I'll see you tomorrow."

CHAPTER
TWENTY-SEVEN

S eve was in the bath when I leapt into my perch. I whispered
every Nacean name I could remember into the night. He
would know why I'd come for him.

And then he had to die quietly.

A dead lord in the middle of Left Hand auditions would be
suspicious. I only had to be less suspicious and they'd never know
it was me.

I'd have to keep him from screaming. Couldn't cut out his
tongue—too much blood, too little words, and a bit suspicious.

I pulled on my gloves, turned my mask inside out to hide
the number, took out my knives, and crept toward his roof.
The servant poured his tea and left, and I dropped onto the roof
as the door shut. I crept around to the side of his little nook,
keeping in the dark across from his chair. A thousand thoughts
flickered through my mind and fidgeted in my fingers. He leaned
into the light.

He was cave-fish pale, blue veins marbling his carefully

maintained white skin. A sheen glistened on his cheeks, catching the light with every movement, and he clutched his silk robe tighter around his long neck. Only one rune marred his hands— the jagged tail of a symbol I didn't know peeking out from under his sleeve. He brushed a hand through his hair and straightened his gold spectacles. His eyes darted to the small mirror hanging on the wall. He checked the wrinkles at the corner of his eyes.

At least I knew how to keep him compliant.

"Apologies, Lord del Seve," I said in Erlenian, coming up behind him and covering his mouth with a hand. "You scream, I carve up your pretty face and leave you for the night crawlers. You stay quiet, I reward you for your time."

Seve nodded. A bead of sweat dripped down his nose, seeping through my glove. I jerked my hand away and rubbed it over my thigh. Disgusting.

"What do you want?" He rolled his neck, fingers drifting to his pocket. "I hold meetings for anyone who asks all day."

Playing it unconcerned, like I wouldn't notice him going for a weapon.

"You wouldn't have agreed to meet me." I tapped his hand with my knife. "Sit. Stay still. Answer my questions and I won't hurt you."

He sat, hands clenched in his lap. "What do you want?"

"Who ordered the withdrawal of troops from Nacea?" I leveled my knife with his neck, the tip nipping his chin, and stared at him through my mask. Let him think I was a shadow come to claim what he owed. If Our Queen had known what he'd done, he'd have died years ago. His death was long overdue. "Your soldiers were there and then they weren't. Same with all the others. Why?"

"Nacea?" His brows furrowed. "That was ages ago."

"Barely a decade." Time must not matter when you were rich and unworried about starving to death or rotting because you couldn't afford a physician. Out of sight, out of mind. "Last chance—names."

"Lord, girl." He threw up his hands and sighed. "I don't even remember what region my troops were in. If you called on me tomorrow, I could look up—"

I slapped his hand away from a teacup—no doubt searing hot and meant for my face—and grabbed his collar. Of course "girl" was an insult when it came from his lips. He made words sound so *wrong*.

"They were in the western farmlands, and you withdrew them soon as you knew shadows were heading your way. You used Nacea to stall the monsters you created, and I want the names of the people who came up with the idea. I know it wasn't you." I tightened my grip, blade still pressed to his neck. "What were their names?"

"I don't know!" He shuddered but stilled. At least he knew one wrong move would have him bleeding out quicker than help could arrive. "It was Nacea and I had other troops, other places to worry about."

A cold calm settled over me. My hand was against his throat, but I couldn't feel him. I was numb to the warmth of his skin, panicked fluttering of his pulse, and frantic rise and fall of his chest under my elbow. Like his words had snapped the last knot holding me to this world.

"You don't know?" My voice was low and soft, softer than I felt, softer than I ever thought I could be. Was this even me?

Was that my hand grasping his neck? "You let thousands be massacred, and you don't know who told you to do it? Why you did it?"

I dragged my knife up his neck, over his lips, to the paper-thin flesh of his nostril. He stilled.

"Stand up." I pressed the knife deeper, and he rose, watery eyes and jutting chin a full head above me. "Remember—you do as I say, your face stays in one piece."

I led him into the moonlight. Let The Lady witness him. He might not have killed anyone with his hands, but his apathy was as guilty as the shadows.

"No, no. We used secret names. We all got letters." He sniffled and stumbled, blood dripping down his chin. "Let me go. I'll get them for you."

"The names." My face—my mask—was black in the reflection of his glasses. A shadow blocking the stars. "You have nothing I want but names and blood. I know they used secret names. What were they and what were their real names?"

A debt of flesh repaid in blood.

"Winter! Winter was the first to agree." He ripped open his sleeve, baring his wrist to me. "Naceans take blood, don't you? To pay debts to your lady? Take it. Take it please. I won't—"

"The other names?"

"I can't. He'll kill me," Seve whispered. "I can't."

At least I owned what I was. They'd rather die than admit they'd done wrong.

I let him kneel in a shaft of moonlight on the edge of the roof. "You stop raising your voice and give me his name or you get a new nose."

He dropped his arm.

"You kept the letters, didn't you? A clever little magpie like you?" I thought I'd be angry, that the rage smoldering within me for so long would burst free, but I was quiet. Still. How clear everything was. "In case they ever tried to move against you? Tell me the name or give me the letters. He can't kill you if he's dead. Who's to ever know you told me?"

"North Star," he whispered. "He sent letters to Winter, Caldera, Riparian, Deadfall, and me after Nicolas del Contes sided with the queen, telling us to withdraw from the fal—Nacea."

"What was your name?" I lowered my blade to his throat.

"Coachwhip. I was Coachwhip." He gripped the roof's ledge. "We'd no other choice with Nicolas gone. The shadows—they'd have killed us. He was the only one who could contain them."

I nodded, staring beyond him to the branch-streaked horizon and glaring stars. The Lady's stars were bright and damning, demanding my attention. "No mage, no way to stop the shadows."

"Exactly! I'd have been sentencing all those soldiers to death. Hundreds!"

Instead, he killed thousands, but it didn't matter. They weren't Erlends. They didn't matter.

"North Star, Winter, Caldera, Riparian, and Deadfall." I waited for the familiar rush of vengeance, memories of stitched faces I couldn't recognize and gurgling screams in my ears. I waited for the rage and terror that woke me every month. Nothing. "What was it you almost called Nacea?"

He paled. "What?"

"It started with 'fal.'"

"North Star used to—" Seve cleared his throat, hands trembling. "North Star calls it the Fallow."

I saw red—blood streaking the farmlands, handprints pressed to shattered doors, stains beneath my nails I couldn't scrub free no matter how many years I scoured my skin. The rush of my blood roared in my ears and raced in my veins. I flipped my knife around.

"We are only what you made us."

I rammed it hilt first against his temple.

He slumped forward, head lolling, and collapsed over my feet.

Fallow.

We weren't fallow. Our home wasn't a field left bare so they could profit. I squeezed my eyes shut as the word ripped its way through my chest and burrowed into my heart. They killed us and had the arrogance to call our blood-soaked lands "fallow." I crumbled, sure I'd split in two with each shuddering gasp. My mask caught in my mouth.

I ripped it off. The weight of everything—Nacea, the shadows, Seve, his information—pressed into my back, digging into my bones like burrs I'd never be able to unhook. I curled up in the garden, muffling the sobs with my arms.

I didn't feel better. I didn't feel better at all. I had their names, but Nacea was still there, looming at the edge of my mind, threatening to remind me of pain and fear and blood with each glance toward Seve's still hands. I couldn't leave him here.

He didn't deserve dying in the comfort of his own home, and I couldn't leave it looking like a murder.

I dragged myself to his belongings and found a bottle of vile-smelling brandy wine. I poured out a measure in the glass next to the bottle and dribbled more into his open mouth. A fall would snap a neck.

He drank. He fell. He died.

It could happen to anyone.

I set everything up to look like a late night drink, fingers trembling as I straightened his sleeve and pulled him back up to the ledge.

"You'd best hope your Triad are more merciful than me," I said and shoved.

He landed headfirst with a bone-snapping *thunk*. I leapt down next to him and sprang to my feet. The guards pacing around the area didn't change course, no footsteps running toward me. I stared down at Seve, legs splayed and neck bent unnaturally. His neck was caught in the ivy scaling the bricks, tangled leaves holding tight to his slack face. Red spittle leaked from the corner of his mouth.

I checked his pulse and found nothing. "Blood owed, blood paid."

The forest felt like home. Lights flickered from above, filtering down through the leaves, and guards patrolled the other edges of the forest with lanterns no larger than my hands. The familiarity of the leaves crunching beneath my boots, the darkness pressing down around me as I fled, ached in my chest, and I hid behind an old creaking oak, tears and laughter burning in my chest.

I'd done it.

I didn't feel better, but it was done. Surely the terrible memories would ease the closer I got to the others. Seve was only one among many.

And I was still in the running to be Opal.

I stumbled toward my room, exhaustion crashing into me. Only Four was about, walking down the path from Emerald's residences. The sound grated, and I groaned. My head ached with all that had happened tonight.

Four spun around. I dove to the side of the path. I couldn't be seen, couldn't let anyone know I'd been awake while a lord was murdered. They'd suspect the killers first, never one of their own, and they'd be right, but I couldn't let them have me. Seve was only one.

North Star. Winter. Caldera. Riparian. Deadfall.

Four moved on down the path. I pulled myself from the underbrush, thorns stuck in my hands and the rotten scent of molded leaves clogging my throat. I shuddered.

The shiver stayed in my bones till long after I was curled up under the blankets in my bed, shadows with Seve's hands clawing at my back.

CHAPTER
TWENTY-EIGHT

A streak of sunlight from the finger-thin slats in the ceiling seared my arm. I rose slowly, arms and legs heavy with sleep. The jaw-cracking yawn of a deep night's sleep rattled me awake and cut Maud's morning knock in half. I took my time telling her to come in, limbs wobbly as a kitten's, and rolled out of bed. The moment she entered, mouth set in a sober line, I knew.

"What's wrong?" I pulled on clean clothes and hoped my nonchalance sounded honest. "You've got that gossipy look about you."

Maud glanced at the door and the slats in the ceiling before ducking her head down to speak—everyone did it when sharing secrets. "Lord del Seve died last night—fell off his roof."

"What was he doing on the roof?" I pulled on my boots, furrowing my brows enough for her to see. "Thought all the people here had parlors and such?"

"Roof gardens are popular. Our Queen started using them when the school was besieged and they'd nowhere to grow food.

The habit stuck." Maud gathered up my clothes, eyes narrowed on my face, and looked me up and down. "You need to bathe eventually."

"Do I?" I sniffed my shirt. "Smell like soap."

"Disgusting," Maud said. "I'll draw a bath after breakfast. You're not going to all your training, are you?"

"How'd you know that?"

She glanced at me over her shoulder. "It's my job to know where you are and anticipate what you'll want."

"You should think about auditioning for Opal," I said.

She laughed till we parted ways, and I ducked into the breakfast hall.

Only Amethyst was there, working her way through a stack of papers and a cup of tea. I sat at the other end of the table. Might as well let her drink in peace.

Eating with the mask on was a trick. I'd not caught them doing it yet, only the moments after.

"Your eating habits are worse than my brother's," Four said as he poured himself a cup of strong tea before he sat across from me, "and he's barely five."

I scowled, my third fat-fried flat cake hanging out of my mouth.

Two sprinkled a bowl of grits with butter and laid a thick slice of fried ham over it—comfort food if I ever saw it. Her hands shook. Four didn't eat.

Something was off. I swallowed my last cake, unfurling my legs and sitting up straighter. Ten and Eleven showed up next, bandages on their arms from Isidora's training, and Fifteen strolled in well after they were done eating. Five entered last.

Charcoal dust spotted his clothes and gathered in his chair.

Crescents dark as the new moon shadowed his pale eyes. The whites were spotted with pink.

Good. He was exhausted and scared, and he'd make a mistake.

"I had thought," Emerald said loudly, sweeping into the room, "we were teaching you all how to kill in secret, but you continue to disappoint me."

My nails tore through the cheese bun. They couldn't know.

"Six is dead." Ruby sat next to Amethyst and let out an exaggerated sigh. "Someone better have an alibi."

I glanced around, and only Four wasn't watching the Left Hand.

"So," Amethyst said as she laid down her papers, "do you have one, Twenty-Three?"

Everyone turned to me.

"What?" The world dropped out from under me. All the happiness, all the joy at Seve's death left me in a breath, and Amethyst's words burned in my ears. I'd forgotten Six was even still alive. "I didn't kill Six."

"A denial is not an alibi." Emerald gestured for me to stand, brass nails glinting in the light.

I'd been set up.

"I can't have an alibi for something I didn't do." I stood and braced myself against the table. "I can't prove I wasn't somewhere at some secret time if I don't know when and where it happened."

"The proof of your innocence is your business." Ruby shrugged. "Where were you last night?"

I gritted my teeth together. I'd only passed one other auditioner last night, and he wouldn't meet my eyes. "Sleeping."

"Alone?" Emerald asked. "Did anyone see you?"

"No." I shook my head, every thought and hope crashing in

my mind. They couldn't disqualify me. They couldn't. I'd given up everything. I'd no money, no way back south, and no home left. I couldn't face Rath if I failed. "I sleep alone. My servant didn't see me till the morning."

"Unfortunate." Ruby clucked and beckoned a guard near the door.

I was enough for Opal.

"You lying little meddler." I clenched my hands into fists to keep from leaping across the table and punching Four. "You're using me as your cover, and it'll come back to bite you."

I'd only one way out of this, one possible way to keep them from disqualifying me. I might die outright for even trying it, but that was hardly worse than disqualification.

Emerald tilted her head to the side. "How do you know it was Four if you were asleep?"

"Because he's the only one fiddling with his hands and not watching on with glee," I said.

"I saw you." Four nodded to me, still not meeting my eyes. "It's a better way to go than dying."

Ruby's hand closed around my arm.

I flinched and turned toward Ruby. "I thought you were better than them."

"What?" Ruby dragged me out the door, nails digging into the thin flesh of my upper arm, and motioned for Emerald to wait. "Better than who?"

"Your noble friends." I pried myself from his grip. "None of them would get tossed out or sent to jail with no evidence of their crime. Would you disqualify Five and all your invited noble favorites on nothing more than heresy and lies?"

This always happened. I should've known. Two and Four weren't as rich or as noble-blooded as Five, but they were hand-picked, and nobles never let their kids or favorites wait for a real verdict in court. They got lawyers and trials and motions and apologies. People like me got court-paid folks who couldn't tell the judge from their chair. We got punished.

Truth and justice be damned.

Ruby shoved me against the door, slamming it shut and looming over me till his chest hit mine with each unsteady breath. A knife slipped from his sleeve to his hand and nicked my chin. Blood dripped between us. "Let's clear up whatever misconceptions you have rattling around that cracked skull of yours—you don't know me. That's the point. You don't know me, what I've done, or what I did. So don't come whining to me about the fairness of courts and the priority of laws. I know. I gave up everything I'd ever worked for to make sure all those nobles and their favorites received their dues. I lost my life to see justice done. Do you understand?"

I nodded.

The silence between us tightened till it snapped. Ruby laughed.

"Delightful." He sheathed his knife. "And you do bring up a good point."

I swallowed, heart racing. Ruby had been many things, but he'd never been cold like that—voice low and hands calm while ready to slit my throat from ear to ear.

"What?" I said, wincing as my voice cracked.

"Your disqualification." He patted my head like some bemused master consoling a dog who'd lost their stick. "Do you want to have some fun?"

"It involve me getting stabbed?"

"Probably." He opened the door and nodded me through it. "But not by me."

I slunk through the door, back of my neck prickling at the echo of his footsteps behind me, and Emerald cleared her throat. Amethyst set down her tea.

"New plan!" Ruby clapped his hands and tilted his head to Emerald. "Because none of us saw the alleged murder and we're who matters—not the singular account of someone who wants the other auditioners dead and gone—Twenty-Three is on probation."

The cup in Five's hand cracked.

Probation. I could work with that. I'd get back to being Twenty-Three and the Left Hand would be all the more impressed for it. No hard feelings.

Ruby and I were even.

Emerald and Amethyst looked at each other. Emerald sighed, long and loud and annoyed.

"Twenty-Three will be banned from killing other auditioners and will have until tomorrow at sundown to prove his innocence—exactly like a real court of law would work." Ruby gestured to Emerald, some secret hand signal I'd not seen them use before now, and turned back to me. "And anyone who kills Twenty-Three before then, with proof provided, will be granted immunity for one day—no one will be allowed to harm them."

I swallowed down the shuddering fear taking root in my spine. Chin up, shoulders back. I would never let them see me tremble.

I stared down Four till he looked away.

"You're dismissed," Ruby said with a wave of his hand.

I slipped back outside and touched my blood-damp chin.

Ruby's words lingered. He could threaten me all he liked as long as he followed through on probation. Whoever he'd been before he was Ruby would've been a good person to know though. He wasn't nice, but I was fine with that.

Except now there was a price on my head.

I'd killed Seve and gotten blamed for Six.

And if I couldn't prove Four was lying, nothing mattered.

I'd done everything as planned, and it was all for nothing. Maud had trusted me to be Opal, and I'd let her down, not just me. I might as well be dead to Elise because I'd no chance of seeing her again.

No Opal, no Elise, no Maud, and nowhere to go that was safe.

I needed a place to hide—a place the others wouldn't look. I sprinted from the inner circle of the grounds, through the woods and over the river, back into the buildings where we'd slept on our first night here. The guards only glanced as I raced past, and the burn in my legs overpowered the spreading panic in my chest. I need to live, and Twenty-Three wasn't going to. I had to be someone else.

I could panic later.

Steam clouded the horizon to my left. I took off toward it, clawing my way onto the roof of a neighboring building. The little pathways and alleys around the laundry were crowded and well lit, servants scurrying about, and I circled the roof till I spotted the carts full of dirty clothes at the back of the building. I darted to the unguarded carts near the edge and fished out clothes that looked like they'd fit me. Red spotted the shirtfront and dirt hemmed the pants. I climbed back onto the safety of the roof when no one was looking.

"Thank you," I muttered and checked the name sewn on each sleeve. "Lind."

Noon came and went. Footsteps and laughter drifted up through the air and lulled me into an uneasy half sleep in the shade of a chimney. The other auditioners wouldn't come here, and even if they did, none would scour every nook and cranny of these buildings to find me. I'd no way to prove I'd not killed Six and no way to find the other lords if I wasn't Opal. A cold emptiness twined between my ribs like the ivy around Seve's neck.

All because Four wanted me gone but not dead for some half-brained reason.

At least I could've fought back if he'd tried to kill me.

Except now, I had a chance to prove my worth, to prove exactly how good I was. If Ruby wanted fun, I'd give him fun.

I'd make him proud in the worst possible way.

By proving him wrong.

By surviving.

Maud would know about my probation by now, know that if I failed, she'd be back to her old job, no higher pay and no new title. I had to apologize to her for losing it if this failed.

And Elise—I needed to apologize to her for lying. I'd lied to her for nothing.

She'd be in the parlor, and I owed her the truth about who she'd been tutoring at least.

CHAPTER
TWENTY-NINE

I strolled right past the guards and servants, face bare so the auditioners wouldn't know it was me if they were watching, and none of them spared me a second look. Getting across the Caracol bridge had been tricky, but I squared my shoulders, walked with purpose, and told the guards I'd information for the Left Hand about an auditioner while gesturing toward the blood on my shirt. They paled and let me through.

The paths were empty of auditioners. An odd, anxious fear bubbled up in my chest the closer I got to the parlor. I shook out my arms, ignoring the flash of purple in my periphery and bowing like soldiers did when Amethyst passed me by. She didn't even spare me a glance.

Maybe Elise wouldn't either.

"You're early, Fifteen." Elise didn't look up, brush pen gliding across her paper and lips rolling into an ever more severe line. Her hair was bound today, braided tight and coiling down her back. Silver pins cluttered her dark hair like stars, and her long purple tunic glittered with silver thread. A constellation incarnate. "While I appreciate your eagerness, I'm not beginning your lesson until it's time."

"What about mine?" I clenched my hands together, trying to hide my shaking.

Elise's head snapped up. Even through the thick glass of her spectacles, the redness of her eyes and puffy tinge to her cheeks were clear. "What?"

I half-bowed and my heart leapt in my throat. The words didn't come. She didn't recognize me. Of course she didn't recognize me.

"Explain yourself, or I will have you removed and reassigned to the coldest, barest outpost in Igna."

"I doubt you could reassign me." I straightened up. "You couldn't even have me arrested for robbing you."

She didn't answer. She might not want to see me at all. She might not have cared a lick about me lying to her. Lady, what if she'd been playing me? Pretending to like me and getting in my good graces like Maud had said, and I'd played her right back and neither of us wanted to be here—

"Twenty-Three?" Elise whispered, pen clattering to the floor and ink speckling her hands. She rose slowly to her feet.

"I wanted to apologize." I licked my lips, cheeks warm—she was staring at me, wide-eyed and lost, like travelers finally finding their way home, the look burning within me. I could only nod. She wasn't mad, but she wasn't saying anything. I was too hot, too tight, and everything was new and odd. My own skin was ill fitting. I wanted to strip off the coat, put on a mask, and go back to yesterday. I didn't know why I was here. "But I can go if you like."

"No!" Elise dashed toward me, catching my shoulders in her hands. She ran her hand down my arm, silver ring pressing into my skin. "They said you were gone. I thought they meant dead. An auditioner died, and you were gone."

"Probation." The word came out like a curse, and I turned my hand over for Elise to see. No one had ever looked at me like this, stuttered over their words in their eagerness to see me alive. And certainly not an Erlend. "Basically dead."

"Not at all." She traced the callouses and scars crisscrossing my skin. My hands looked ragged next to hers as her nails trailed over my crooked knuckles and bony fingers. Drips of ink from her freckled hands stained mine. "Sorry."

I tried to speak, but my words were gone, replaced with the impressions of her fingerprints on my hand, ink on my skin, and lemons on my lips. She was everywhere.

She gripped me so tight that I was sure I'd bear the marks forever.

And I didn't mind.

"Are you all right?" She leaned back, eyes narrowing and smile falling. "What's wrong?"

I took a breath, and a small voice I couldn't stand to know was mine asked, "Why are you being so nice?"

I fought the urge to pull her back into the circle of my arms, to place myself back in the tight grip of hers. She'd hugged me— she hardly knew me and she'd leapt out of her chair to hug me.

She'd worried about me.

"I thought you were dead," she said as if the words made any sense.

"Tons of people have thought that." I stared at the stray curl bouncing against her cheek, unable to meet her eyes with that lost-and-now-found look. The aching, longing sense of wanting a life where I was *me* flared—one where I was known as me even if my name was Opal and I could be me. No one had ever worried about me. "But you've been crying."

Rath had thought me dead once and clapped me on the shoulder when I reappeared. He'd never cried—another dead friend, another funeral pyre we couldn't afford, another memory to dissolve as the years went on. I was always *another*.

Elise laughed. "I thought you were dead, and half of what I've been saying to you is how you're too dangerous and wild. Last time we spoke, I insulted you."

"Not more than anyone else." I shrugged, dropping my shoulder so her hand fit more easily around my neck. This was new, terrifying, and I'd no idea what to do.

"People flirt with the Left Hand all the time." Elise slid her fingers from my shoulder to the curve of my neck to my jaw, heat trailing wherever she touched. "I didn't want you to think I was doing that. That I was lying or being insincere. I was keeping you at a distance but not lying. And then you were cross and dead, and you didn't know."

Lady bless, I couldn't tell her I was the one who was lying now. Especially not when she'd been doing what I had—playing it safe, keeping her real meaning guarded.

Elise wasn't like I'd thought at all.

She wasn't her nation or an idea.

She was Elise, and I'd not been paying attention.

"Come." She tugged me toward the table, pushing me into the seat. "You look like you're the one who's seen a ghost."

"You cried." I couldn't reach out to her, not yet, not while all this was so new. "No one's ever worried that much over me."

Elise sniffed and closed the distance between us. "You haven't known the right people. I thought you were likable even when you were robbing me—funny, nice about it, apologized eventually."

"Only because you were a bully." I smiled. "You thought I was funny?"

She looked at me over her spectacles. "In that mask? Funny looking."

"I'll get a new mask."

"Works for me." She touched my blood-spotted coat. "What happened?"

"A liar—an auditioner accused me of killing another auditioner, and I couldn't prove it wasn't me. Didn't have an alibi." I slowly took her hand, torn between keeping her close and running away fast as I could so I could sort through whatever feelings Elise had awoken. Out of all the things I'd done, how was this the newest, strangest thing to happen to me?

Elise straightened my collar, studying my face. Her hand fluttered next to my cheek. She didn't touch me and didn't pull away, only lingered. "I can't picture you as a new recruit."

I leaned very slowly against her hand.

"I'm glad you're not." Elise tucked a strand of my hair behind my ears. "They would've sent you somewhere far, far away."

"Can ladies have affairs with common soldiers?"

"We can do anything we please," Elise said softly. "Even if we should know better."

"Like kissing people who could kill you?" I couldn't keep the catch from my voice.

"Oh yes." Elise slid her arms around my neck again, pulling me into a half hug. "Is this the last time I'll see you?"

"No." I tangled my fingers in her tunic till I could feel her warm skin and heartbeat fluttering in her veins. "I'll come back tomorrow, if I'm still alive. I need to take care of a few other things."

She hugged me, arms tight enough to break, and tucked her face into the side of my neck. I slid my hands around her waist, unable to stop the hesitant shaking that had taken over my limbs.

"Don't die," she muttered into my neck, lips hot against my skin. "I'll stay here all night. Come back *before* you die."

I didn't want to die, but the idea of someone hoping I didn't, asking me not to, made the prospect of tomorrow brighter. "I'll try."

"Good." She pulled away from me, rubbed her eyes, and straightened up.

I leaned forward and pressed my lips to hers. She blinked up at me, eyes half-shut behind her spectacles, and I kissed her more gently than I'd done anything else in my life. Her hand closed around my wrist. I pulled back. "Here." She slid her silver ring over my finger. "Now you have to come back—to return it."

I nodded. "Wouldn't be like me to steal something like this."

Without another word or touch, sure I'd be unable to leave if I lingered too long on how her mouth felt against mine, how her fingers curled just so around my wrist, how her eyelids fluttered shut over her dark, dark eyes with each shuddering breath, I turned my back on Elise de Farone and walked away.

CHAPTER
THIRTY

With a confused weariness tugging at my bones, I wandered back to my room and crawled into the perfectly made bed. The cleanliness of it all only made the loneliness more gaping. Maud must've thought I wasn't coming back.

I glanced at the little constellation of ink that Elise's stained hands had left on my skin, breathed in the leftover scents of lemons and paper, and sighed. She'd haunt my dreams longer than ink could stain my skin, and both thoughts eased the hollow chill in my chest.

"This punishment?" I asked the night sky, staring at The Lady's stars through the open slats in the ceiling. "Retribution for killing? Losing my temper with Seve?"

Her stars twinkled back. I raised a hand to trace the line of her armor, the runes dripping from her fingertips, and the vine leaves curled around the roof shifted in the breeze. She vanished.

"I was doing it for funeral rites." I took a deep breath and threw my ink-splattered arm over my head. "All those lords who spilled blood—your blood—and let it lie are here, and I'm returning them to you. Repayment for their debts."

It would be an easy run for the ones left—I'd bet anything Two, Four, and Five would be the last three. It had better be Two. I'd smack Four if he was named Opal and I was still alive, and I'd not mind the punishment for assaulting a noble.

I'd have to see him in court, but that would be another chance to hit him.

Courts. The audition followed the same rules as courts, and witnesses recanted all the time. Grell used to stare down law-abiding folks till they ran out trembling and the charges were dropped. If Four recanted, I'd have proof it wasn't me.

And I could make it fun.

The lock on the door clicked. I dove aside, darting to the wall and tucking myself where the door would hide me. The person let out a long sigh, stepping into the room with a shuffle, and adjusted the basket on their arm. A familiar plait of shiny black hair tied with gray ribbon flopped over one shoulder. The person shut the door and turned.

"Maud?"

She shrieked and tossed her basket at me. I caught it.

"Maud, Maud, stop." I held out the basket. "It's me, Twenty-Three."

She stopped shrieking. Her eyes widened, and she flew at me. I took the first punch to my shoulder, falling with it onto the floor. She smacked my uninjured side, never hitting anywhere near my stitches, and rained a series of ill-done punches on my chest and arms.

"You ass." Maud pulled her arms so far back that she tangled her fingers in her hair. "You were disqualified!"

"I wasn't! I'm just on probation." I took her hand, tugged her thumb from inside her fist, and patted her knuckles. "You'll break your thumb that way, and you should always go for the throat, nose, or ears."

Maud rolled her eyes, sitting on the edge of my bed. "I'm not one to start fights."

"No." I smiled. "But you should know how to finish them."

"I'll finish you," Maud muttered. She bumped her fist—properly folded—against my cheek. "You're plainer than I thought you'd be."

"I deserved that." I nodded to her hair. "You're all out of sorts."

"All thanks to you."

She deserved more than an auditioner doomed to die. Like Grell's bounty. It had to go to someone, and she'd get more use out of it than I would. I'd have to will it to her later.

"I am sorry though. I'm trying to stay in, but I'm probably going to die and lose you your job—"

"You know how long I worked trying to get out from under Dimas?" Maud asked, throwing her hands up and interrupting me. "And cleaning! I don't like it, but I'm good at it, and everyone says an eye for detail like mine can't be wasted on some wealthy merchant coming to town and keeping me around to run the guests rooms, but this was finally something they couldn't stop me from doing."

I stopped smiling, completely done with being interrupted and ready to be Twenty-Three again.

"I'm on probation and all the auditioners are out to kill me," I said. "Sorry if that disrupts your business plans, but I have to get a killer to recant in order to prove my innocence. So I'm going to focus on that."

She sucked in a breath, walked to the tub, and started going through the chest of drawers next to it. She returned with a tiny jar. "Shirt up—you can't do anything if you pull your stitches out."

She washed her hands with a bottle of watered-down witch hazel and opened Isidora's salve. The spicy scent of hot peppers wafted around us, burning my nose.

"What do you need?" she asked.

"You'll be breaking the rules."

"Those rules were made for auditioners not on probation." Maud sniffed and patted the salve down my side. "They never specified rules for this."

"I knew I liked you." I grinned and saluted her. If I died, she didn't get paid. Helping me, even if it was slightly wrong, helped her. "I need to know what the others are up to, and there's only one sort of person they won't attack—a servant."

She nodded and said, "I'll have to get you a uniform. What else?"

"It's about time for another test, isn't it?" I tested the edges of my wound, wincing with each pinch of pain as I twisted. "You heard about that?"

"I thought you'd never ask." She sighed. "It's breakfast."

"So you're fine with helping me win but not fine with telling me stuff like that outright?"

She frowned.

"Your face will stick like that one day." I laid out my mask, knives, and lock picks on the bed. Best take stock of what I had and what I needed. "Ruby's been teaching us manners, and you need those at the breakfast table. The meal's poisoned—there's Emerald's lessons—and they're seeing if we paid enough attention to Amethyst and Isidora to know how to counter it. They using servants?"

Maud nodded. "I volunteered to serve drinks."

"Think the Left Hand will notice if I take your place?"

"Probably not. Their servants recruited us." She shrugged. "They'll be too busy with the food to check."

The door handle twisted. I threw a hand over Maud's mouth, dragging her to the other side of the room.

"Someone picked it," I whispered. "Be quiet and still."

No one had seen me enter. I'd made sure of it. So this was meant for me the next time I opened the door. I let go of Maud and lowered myself to the floor as quiet as I could, cheek pressing into the floorboards. Small feet—too small to be Four, Five, or Fifteen—tapped against the entrance steps. Gloved hands fluttered around the bolt keep.

Eleven.

She had to be trapping my door. I knew a few common ones: packets that blew powder and vials filled with oils that ignited as soon as the air hit them. I could disarm one of those without killing myself. Probably.

I'd done it once, and Rath had only lost some knuckle hair.

Eleven shut the door and hurried away.

I tested the handle, wincing at the pressure. The trap was inside the bolt keep and probably a packet of something nasty. Sliding one of my finer, thinner picks between the keep and the door, I wedged the pick in place. Silver shone in the crack between the door and the jamb. I took a small breath.

A mealy, slightly acidic scent hit my nose.

"It's Lady's Palm." Fresh from the earth and potent enough to kill a grown man. Emerald had shown us the mushroom in a dark, damp corner of her greenhouse. I'd only ever seen it dried before coming here. "I mess this up, don't touch anything. Just go get Emerald and Isidora."

This wasn't clever. Eleven's trap didn't discriminate between auditioner and servant. Lady's Palm was the easiest poison to use and the hardest to counter. The antidote only worked if you knew how much to take.

And Lady knew no one wanted to guess how much nightshade extract to drink.

I eased another three picks into the crack and opened the door. No click, no puff, and no white cloud of death.

A small white ball of Mizuho rice paper—thin enough to fold and thick enough that the powder didn't seep out—sat in the keep. If I'd opened the door as normal, the ball would've rolled out and the needle glued above it would've torn a hole in the rice paper. It was crude but effective.

"That's it?"

I glanced at Maud. "Killing people isn't hard."

And wasn't that how everyone died? Not expecting death from something simple.

"You all need better locks." I studied the ball, gently turning it over in my hands.

"You really don't trust anyone, do you?" she asked, crossing her arms over her chest. "It's impossible to cross the river and get here—"

"I did it."

"—normally." She stepped around me and peered out the door, blocking me from view with her skirts. "They changed security for the auditions."

"Handkerchief." I held out my hand, and Maud handed hers over. "What do you mean?"

"Most of the guards are new recruits," Maud said. "They switched them up for auditions."

I'd not thought of that. I pried the needle off the door, tossing it aside. The ball was trickier, and I wrapped the handkerchief twice around it. If Eleven had used rice paper, the powder was too big to fall through the holes, and she'd surely not put herself in danger with a leaking trap. Maud took a step back from me, eyes on my hands. I nodded to the door.

"Shut it." I weighed the bundle in my palm. This could work. "Know where I could get nightshade extract?"

"Lady dal Abreu has everything in her laboratory." She shook her head a breath later when she realized why I'd asked. "You can't—she has everyone searched before they enter and again when they leave."

"That's fine." I pictured the building for healing training in my mind, trying to remember how many doors and windows it had. "I'll just go in properly and leave some other way."

"The window," she said softly. "Go out the window."

"What?"

"The orphanage masters searched us when we left and when we returned." Maud shrugged. "So we used the window."

Of course—concerned more with if their charges were stealing than why.

"We used to break our falls with this old hay cart. It worked fine as long as you landed properly." She nodded slowly, spreading her arms out wide, as if to prove all her jumping had left her in one piece and I'd be fine. "I'll leave a laundry cart there, and you can land in it. That might work."

She arched her brow and tapped her foot when I didn't agree immediately, as if jumping out of windows was normal.

"Trust me," she said. "We've got nothing left to lose."

I snorted. Trust got people like me killed.

But she'd used "we." Maud was in this too.

"All right." I clapped her on the shoulder. "Let's jump out a window."

CHAPTER
THIRTY-ONE

M aud was quick to remind me that she wasn't jumping out of any windows.

She left to get me a uniform. I double-checked my stitches and bandaged up the rest of my hurts so they couldn't be seen while I was playing servant. She returned with a sharp-looking set of clothes identical to Dimas's fitted shirt, flared coat, and matching gray pants. I tucked the soldier's uniform away for later and got dressed. Maud looked me over with her critical gaze.

"Passable." She buttoned the collar up to my chin. "Now how to serve drinks."

I shifted about in the stiff coat. "Pour when the glass is empty?"

"Just be quiet and pay attention."

It was boring. Exhausting for sure but mostly boring, and the fact that Maud had a strong enough will to stand around waiting for folks to order her about made her all the more interesting. Anticipating people's needs was a whole different kind of spying.

It took me till dawn to get the hang of all the little rules. I even had to stand a certain way.

Maud straightened my clothes one last time and wrinkled her nose at my less-than-polished boots. "Go now—the guards will switch shifts after you get there. It should buy you some more time."

"You sure you're not a criminal mastermind?" I muttered as I left.

Maud only scowled.

But she was right. Two yawning guards patted me down as soon as I crossed the threshold. I'd not stayed in training long enough to study the building, but it was larger and taller than it looked. The first floor dropped into the ground—more basement than anything else—and gave the guards their own little room for checking people as they came and went. I adopted Maud's passive stance while they looked over me.

"I only need something stronger to clean up my auditioner's mess." I shrugged while he patted down where I'd hidden my lock picks and dropped my voice into the soft, resigned tone of someone forced to do something out of their control. "You know how they are."

The explanation had been Maud's idea.

He huffed and waved me through, laughing when his partner saluted me through her yawn. I smiled back at her.

"I appreciate it."

The building was mostly deserted. Only two servants paced the halls, scrubbing the floors by the dim dawn light. I fiddled with my heavy coat, high collar noose-tight and stiff sleeves confining as shackles. It didn't take long to find Isidora dal Abreu's laboratory.

I wasn't keen to leap out a window though. Not one I'd never seen. Worst-case scenario was that Maud misplaced the cart and I broke my legs, tumbling ass over shattered feet to the hard-packed dirt.

I slipped my lock picks out, fumbled on my first attempt, but popped open the door on my second.

None of this mattered; fear didn't matter. I had to do this.

I slipped into the laboratory. Shelves lined the walls from floor to ceiling, and glassware glittering in the dim light of one dying lamp littered the tables. A few chairs were scattered throughout—one covered by a fancy yellow coat with obnoxious black stitching had a sheathed sword with a melon-shaped pommel resting on the table before it. I slipped off my own coat and scanned the walls. I only needed a little nightshade.

Any more and I'd be poisoning Four instead of fixing him.

A sketch of the bell-shaped flowers covered a label halfway up the far wall. I picked the lock on the cabinet.

Among the dozens of vials inside sat the one I needed. The small white crystals that countered Lady's Palm were hard to create unless you were a proper physician, and they were usually too expensive to buy if you were a thief unlucky enough to need them. I carefully picked it up.

I might actually pull this off.

"You couldn't ask me this last night?" The sharp, sleep-husky voice of Isidora slipped through the door. "Or literally any other time that wasn't now?"

I paused. A muffled laugh answered her.

"Triad bless, you've not grown up at all." The tap of her graceful footsteps neared.

Only one thing left to do. No more time to stall.

I backed up against a counter, kissed Elise's ring, and leapt.

Air hit my face. I bent my knees, vial of nightshade safe in my chest pocket. The world blurred, a smear of greens and browns ripping through my sight, and I clenched my teeth and looked down. A white smudge rushed toward me. A jolt shuddered up my heels.

I collapsed, breath knocked out of me. A puff of down feathers fluttered over my shoulders. I checked the vial.

Safe.

Maud plucked a feather from my hair. "You're welcome."

I opened my mouth but could only gulp down the breaths that my landing had smacked out of me.

"I do love leaving my employers speechless." She clicked something on the cart and shoved it down the path. "Did you get it?"

I nodded.

She'd caught me. She'd kept her word. I patted one of the pillows she'd tied around the edges of the cart.

"Good." She pulled a string and the knots holding the pillows in place fell. Quick release. Clever. "I'd have had a bigger mess to clean if I'd placed this incorrectly. It might be my job, but I loathe extra work."

I couldn't stop myself from grinning even though my heart was still beating like horse's hooves pounding my ribs to dust. My backside would be bruised, but it was worth it. I could bribe Four into recanting.

"It was fun to watch too." Maud shoved the cart across the little lip of the bridge. "You know what you remind me of?"

Not a cat. Everyone said cat.

Rath always said, "The slinking and staring and general air of arrogance only you and cats have mastered." Then he'd point to the ratty-eared street cats with dark fur and feral eyes. The sort that hissed and clawed when people got too close.

It made my skin crawl.

"One of those mountain goats." Maud raised her hands to her head, fingers curling into little horns, and scrunched up her nose. "The climbing ones."

I scowled. "A goat?"

"Only the mountain ones." She nodded. "They can stand on air, the good ones. Stroll right up cliff sides sleek as glass and never fall."

"How do I remind you of a climbing goat after falling out a window?" I kicked a dirty blanket off my legs and groaned. A goat.

She laughed. "I saw one fall once. Made the funniest sound when it hit the ground—like the ground was the one in the wrong, not the goat."

I smacked her hand.

"Trust me," she said without flinching. "You're a mountain goat."

I wasn't a mountain goat, but she did catch me. I'd the night-shade in my grasp, and Four would soon recant. I settled back into the cart and watched the sky roll past overhead.

"I trust you."

Maud taught me the last little tricks of serving—pour Emerald's drinks from the left while everyone else was from the right and keep your head ducked to avoid meeting gazes. I practiced slipping Lady's Palm into a glass.

Using dirt instead of the powder, of course. I wasn't dealing with the real thing till I had to.

So long as there was nothing else weird in his drinks, I could slip the Lady's Palm to Four easily. All I had to do was be there on time.

Which left me plenty of time to see Elise.

I checked my uniform one last time, opened the door to the nook, and grinned. Elise sucked in a breath.

"I will admit," she said, rising from her chair and gliding across the floor to me, the fresh bite of lemon coming with her. She'd a stack of papers nearly tall as her, and she must've been working the night away while waiting for me. "While I would love for you to be Opal, I am very fond of your face."

She touched my cheek, fingertips clean but a few stubborn smears clinging to her palm. I smiled and ducked. I'd no mask to hide my blushing now.

"Thank you for waiting for me. You must be tired." I picked up her other hand and took a breath, ready to tell her everything she deserved to know.

"I'm used to it." She ran a thumb along the back of my hand where she'd splattered ink last night, little dots still visible. "I'm sorry. I try to keep my mess to myself most times."

I gestured to the smudge on the tip of her nose. "You can leave whatever marks you want on me."

"I can't say no to that." She laced her fingers through mine and tugged me to the table. "One last chance to talk."

I shuffled after her, gaze stuck on my hand in hers, and cleared my throat. "If I don't die, I'll find a way to talk to you again, even if it's just a letter. You taught me to read and write, and I owe you for that."

"You don't owe me anything." She hummed deep in the back of her throat and pushed me into the chair. I curled my fingers around my palm, desperate to keep her warmth on my skin, and she picked up her pen. "But I would be upset if you didn't at least write to tell me you'd lived."

I'd come here looking for revenge and found a home. I could have both.

I wanted both.

"I'm assuming you've not joined the noble ranks of our servants?" Elise dipped her pen and gently—always gently, always soft—pried my hands apart, turning one over in her palm.

"No, have to look the part today." I tensed my fingers till the black line she'd drawn across my palm danced. "A meek little servant in a spotless uniform."

"Then I won't ruin it." Elise smiled and tucked the top button of the collar. "Relax."

"Ruin it?" My heart cracked against my ribs as her fingers slipped the buttons of the coat undone, one after the other, fingertips sliding down my chest. I held ramrod straight, painfully aware of her hands drifting lower and lower, the heat of her seeping through my thin shirt, and the brush of her hair against my chin.

"That's better," she murmured, pushing the coat off my shoulders and pulling my arms free. She smoothed a hand down my shirt and rolled up the sleeves to my elbows. "I'll keep the ink under your clothes too. Just in case."

I nodded, completely at a loss. Elise's breathing quickened, and she dragged her nails down the inside of my arm. Her fingers paused above my racing pulse.

"What have the auditions been like?" she asked. "The transition here? I've wondered how you ended up a thief in an auditioner's mask."

"Exhausting." I should've let Five kill me in the forest. At least it would've been faster than this slow death under Elise's steady hands. "Life here's better."

"Even with all the death?" She wrinkled her nose, and I'd a vivid flash of her face the first time we'd met as tutor and auditioner. I was so foolish—of course she didn't like me for my dangerous mystery. Maybe a little, but after I'd become Twenty-Three, she'd preferred me. "I heard about the forest."

"The shadow kill?" I shuddered and gripped the table's edge

with my free hand. This was tender, intimate, and totally new. "I saw it. How'd you hear about it?"

Elise glanced up, brush dripping ink into the pot. The sound slithered into my ears, and I shivered. She ran a warm hand up my arm.

"The whole court heard about it. It's an assault against Our Queen's promise of safety. If she can't keep the children sent to learn in her court safe, then no one will trust us. It's only one step from visitors killing visitors to visitors killing nobles, and if word got out—even if it were false—that the shadows were back, she'd lose her right to the throne." She pushed her glasses up her nose with her wrist and sighed. "I was worried it was you."

I shook my head. "Harder to get rid of me than a boy with some knives playing shadow."

She tapped her pen once and slid the brush over my arm, ink raising gooseflesh up my arms. She swirled the thin black line into a delicate curl of letters and flourishes, her other hand holding my arm firmly in place as I tried to hide my trembling. She finished off the word with a long twisting tail circling my elbow, raised my arm to her lips, and blew the damp ink dry.

Heat blossomed in the pit of my stomach, writhing in my chest till I was sure it would burst from my skin. I stared at the crown of her head—jeweled pins placed like river stones next to the sea-green ribbon running through her curls—and squeezed my eyes shut. I needed to remember all this, every touch and every breath, in case it was my last good memory.

It was certainly one of few.

I shifted, arm still in Elise's grasp, and managed to mutter, "What did you write?"

"Opal."

I laughed, the low pitch catching me off guard. "Optimistic of you."

"I'm an optimistic person—the thief who would be Opal." Elise pulled my arm into her lap again and leaned out of her chair till our knees were pressed together. I could taste the sharp black tea on her breath. "And if you die today, I want to remember you in every way I can. Especially since I don't even know your name."

"Sallot." It escaped me in a rush. She wanted to think of me when all was said and done, whether I was Opal or not. It filled me with a desperate need to move and speak and scream it to the rising sun. "Remember me as Sallot."

"A name and a face," said Elise. "Good farewell presents."

I laughed again, and Elise raised a hand to my face, fingers skimming my jaw. The sound died in my throat.

"I wish I'd met you properly." We'd met days ago, and I'd thrown all that time away. I wanted to close the gap between us and know if she tasted like tea, memorize the line of her fingers and subtle flick of her wrist as she wrote, listen to the soft, delicate sound of her breath between each word. I wanted all the things I thought I could never have.

"Sallot."

The sound of my name on her lips cut through every last barrier keeping my words inside my head. "Elise, I like you."

Her eyes widened. "I would hope so, or I'd be rather embarrassed."

"No, you don't—" I said and stopped. I grabbed her hand, pressing my forehead to hers so the words would reach her even if my voice softened and fled. "You don't understand. I hate Erlend. My entire life's been stuck in the shadow of Erlend's crimes, and I didn't like you. I did, but I didn't realize it. I kept trying to think of you as the same as the others, the lords and the ladies who started the war and razed my home, but you're not like them. Not at all. And I've waited for so long for some chance to show them up and help Our Queen, and it's here, but you're here too, and I—"

Elise closed the distance between us and pressed a light, chaste kiss against the corner of my mouth.

"You shouldn't kiss people who could kill you," I whispered, all the blood in my veins singing her name and urging me to kiss her.

"Don't presume to know what I should or shouldn't do," she whispered back. "I know what I want, and that was a kiss for good luck. Do not die—you've an awful lot left to do and even more to explain to me."

I nodded. "I do owe you some explanations."

"Tonight then." She turned in her chair till her back was flush against my chest and her hair brushed my chin with every breath. "Until then, something to remember me by."

Elise picked up her brush again. She dragged the ink across my arm in small sharp strokes. Drips turned into wispy letters under her fingers, and illegible scrawls bloomed into words I knew I'd seen but couldn't place, blackening my skin from fingertips to elbow. She curled over my arm, and her lips seared my palm.

"There." She leaned against my shoulder instead of moving aside, ear pressed to my chest, and sighed.

A faint black lip print shone in the center of my hand, her words spiraling out around it.

"What's it say?" I asked, resisting every desire to tilt my head and taste the answer on her lips.

Tonight. If I lived.

Elise chuckled, the sound ringing in my ears. She blushed and rubbed the ink from her lips with a thumb. "It's a poem."

"But what's it say?"

"All the more reason for you to survive tonight." Elise stared at me over her shoulder, lips set in a mock-serious, ink-smeared smirk. "It'll keep me in your thoughts. I'm very selfish, you see."

"Not even a little bit." I grinned. I wasn't likely to stop thinking of her unless I got dumped in the Caracol. "Least tell me the book."

"*The Way of Melting Snow*. Isidora let me borrow it." She glanced at the clock and shoved the pen into my hands. "Quick—your name."

I flexed my fingers, afraid the ink would crumble like ash. She wanted some part of me on her for longer than a heartbeat, and the thought rendered me senseless, unable to even recall what letters made up my name. "It won't be pretty."

"I don't want it to be pretty. I want it to be yours."

I picked up the pen with a shaking hand and wrote my name on her arm, splattering extra ink across her wrist and leaving a spotty trail of black from letter to letter. I was sloppy and sharp, none of Elise's soft curves. She smiled down at it.

I held our last glance in my mind as close as the ink on my skin.

CHAPTER
THIRTY-THREE

The second test was a tense affair. Two was first, eyes darting over every dish and cup placed in front of her. The Left Hand watched from across the table, and Ruby tapped Two's fingers with his spoon each time she raised a piece of food to her nose to sniff.

"Subtly," he drawled. "It's very rude to insinuate your host is attempting to kill you."

Ruby glanced at me when he said it or at least turned his face to my corner. The Left Hand hadn't told the guards to stop me when they let me enter. I stood in the corner meant for Maud, arms trembling after holding a pitcher of wine still for so long, and they let me be. Except for Ruby.

He kept dumping his wine in the potted plant behind him and demanding I refill his cup. Dying by his hand might've been better than this.

He must've recognized me.

Two ate enough to be polite. She spat the poisonous mushrooms from the first dish into a handkerchief; took the wine but wisely refused the poisoned tea; and palmed the candied plums dusted with extra sugar and deadly sunrise trumpet. The servants moved only when called.

By the time Two was done—alive but chastised for her posture—I was tired of holding a half-full pitcher of wine. This was too boring to be bearable.

Four entered. Finally.

I straightened. He was only two steps away and laughing. I gripped the handle of my pitcher tighter, the weight of Elise's words on my skin giving me courage, and waited to pour his wine. The other servers fluttered around him, taking twice the time to set up his first plate so Emerald could slip white powder into his grits. He saw, smiled, and motioned to me. He never looked away from the Left Hand.

Perfect.

I bowed next to Four with my hand holding the packet of Lady's Palm on top of the pitcher to keep it still while I poured a steady stream of poison into his glass. The poison dissolved on contact—odorless and tasteless once in liquid. Four must have assumed that if the Left Hand hadn't touched the wine that it would be safe. Perfect.

I waited for him to take a few sips and whispered, "You should recant."

He spat what was left of his wine back into the glass. "What did you give me?"

Everyone stopped.

"Lady's Palm." I straightened and let the silence hang between us. The nightshade was safe in an extra pocket Maud had sewn into my shirt. "And I can't recall killing Six or where I put the nightshade extract."

"Finally!" Ruby tapped a butter knife against his wrist. "I thought you'd never get to the point."

Emerald leaned back in her chair, fingers tightening around her glass. "A condition of your probation was not killing the other auditioners."

"Dying's up to him," I said, hoping my voice was steady. I was giving them enough reason to name me Opal or kill me on the spot. "Four lied to cover up killing Six."

"I didn't kill Six." Beneath the table, Four rubbed his palms along his pants. Sweating—the first symptom.

"Auditions are like court, right?" I set my pitcher down, arms shaking, and glanced at Ruby. His mask gave nothing away. "A witness recants in court, they strike it from record. You can't be tried if they've got nothing."

"This would've been simpler if you'd had an alibi." Emerald took Four's poisoned wine and held it up to the light. "Where'd you get this?"

I shrugged. Let Eleven do as she pleased as long as I got reinstated. If she messed up and hurt a servant, all the better. I'd given Maud the warning and extract. They'd be fine, and Eleven would be gone.

"I'll leave a little trail of witnesses everywhere I go next time." I leaned in front of Four till our eyes were level. The Left Hand only watched. Good. If they weren't stopping me, they were all right with this. "You feeling it yet?"

Four swallowed. Second sign. Slobbering and sweating, the

death marks of Lady's Palm. "I saw you walking in the opposite direction alone when I went to kill Six. Happy?"

"Very." I ignored Emerald's snort. "So?"

Ruby and Amethyst shared a look, and he inclined his head to Emerald. She shifted, the start of a word echoing behind her mask, and a shout outside the door stopped her. We all turned.

"What else did you do?" Emerald asked sharply.

"Nothing." I shook my head. "I was only after Four."

The door crashed open. Fifteen stumbled inside, mask torn and face bloody. Sweat dripped down his broken nose, cutting through the pale yellow dust coating his skin, and he raised his trembling hands. A servant hung limp in his grip, blood trickling out of her mouth. He tossed her into the room.

Amethyst dove for her. Emerald leapt to her feet, drawing a pair of knives from her dress, and I lurched backward. Fifteen's huge frame and glazed eyes shook me to my bones. He wouldn't go down easy.

Ruby jumped the table and grabbed my throat, ramming my back against the wall. A blade bit into my neck.

"What did you do?" he asked, voice cold and dead. As much as I looked up to him, I'd no love for this end of his blade.

"Nothing." I stilled. "Eleven trapped my door. That's how I got the Lady's Palm. I didn't do anything else."

Ruby's fingers twitched, the raspy sound of his rapid breathing all that hinted at his feelings. He dropped me. "And stole the nightshade from Isidora, I imagine? Good. That's not too bad."

"Spies!" Fifteen grasped at everything in sight and threw a pitcher.

I shoved Ruby in front of me. The pitcher caught him in the

stomach, sloshing water down his front. He kicked the pitcher at me, soaking my shoes, and circled around the table to Emerald. They stood guard over Amethyst and the servant.

Probably shouldn't have done that. If Ruby was mad at me before, using him as a shield wasn't going to help his mood.

"You turned us in. I saw you." Fifteen howled and caught Four's collar. Four—skin ashen and reactions slowed by the Lady's Palm—flailed in Fifteen's grasp. "You were there."

Four would've stood a chance if I'd not poisoned him.

Fifteen hoisted Four higher, large hands around his throat. I couldn't find an opening, not with Four struggling like he was. Fifteen's eyes were blown out, the pupils too wide to be natural, and he slurred every word, running his accusations into each other.

Spy. Liar. Murderer. Could've been any of us, but why was he going after Four now?

Four might've almost ruined everything, but he didn't deserve this. Fifteen was too far gone for a decent kill.

I shot forward and sliced Fifteen's arm. He tossed Four into a chair easy as anything and swung at me. I stumbled back, knife flying from my hand.

Four shrieked. The shattered remains of the chair crunched under him, splintering into a hundred pieces sharp as knives. Fifteen didn't turn to me, didn't even wince at the muscle-deep gash in his arm. He only picked up a chair. I tried to stab him again, but he swung the chair at me. I ducked behind him, nicking the soft skin on the back of his calves. He swatted me away like a fly.

Fifteen slammed the chair into Four. The ornate wood shattered, breaking off in Four's unprotected legs and raised arms. He cried out, and I slammed into Fifteen while his guard was down, jabbing the backs of his knees. He stumbled out of the way, grabbing a servant for support.

Emerald moved faster than I could follow, clearing the table and burying a knife into the back of Fifteen's neck. He crumbled.

Good. Done.

I dropped to my knees before Four. "You look ready for nightshade."

"Bit late." He laughed, the rasp filling my head, and nodded to his legs. His left one was torn open, groin to knee, by jagged wooden splinters, and a ribbon of blood streamed down his calf. His fingers trembled in his lap. "Beaten by a chair—original."

"Shit." I pulled off his sweat-soaked mask so he could breathe. He wasn't handsome, but he was something—strong nose broken countless times, black eyes hazy with poison, and bushy eyebrows drooping. "Didn't mean for that to happen."

"Doubt anyone meant for that to happen." He waved weakly to Fifteen's corpse and grabbed my hand, grip weak and dying. "You were supposed to leave."

"I played a dangerous hand and won." I glanced over my shoulder, but the Left Hand was unmoving and silent. Just another auditioner dying.

"You'll have to tell me about it next time we meet." He reached for me, hands trembling, and fell short. "I didn't want to watch it—not after seeing Three dead. You'd have liked her."

"That all it took for you to get me on probation? You get squeamish over seeing people die?" I settled down next to him and shrugged off my servant's jacket, tucking it behind his head. Bleeding out wasn't the quickest, but it wasn't the worst. I gently tugged his hands into mine. "You shouldn't have come here, invited or not."

I was unsure of what to do in the face of his death. I'd wanted revenge, but I couldn't keep the chill from my chest.

"Probably not, but it's hard to turn down those invitations." He wheezed. "I'm not sorry I tried to disqualify you. I didn't mean to like you, but I did, and seeing folks die hurt worse than I thought it would. I don't really give a lick what happens to any of the others, and Two can take care of herself, but you're—"

"Not a sibling of yours to protect. Not even a friend." I wanted to be Opal just like he did. "You want me to get Two?"

I could only see gaping servants through the door, but Two and the rest couldn't have been far off.

"Think I've annoyed her enough for one lifetime." He smiled and coughed, blood speckling his crooked teeth. "Five years."

"What?"

"Took me five years to get this good. Two did it in three. Show off. Course, she's got the best motivator." He pressed his satchel of throwing knives into my hands. "She hasn't missed a target as big as you since she was twelve, so start practicing."

"I'll do it in two years." I tucked them into my pocket, squeezing his fingers.

He snorted. His head fell forward and his fingers fell limp. I sniffed and squeezed his hands again, but he didn't respond. The pulse fluttering in his wrist stopped, and his shallow breathing ceased. I laid his hands across his chest, wiping the blood from his hands. He was still warm, still smiling.

He might've only been sleeping.

CHAPTER
THIRTY-FOUR

W ell," Ruby drawled, footsteps drowned out by the chaos in the hall. He leaned over my shoulder and cocked his head at Four, words whistling through his mask. It made me shudder. "That was nice of you. For someone so bitter, you're not big on plucky revenge."

"He recanted." I pulled the nightshade extract from my pocket and shook the vial. "It's not worth it."

Ruby took the vial and pocketed it. "Because killing doesn't bother you."

I nodded. I'd never killed before auditions—all those people I'd robbed and fought could bounce back from boxed ears and a few missing jewels—but I wasn't killing because I liked it. It was a job. Eight, Seven, and Four had all signed up to die, and we all knew the risk. We'd agreed to serve Our Queen in any way she saw fit. We were keeping her on the throne.

Peace had a cost, and we collected.

"Delightful." He straightened up and flicked his fingers at me, tapping his foot on the floor. "Pity you didn't have a real alibi the first time around—could've saved us all this trouble."

"You knew?" I rounded on Ruby, blood rushing in my ears. I'd blackmailed Four for nothing. Threatened him for nothing. "You knew it wasn't me without a doubt the whole time?"

"Of course we knew. It's our business to know. It's why Nicolas is involved, why we know who's seen and who's set up." Ruby picked his way over the shattered remains of the room and picked up my knife, missing my shudder—they couldn't know about Seve, they couldn't. "Next time, have an alibi and keep your arm loose but your grip tight."

"Oh yes, I'll get right on that, my lord." I tore myself away from Four. Of course the Left Hand knew. They'd even had their spy Nicolas del Contes investigate my past. I might break my hand punching Ruby in the face, but it would be worth it if I broke his nose. "Next audition, I'll have an alibi for every day. I'll look good in red."

Ruby laughed and said to his servant, "Get the other auditioners. Don't tell them what's happened." He twisted back to me soon as they were gone. "Using me as a human shield? Really?"

"It was a pitcher." I shrugged. "I was improvising."

He snorted. I leaned against the back wall, pulling my mask over my face. The bitter scent of sweat and blood, musty dirt and dry forest, clung to the linen, and I sucked in a deep breath. Back where I belonged.

Where I needed to be.

No need to let Two and Five know what I looked like now that I was back in the audition. Amethyst helped the servant, now awake and confused, into a chair and looked me over. Emerald didn't spare me a glance.

Eleven entered first, stepping through the broken door skittish as a deer. She was forgettable like me. I hadn't paid her any attention.

She could've killed everyone.

She caught me staring and glared. I glared right back. She'd no right endangering the servants.

Five slipped into the room. His gaze darted from Eleven to Four's body, to the Left Hand and the servant recovering between them. He put his back to a corner and fidgeted. Good.

At least I'd gotten that right. He was still finding my eyes.

Two came in last, saw Four, and stopped. She stayed in the doorway, raised on her toes and ready to run.

"Four and Fifteen are dead." Emerald stalked around us terrifying as a storm rolling in from the sea, voice barely rising over a breathy whisper. She rolled her neck and cracked her knuckles. "All of you, at the table."

Two, Five, and Eleven lined up alongside the table. Ruby circled behind them, huffing at the smears of charcoal that Five's dirty hands left on the wood. Amethyst beckoned the servants into the room. Maud glanced at me as she entered.

"Which of you rigged the doors with Lady's Palm? The doors to the rooms frequented by people we specifically told you were not to be harmed? With poisons that cause violence and delusions?" Emerald slid behind Eleven. "Admit it, and I'll be less likely to kill you despite our well-stated rules."

Eleven shivered and raised her hand. "It was only the auditioners' rooms after their servants had cleaned."

Emerald slammed Eleven into the table, smashing her face through a ceramic kettle and grinding her cheek into the slivers. Blood and tea pooled beneath Eleven's face. She whimpered.

"When we said the servants were not to be harmed, we meant it." Emerald's voice was muffled and low. "No harm—not a chance, not even a little. Your disregard for the lives of the people you would have served as Opal is clear. So show me every trap and then get out of my sight. You are lucky no one else was seriously hurt."

She yanked Eleven up and pieces of the kettle tumbled from her bloody mask. Five edged away. I bowed my head, not the least bit sorry. She could've killed Maud.

"And you are very, very lucky." Emerald rounded on me. "This," she said, gesturing toward the wreckage around us and nodding to Ruby, "wasn't well done."

I gritted my teeth, unwilling to let them see the disappointment so stinging that I was sure my bones were on fire. I nodded.

"But he recanted." Emerald nodded to Amethyst. "And you were correct about the courts."

Amethyst shook her head at me. "Although the extortion was a nice touch, if not sloppy."

"You lot have an odd definition of nice." My breath caught in my throat, choking me and burning in my chest. It had worked. It had all paid off. "Really?"

"Four's witness against you would no longer hold in court, so it no longer holds here." Ruby sidled up next to me, peering over my shoulder.

Ruby then strolled to the table, ignoring Five's furious glares at me. I smiled, sure my lips would never drop the look again. Meeting his gaze only made him scowl more.

"Congratulations." Ruby raised a broken teacup handle to us and bowed. "To our final three auditioners—Two, Five, and Twenty-Three."

Ten must've died while I was plotting. Good.

"She's disqualified!" Five gestured wildly to Ruby. "You can't bring her back."

I stiffened. I'd uppercut Five if he ever spoke wrong about my gender again or spoke to me at all. I was dressed as a man. I was clear as day.

And I hadn't been disqualified.

"I can do whatever I like. I'm Ruby, and you still have a big number on your face." Ruby shooed Five away from him and waved at me. "Twenty-Three was never disqualified. He was on probation. Four admitted to lying about the kill, so Twenty-Three is reinstated. End of discussion." He turned Five around by the shoulders and pushed him into a chair. "Also, because we said so and our word is law."

Five clenched his jaw shut, flinching from Ruby's touch. I grinned, the stress Ruby had placed on "he" warm and comfortable in my ears. Almost regretted tossing him in front of that pitcher.

Amethyst beckoned Maud. She tried to do her best to look surprised, but Amethyst laughed softly behind her mask.

"Due to recent events, let us reiterate the rules." Amethyst put the broken door back on its hinges best as she could. "The servants, soldiers, courtiers, guards, nobles, and whoever else isn't one of you three are off limits. That includes indirect injuries caused by your actions."

"Use discretion." Ruby splayed his hands over the broken table, head tilted toward me. "Your first test was about physicality.

This one was about subtlety. Your last one will require both. Only those capable of the two will succeed."

"For lack of a better phrase, you are the best auditioners." Amethyst was rigid under her armor. "Though you have arrived here sooner than expected."

No doubt—Four, Eleven, and Fifteen would've been safe if Eleven had thought through her plan.

"Whether that is through your own skill or the skill of others, it doesn't matter." Ruby twisted to look at us each in turn. "We prefer shorter auditions because they are more efficient." He gestured to me. "And unless you think Twenty-Three is a better Opal than you, his presence here is of no consequence."

That smacked the smile off my face.

"As such, we must bring the auditions to a pause," said Ruby. "Right now, your goal is no longer to eliminate the competition. It's to do exactly as we say when we say it. Your servants will be briefed, and at dinner tonight, we will provide you with your final test. You will succeed, or you will forfeit your place in the Left Hand."

At least I wouldn't have to worry about Five creeping through my door and putting a knife in my neck.

Probably.

"Further rules will be provided over dinner." Emerald shoved the door out of her way, voice still quietly angry. "Make no attempts on each other's lives and set up no traps. Your rooms have been cleaned and baths drawn with special soap. Use it. Your servants will dispose of your clothes. Five, with me."

Ruby and Emerald swept out of the room, the crowd of servants outside the door scattering, and Five followed. Amethyst looked around the destroyed table.

"It would be best if you ate and rested. The audition is designed to test you and wear you down. We must know how you act under exhaustion and pressure. You should be proud of yourselves for getting here, but it isn't over yet. There is still much to do."

She left us in silence.

CHAPTER
THIRTY-FIVE

I collapsed over a chair, laughing into my mask, heart bursting at the muffled sound I'd grown used to.

"How'd you last?" Two turned to me, hands shaking. She was young, younger than me by maybe a year, and bone-tired by the shadows under her eyes. Blood dotted the whites. "Four's a better fighter than you. We all are."

Were better fighters. Lady help Two when that fact hit her.

"So far as you know." I salvaged a cup of water from the unpoisoned pitcher and took a sip. "I've been fighting for years."

She made an odd sound in the back of her throat. "He thought you were only a thief. Death doesn't settle well when you're not used to it."

Erlend forced me to be used to it. "Says the circus performers."

"And look how well we fared." She opened her arms wide and shot me a funeral smile. "See you at dinner."

"See you at dinner."

She wasn't handling this well.

"Twenty-Three?" Maud appeared at my elbow. She was perfectly Maud again. Every hair was in place and her face showed the emotionless passivity all servants had, but she'd bitten her nails to the quick. "If you'd like to go to your room?"

"I'd love to."

Maud didn't speak, didn't even look at me, till she shut the door to my room. I sat on the bed, ripping off my coat. Elise's ink crinkled on my arms.

"The bath is hot. Don't soak your stitches."

I flashed Maud a weak smile. Trusting people was nice—no wasting thoughts on second-guessing. "Thanks."

I sunk into the bath behind the screen, and Maud fiddled around the room, washing my mask in a small basin and hanging it up. I kept my inked arms out of the water and crawled into bed still damp, laughing as Maud left with a huff. I fell asleep to the midmorning sun slipping through the slats above me.

I awoke to the sounds of clattering plates, mouth dry as cotton and head filled with sand. I rolled onto my stomach.

"Time?" My voice cracked, and my shirt clung to the fresh salve on my side. "You change my bandages?"

"Early evening—and yes." Maud pulled me up into a sitting position and pressed a tin cup into my hands. "We need to talk about dinner."

I glanced at the tray of food filling my room with the savory scents of browned onions and olives. "Looks good."

"Not this. The real one." She rose and crossed to the clothes in the corner. "You're meeting with the Left Hand, and Two's servant, Catia, was prepping an elaborate outfit in the washing rooms."

I sipped the tea. The tang of lemon snapped me awake and

warmed me from the inside out. The ink on my arms had dulled to storm gray. "What am I supposed to do? Steal a nice outfit before dinner?"

"Play to your strengths." Maud set the tray onto my lap. "I washed the clothes you wore here, but I wouldn't suggest wearing them tonight. Or ever again."

"For the best." I traced the lip print on my palm. "What are Two and Five wearing?"

She wrinkled her nose. "Catia had a leather uniform with bracers. Dinah didn't bother washing Five's clothes before tonight, and officer's uniforms always dye the water blue anyway. They're only for parties. Completely useless."

I speared a boiled egg with my knife. Of course Five was an officer. He'd been trained with a spear, sword, and bow since childhood, and killing came easy when it was all you knew. The war was still alive but in skirmishes and courts. Unrest was rampant in the north where the lords who'd ruled Erlend still loomed. He'd grown up thinking civilians were the enemy.

Such a surprise.

"I was going to enlist, you know." I plucked up an olive and squished it between my teeth. "But I'd have been a foot soldier. Nothing fancy."

She sighed, spirals of steam from the food flushing her cheeks. "My orphanage sells work contracts to the highest bidder. You can't leave till you work enough to pay back the bid."

"Five pearls are enough to keep four fed and housed." I tucked into the meal and offered her a slice of bread. She shook her head. "So how many orphans you trying to buy?"

"Three." She picked at her nails and took a deep breath. "My mother died when my siblings were born—triplets—and the orphanage will sell their contracts to whoever needs a servant soon as they turn nine. I have to buy them first."

That would do it. No wonder she liked rules after living in an orphanage and being responsible for a trio of toddlers.

"That's it though." She stood and walked toward the door, fixing me with a stare.

"How about your name for mine?" I asked. It wasn't worth asking what she meant about papers. She must've lied about her age when they took her in so she could get out and buy her way out sooner. "Our real ones?"

She paused.

"Knowing my face could do more harm than me knowing your name." I tapped my nose.

"Maud de Pavo." She smiled at me over her shoulder. "And your face was more punishment than privilege."

"How can you be afraid to tell me your name and be so mean to me?" I tried to frown, look at least a little threatening, but she kept smiling. "Sallot, but you can call me Sal in private till I'm Opal."

"You'd better be Opal after all we've gone through." She gestured to the food. "Eat. I'll find acceptable clothes. You have tutoring with your lady after all."

I froze.

I turned my arms over and shoved my sleeves up. The ink was crinkled and cracked, and the lines blurred on my fingers. My gloves had saved most of it, but it was fading. I kissed my palm with the memory of Elise's lips still seared into my skin.

I was fishing the amber dregs of honey from my tea when

Maud came back. She set the tray by the door and herded me toward the washbasin. I tugged my mask off.

"New mask." Maud held up a new mask with a pearl-white "23" stitched on the forehead. The number was small and unobtrusive, completely unlike the giant ribbon on my face now. She pulled a brush out of her pocket. "Two's outfit is armor. It's red and gold, and it's got an insignia—an arrow shooting through flames."

"Of course it is." I sucked on my teeth, wincing at Maud's rough hairbrush ripping through my hair. "Carnival of Cheats—a family of fighters and thieves and daredevils."

What other circus taught people how to throw knives as easily as punches? A traveling carnival full of people doing dangerous things, most putting their more dangerous pasts to use and teaching their kids every trick of every trade, was the perfect breeding ground for assassins. And trust.

Perform together, die together.

"Five's wearing his officer's uniform, isn't he?" I asked.

Maud nodded. "He must have torn the pin off tonight, but I saw it when he arrived. Lukan was his last name."

"Lukan?" I patted down my untangled hair, trying to think of an outfit I could wear to compete with Two and Five. "That's not a noble name."

And everything about him screamed noble.

"No, but Dimas has heard of him. He killed his valet. They only found out after they'd invited him, and Dimas nearly quit. Emerald said the rules would be enough to keep Five from hurting us, but I wouldn't have kept on if I'd drawn his lot." Maud sat next to me, grabbed my hands, and cleaned my nails, careful to avoid Elise's ink. "I hope you've got an impressive costume to break out."

"Street fighters and road agents don't get costumes." I washed my face with my free hand best I could without touching Elise's words. The lifetime of wounds I'd collected were a map of bumps and pits under the ink. "We get fancy scars."

"Have you got enough to justify going to dinner naked?" Maud grabbed my other hand.

"Is it too late for you to find me something?" If I was going to dress to impress tonight, I wanted to be like Ruby. Power and grace, a figure fit to be noble and deadly. "Can you make me look like Ruby but in white?"

No reason to dress as the past when Opal was my future.

"No," Maud said but stopped, hands drifting to her pocket. "How much like Opal?"

"Close as can be without being rude." I pulled my new mask on and sighed. Soft cotton and silk lining the eyes. So much better. "Let the others be themselves. I want to be Opal."

She stood, nodding to herself. "I think I can do that. You go to tutoring, and I'll get your clothes."

No more mistakes, no more close calls, and no more deaths like Seve. I could put those lords to rest when I was Opal.

And I had to be Opal because I was fairly sure the only way out of the final three was death.

CHAPTER
THIRTY-SIX

I knocked, straightened my mask, and opened the door. "Sallot!" I startled, not used to hearing my full name, and Elise barreled into my chest. We fell back against the closed door.

"How are you?" Her arms hooked around my neck, warm and heavy, and she tucked her face against my shoulder. She wore mourning colors—an ash-gray bodice trimmed in black and laced with opalescent ribbon—and had bound her coiled hair in a silver net. She touched my mask. "You're Twenty-Three again."

I nodded, not sure about what to do with my arms but entirely sure I could not do this.

"Plan worked, and I didn't die." I splayed my fingers over the wide curve of her hips, blood rushing in my ears, and curled my other arm around her back. "So here I am."

Elise traced my collar, fingertips skimming my neck. "I'll miss calling you Sallot."

"You can call me Sallot." I rubbed my thumb along the dip

between her hips and ribs. She'd liked me for days—I had to catch up. "In private. Probably best not to do it in public."

"Yes, I'll call you Honorable Opal like everyone else." She drifted out of my arms, dragging her fingers over the words on my arm and letting the cold sweep into the space she'd left behind. "I admit I have nothing to teach you today. I wanted to talk."

I nodded and trailed after her, too pleased to say much more. She sat and gestured to the chair across from her. I took it.

"Yesterday," Elise said, fiddling with her locket, "you gave a very rambling rant about how much you hated Erlend, and I am less interested in that and more in you, but what did you mean?"

I swallowed. "Just what I said—never had much good to say about Erlend."

"Well, I wasn't too fond of you when we first met either. I suppose we're even." She closed her fingers around the locket and shrugged one shoulder. "And now?"

"You proved me wrong." I reached between us and took her hand, studying the lines of her palm and faded ink stains on her fingers. "I thought you were clever and pretty, but I expected you'd be like every other northern noble and dislike my sort. Then you didn't do any of their sneering, and I moved on to thinking you liked me because I was mysterious and dangerous."

Elise tapped the imprint of her lips on my palm. "I didn't like you until you corrected me about sounding literate."

"What?" Speechless, I let her lace our fingers together while I found my words. That was ages ago, back when I'd slipped with my pretending and called her on how I sounded. "I snapped at you."

"You were honest with me, and I was wrong. You hardly snapped," she said. "People are rarely honest with me. You couldn't rob me, couldn't be angry without softening it with a joke, and you always showed up to tutoring on time and ready to work."

Elise leaned in front of me and added, "You look like I've shifted your world."

"Just about." I tapped my forehead against hers, slipping an arm around her waist. "Thought coming here would be different but didn't expect you."

"You kept my ring." Her gaze dropped to my lips, and my heart leapt into my throat.

"It was pretty, and Our Queen had touched it. Never had anything nice I could get away with wearing." I nudged her with my nose and tugged her closer.

"Come here." Elise pulled away, and I swallowed back my protest when she slid from her chair and onto the floor near my feet. I sat next to her, back to the sturdy table legs, and she settled into the curve of my side, legs stretched out and pressed to mine, cheek on my shoulder and arm tangled around me. All the warmth in the world couldn't have compared to her. "How did Sallot end up as auditioner Twenty-Three?"

"Easily." I traced the curves of her thigh through her dress and pulled her legs across my lap till there were no gaps between us, the press of her steady and sure as the sun rising. "You had a poster in your purse, and I wanted out of Kursk."

She hummed, the sound shuddering from her chest to mine. "Opal is a long leap from road agent."

"I like Our Queen, and if she needs me, I'll answer." And I

wanted to kill those she'd let run free. I reached onto the table above us and grabbed a stick of charcoal. "My turn."

Rath used to do this trick where he'd place a seed in his palm and flick a hidden flower out from between his fingers like magic. I'd never asked how to do it and had no flowers. I took her hand in mine.

"How'd you get on the high court so young?" I dragged the charcoal down the underside of her wrist, slowly drawing an orange blossom over her fluttering pulse. I leaned my cheek against her scalp.

She took a shuddering breath and steeled herself. "I was invited to court after the war—something political involving my father, I'm sure—but Isidora took me in. When Our Queen asked for a list of trustworthy Erlends, they gave her my name. The war was built on half truths and omissions. History is simply what the winner writes, and Our Queen has a host of scribes to keep our histories varied. I am the Erlend scribe."

"You're keeping them honest." I trailed the stem up to her elbow and very carefully laid her arm over her lap. "How noble of you."

She laughed and touched the tip of one petal, finger coming away black. "You're supposed to put it behind my ear."

"What?"

"People tuck a flower behind the ear of the person they're courting." Elise arched her neck and bared the soft spot of flesh behind her ear to me. "But since it's not a real flower, I'll settle for a kiss."

She grinned.

I swallowed. We were both at the same place then. "Settle?"

Elise took a breath and rolled her eyes, rising to her knees. With one leg between mine and the other pressed firmly to my hip, she pinned me to the table and knelt in front of me to cup my face in her hands. My breath was caught behind the hollow of my throat, painful and demanding, heart pounding at the pressure of her thighs against my hips, the warmth of her fingers tickling the curves of my ears. I raised my hands to her waist and pulled. Her lips crashed against mine.

My eyes fluttered shut. She threaded her fingers through the hair at the nape of my neck, tugged me closer, the curve of her hips hot against mine, the flutter of her pulse fast and demanding against my lips. She made a small pleased sound and combed her fingers through my hair. I shuddered.

"If you become Opal," she said softly, voice raspy and out of breath, "you can court me."

I licked my lips, the taste of her tea filling my mouth. "Yes please."

"Good." She shook her head and leaned back, hands falling from my neck, down my chest, pricking the buttons of my shirt. "Go to dinner, Sallot."

"Of course, my lady." I watched her rise to her feet, graceful as ever but flushed. My own legs were weak, and a tingling, dreamlike sensation raced across my skin. I stumbled to my feet. "Thought you didn't kiss people who could kill you just as easily."

I'd so much blood on my hands, seeped into my soul and heavy as lead, and she was light as air, a breeze through ocean sands. She was summer and heat, the taste of salt on white crests, the shade of storm clouds before late spring rains. She was everything I wasn't.

"Hush." Elise darted forward and kissed my cheek, my mask stuck between us. "I'll kiss whomever I like. There's not enough innocence left in this world after all we've done to it."

We'd been children, and we reaped what our parents sowed.

But we were both working toward the balance—her teaching kids to read and paying for physicians for her people and me clearing the land of the nobles still stuck in the past. Protecting Our Queen, the only person who'd given us peace.

"Say my name again," I said and braced myself for the chill of leaving her.

She laughed and smiled. "Sal—"

I kissed her gently, barely brushing my mouth to hers, and memorized the feel of my name on her lips. "I'll see you when I'm Opal."

CHAPTER
THIRTY-SEVEN

M aud grabbed me soon as I stumbled into my room.
"I know it's old-fashioned, but trust me." Maud
grabbed my shirt and started undoing the buttons before I could
even speak. "It's as close to Opal as I can do."

I grabbed her hands and ducked out of her grip. "I trust you,
but I can undress myself."

"Fine." She stepped aside with a sarcastic bow. "Eventually,
you'll have to get used to me helping you."

"I trust you," I said slowly, savoring the words. I grinned. "I'll
work on letting you help me later."

She only laughed and gestured to the bed. A crisp off-white
pair of pants stitched with pale gold laid at one end. A matching
shirt, collar wide and open with shell buttons and stitch work
of golden stars along the hem, rested beside the pants, and a
coat that might have been spun from starlight it was so pale was
folded over the chair. The long coat was silk softer than I'd ever
touched. I shook my head.

"Maud, I can't wear this." I rubbed the hem of the coat. "Where'd you even get it?"

"It was my uncle's. You're about the same size, and the only people who'll buy it want to strip it for pieces. I don't have the heart to let them pay me so little only to take it apart. I'm hoping my brother will grow into it." She rustled through a bag at her feet. "You will give it back to me in one piece. The style's old—coat will hit your knees—but if you leave it unbuttoned, it'll look like one of those new robes that are getting popular."

I nodded, no idea about what was popular.

"Let's make me Opal."

Maud grinned. "Perfect."

She rubbed woody, herb-scented oil through my hair, drew a line of thin rouge across my bottom lip, and lined my eyes with black—to make the dark circles more accent than exhaustion.

"Don't stab me in the eye." I stared up while she worked. "I'm already bad enough at archery without having to relearn how to aim."

Maud finished and fanned my face. "If you wanted to be really fashionable, I could draw the runes like Our Queen's. They look nothing like the real thing, but everyone's doing it."

"No." I shuddered. Words and cosmetics were one thing, but runes were a world I wanted no part of. Magic had no place on my skin, even if it was gone. "No runes."

"No runes." She carefully pulled my mask over my hair and face. "Aren't you glad you trusted me to do my job?"

"You say that like you're insulting me." I wiggled my nose, eyes itching but too afraid of Maud to rub them.

Maud shrugged. She circled me and pinned each spot that

needed it. The shirt was easy, smooth and light against my sore side, and the coat was heavy over my shoulders. Maud didn't mention the ink on my arms and hands, and I didn't wash it off. I straightened the long sleeves of the coat, everything coming together. Ink crackled like fire against my skin.

I was Sallot Leon—one of the last children of Nacea, orphan and street fighter, highway thief and Twenty-Three. I was steps away from being Opal, a figure of power flushing out the Erlend lords. I'd carried the weight of what they'd done for so long, and now I could repay them for the long list of names they'd left me with. I'd take their safety, their homes, their heads. They'd made me an orphan and only child, made my name sound foreign on my own tongue and useless to the ones who'd already forgotten Nacea had lived.

I would make them remember, and only then would I let them die.

"How do I look now?" I asked, loose and sure. I'd made mistakes and I wasn't Opal yet, but Two and Five would not hold me back.

"Needs more thief-turned-rakish-deadly-lord." She pulled a wooden sheath inlaid with a spiral of crushed, jagged shells from her pocket and hooked it to my belt. "Didn't open though, so could be a wooden dagger."

I smiled. "Thank you for thinking of it." Thank you for being patient while I learned to trust you. "Going weaponless would not have been great."

"Nails!" Maud clapped and dropped to her bag, digging to the bottom. She shoved a small pot into my hands. "Hold this."

I unscrewed the lid. "Rakish-deadly lord, not fancy courtier."

"You can be both." She straightened up, a tiny brush in hand. "Nearly everyone does it. It's a miracle anyone's got nails left after all of them trying to copy Emerald." She snatched the pot back and started painting my nails with a smoky orange oil. "Dimas does it all the time, and it looks lovely on him. You've got the same long fingers."

"How much time you spend looking at his hands?"

She lightly pinched my wrist. "Hold still and let it dry. I'll cut the tips from your extra gloves."

I rolled onto my heels, getting used to the feeling of the clothes and going over how to properly eat with nobles in my head. Maud helped me pull the gloves over my fingers.

"But really," I said softly, "how do I look?"

"Good." Maud circled me, lips set in a serious line, and smoothed out the bottom hem of the coat so it flared behind me in a wake of gold and white. "You look like Opal."

CHAPTER
THIRTY-EIGHT

Maud led me to dinner. The scars I'd gained from years of running and fighting were bare under the wide collar of the shirt, and the sheath jostled softly against my thigh, a familiar weight in the middle of everything else. My real knives were tucked into my boots. I looked nothing like the Sal who'd showed up at auditions. Let them see me as more than that.

"You're serving yourself like a casual meal, and the Left Hand has Dimas in charge of the room—no servants until you all leave," Maud said. "It'll just be you six."

"Thank you." I glanced once more at her, swallowing the fluttering in my throat. "I look all right?"

"You won't if you ask me that again." She smiled. "I was joking about the scars, but you're pulling them off. Now stop. It's my job to make you look good, and it's insulting that you think I failed."

I snorted. "See you after."

The dining hall door creaked open. I took a breath, squaring my shoulders and straightening my spine, and took one step over the threshold.

Shit.

I was supposed to wait for them to invite me into the room. I bowed anyway, feet apart and arms at my side. A splash of red light sparkled across my feet.

"Good evening," Ruby said. "Six out of ten—sloppy bow."

I gritted my teeth and stood. Of course he was grading us still. My footsteps echoed over the stone floors, and Ruby gestured to the two empty chairs at the table. I sat across from Amethyst.

"And Twenty-Three." Emerald raised her glass to me, the delicate glass stem green as the silk dress draped around her. She wore a crown of purple oleander. "Welcome."

I bowed my head to her. The tables had been rearranged, pushed together to form one long table with three chairs on each side. I was facing Amethyst, and Two was one seat over. I'd be next to Five.

Dammit.

"Abel, a drink." Amethyst, radiant in a midnight-blue gown with a copper-ribbed corset, beckoned her servant, and he poured me a glass of watered-down wine. The taunt lines of Amethyst's bare muscles were beauty alone.

I grinned. "Thank you."

"We're only waiting on Five." Ruby leaned back in his chair and crossed his legs, the very image of bored relaxation. "We'll begin when he arrives."

A power play. From Five. How unexpected. I'd be unsurprised if he didn't march in here and salute.

Two shifted. Her perfectly tailored, fiery outfit showed off the lean strength in her body from feet to fingertips. The leather vest was old, well worn, and dyed red with flames devouring the arrows burned into the sides. A patchwork of red and orange silk twisted like flames covered her arms.

Before Our Queen devoured the magic in the land, the Carnival of Cheats appeared from the void wreathed in fire and was full of people boasting feats of marksmanship, strength, and bravery without magic—the only rune writers were for show. Two had no magic inked into her skin.

These days, they appeared overnight instead of by magic. I'd seen them once, from afar. An acrobat had walked a high wire strung between two buildings during market day in Kursk, and she'd juggled swords over gawkers' heads without missing a beat. Two would be as in control of her body as that acrobat had been.

"You didn't have to dress up to impress us." Emerald leaned forward, chin balanced on her fingers. She said it in a way that made it clear we should've dressed up and hadn't yet passed her inspection. Her wineglass was empty, but I hadn't caught her drinking. "Don't worry—we've been watching and already have our opinions about you."

"Though your origins and senses of fashion are interesting." Ruby raised his now-full wineglass.

Their sleight of hand was impressive.

"Mostly," said Amethyst. "White's an optimistic choice."

"I'm am optimistic person." They kept talking like they knew everything about us. Should I play all my cards or only part of them? They'd people like Nicolas del Contes spying on us. Couldn't hurt to let them know I was returning the favor. "Two and Five were dressed so nice, I didn't want to be left out."

Two's head cocked toward me. So she hadn't been spying on us like I'd been on her.

Amethyst nodded. We were sharing half our hands then. If only I could see their faces.

"I've always wanted to see the Carnival of Cheats again." Ruby leaned toward Two, voice low and measured. "But three members down must have left them scrambling for new acts. Well, at least they knew you were leaving soon."

Two stiffened. "We had apprentices ready to step into our roles. We won't be missed."

"You must be looking forward to court, Twenty-Three." Emerald raised her glass to me. "You've robbed half of them and all their merchants and business partners."

"Only have to learn their names now." I didn't drink the wine. No accounting for what they'd do since I missed the second-round test.

The door opened and Five's heels clicked behind me. Whenever he stopped to bow, he snapped his boots together. Light from the pins on his chest flickered around the wall opposite of me. He'd commanded people before, and now he was auditioning to kill them.

"And Five makes three." Ruby waved to the chair across from him and next to me. "We were discussing fashion and murder. Join in."

Five sat stiff and rigid. He crossed his right ankle over his left knee, wearing thick woolen pants made for far colder lands, and took up all my space. I stretched my legs out till our knees touched. He jerked away.

Typical.

"It's rare that officers respond to our invitations." Amethyst nodded to Five, dress slipping off her shoulder to reveal a deep scar gouged over her heart. She had to have been a soldier. They'd scars like that to spare. "Their training is typically antithetical to ours."

I'd never wondered what officers were taught. If he was really Fernando de Lukan and Dimas knew it, Nicolas del Contes definitely knew. Why'd they invite him?

"I thought my talents were better suited elsewhere." Five's voice was rough tonight. Dark circles ringed his eyes, and his gaze focused solely on Ruby. "And your invitation suggested the same."

"I doubt the invitation suggested much," said Ruby. "We were mostly impressed with your ability to stay alive. It's rare anyone survives an attack from Lord del Weylin. Not even our dear departed Opal did. The rest of your history was less than satisfactory."

Five stiffened.

Weylin—he was surely one of my secret names. He would never have stationed soldiers in Nacea—too far, too foreign, and too odd—but he'd have supported a withdrawal of troops to save Erlend lives. He hated anything farther south than his borders.

His lands were a maze of icy mountain passes and avalanche traps. He was the last major holdout against Igna and Our Queen, and attacking him was impossible. Our Queen could only keep the border well guarded with soldiers and wait for news. No idea how he kept his army and lands supplied, but he did it.

Drafted everyone he could probably, whether they wanted to fight or not, and kept the rest indentured.

I'd have to ask Maud and Elise for any palace rumors.

"I do wonder," Ruby said as he leaned across the table, elbows on the top and chin on his hands, "did you meet Lord del Weylin?"

Five shook his head.

Ruby dropped a metal pin on the table. Five's hand flew to his chest pocket, fumbling down the front.

"Pity," Ruby said. "You should've told him your real name, Lord Fernando de Lex. He probably would have seen you then."

I gripped the table edge. Emerald tapped her glass, empty face fixed on me. Five wasn't just a noble and an officer—he was the youngest son of one of Erlend's oldest families. A family nipped at the bud during the war. His oldest brother had been the head mage of Erlend and the first Rodolfo da Abreu had killed. Rodolfo had taken the mages' hands, stripping the runed skin from its bones to make sure no one would ever hold the secrets to shadow creation again. A necessary violence.

A bloody, painful violence that Fernando de Lex no doubt remembered.

I glanced at Five, a writhing mix of rage and recognition shaking down my arms. He'd have been six when his brother was slaughtered—old enough to remember and about the same age I'd been when his brother's shadows had flayed Nacea. His parents had died in the war, and he'd vanished. We were both the last of our names.

But my fallen family hadn't ever murdered children.

Fernando de Lukan. The officer who'd killed his valet, survived an attack from Weylin, and ended up invited here under that false identity.

Had he rebuilt himself or returned for darker purposes?

"Do you have a problem with me?" Five shifted in his chair, shoulders back and chin up. "With my old name?"

"That's your question?" Ruby huffed. "Not how I know your real name?"

"At least one of you met my brother," Five said. "We looked very much alike."

The Left Hand exchanged a series of shoulder-shrugged looks. Emerald plucked his name tag from the table. It was almost sad. His brother was taken by forbidden magic and revenge, and all he had left were pieces. If the rumors were true though, he'd been killing long before he got here, and his brother had created the shadows.

Even if Five were executing some half-thought-out scheme of vengeance, he wasn't avenging someone worth it.

And it wasn't like he could take revenge on a dead man.

"I was mostly interested in how you were the only survivor. Your escape from Weylin's lands is unprecedented." Emerald gestured toward the door. "But let's eat."

The color-collared servants slid into the room, arms weighed down with trays—tureens full of steaming black bean stew with balls of cornmeal speckled with green chilies bobbing between mutton slices; peppery shrimp and hominy soup with stewed tomatoes; and little bowls of pickled green tomatoes, braised mustard greens, and corn fritters no bigger than my little finger. I folded my hands in my lap.

Lady, if they'd poisoned this feast, I'd punch them for wasting food.

"Tuck in." Emerald brandished her spoon toward the place

LINSEY MILLER

settings. The meal placed in front of her was identical to Amethyst's and Ruby's plates, but their sleight of hand wouldn't work here. How lonely it was living behind their masks.

I'd rarely been without one since running with Grell, and now I'd found the one profession where I'd be trapped behind a mask forever.

"It's safe," Amethyst said. "Dinner isn't the test."

I grabbed a bit of everything but the chili-braised chicken feet.

At least the bones in Five's room were sentimental, but I couldn't shake them from my head.

"As of right now, your only goal is to find the name on this paper, kill no one but this person without implicating the Left Hand, and bring Our Queen proof of your kill." Ruby fanned out three slips of paper like gambling cards and offered them to us. "No harming their guards, no killing civilians, and no letting anyone know you killed your target."

It was every single one of our lessons rolled into one.

Five sipped wine with one hand and grabbed the target Ruby held out to him with the other. Two took hers, glanced at the name, and pocketed it. I pulled the last slip from Ruby's fingers.

"Your group has been above average in both mortality and ability during these auditions, and several mass events narrowed the playing field." Emerald settled back in her chair. "Which leaves us with you three, and considering all your indiscretions, we're not holding out hope for clean, good kills. But understand this: I don't care how you do it, but you will not get caught and you will not kill anyone else—not a hair on their heads disturbed—or I will end you."

Emerald, as always, managed to terrify and impress me all at once. I wanted to be her, and I never ever wanted to be on her bad side.

"The names and descriptions on your paper represent three minor people who have either caused unrest, committed violent crimes, or supported the instigators in the north." Ruby let out a long bored sigh.

Amethyst continued Ruby's speech. "They need to be eliminated quietly and quickly. These are not to be public executions. Do not treat them as such. Understood?"

"Good." Emerald didn't wait for us to agree. "Your marks are all in Willowknot for the next three days, and we will take into consideration the speed of your success. If you are caught, you are on your own. If you insinuate that this was part of auditions for the Left Hand, you are on your own and dead. Bring us proof of your kill that won't arouse suspicion."

Five finished eating and glanced at the slip of paper. While sipping tawny wine, he shifted, and I caught sight of an extra knife in his boot. It didn't change anything, his true history. Just meant I knew which memories to drag up to hurt him if need be.

"Any questions?" Amethyst slid from her chair as we stayed silent. "Then you're dismissed."

We all waited till the Left Hand stood—I knew that much at least—and Five left the room with a bow to each of them. Two left with less show.

She was too quiet. She could kill me and I'd never be the wiser it was her. I needed to finish this perfectly and avoid her and Five at all costs.

CHAPTER
THIRTY-NINE

M aud wiped the cosmetics from my face and folded the nice clothes on my bed, fingers shaking the whole time.

"How're you so nervous?" I pried my slip of paper from the coat pocket and shook out my arms. "I'm the one who could die."

Maud straightened the collar of my shirt, lips pursed and face carefully blank. She patted my arm. "You die, I don't get promoted."

"Of course." I swallowed. No point in embarrassing us both with emotions. "I'll be sure not to die then."

"I appreciate it." Maud grinned—barely—and handed me a cloak.

"I look boring?" I threw it over my shoulders and fixed my hair, face cold without my mask. I was going into Willowknot, and I'd need to make a friend fast to find my target. "Presentable?"

"Passable." The thought of me wandering out into the world looking "passable" washed away whatever she had been feeling, and she raised her hands to my hair. "If you'd let me—"

"No, passable is what I want." Meant I was forgettable, and I could live with that. It meant no one would remember another person in the crowd. I pulled off the last bit of gilt that marked me as more than a traveler and handed Elise's ring to Maud. "I don't come back, tell Lady de Farone I'm sorry. And I won't fault you if you try to wrangle a better paying job out of it. Sure she won't either."

Elise's attendant was probably too busy getting ink and charcoal stains out of her clothes to do anything else.

Maud tucked the ring into her pocket. "I will. I promise."

"I know. I trust you. Which is why I want you to have the bounty for Grell da Sousa. I killed him, and I won't need it if I'm dead. Amethyst seems nicest. Talk to her about it."

She opened her mouth, and I thrust my slip of paper into her hands.

"Just accept the money and go get your siblings." I could read it—mostly—but I had to be sure. "What's it say?"

She stared at me for a moment too long. "Thorn da Tonin, nineteen hands, shaved head, runes on forearms and back, scar across left side of mouth, lives in Willowknot, runs Quick Silver." She wrinkled her nose and handed it back to me. "He's one of yours."

I checked all four of my knives and pulled on my gloves. "Mine?"

"Street fighter, gambler." She leaned against the tub. "Alibi's this old gambling house. Dimas bans all the new workers from going, but the soldiers still show up beaten to bits every few nights, and it's good money. Thorn tried to buy it out, but they never gave in, so he opened up Quick Silver across from it. Stole half their business."

"And you know all of that how?" I asked. "Don't strike me as the gambling type."

"I was looking for work." She crossed her arms, wincing. "The Triad help whatever poor souls he's got working for him now."

"Well, Our Queen's helping them at least." I tore up my slip and handed it to her. I was Sal again—dressed for a job in mostly fitting clothes and pleasantly buzzed with the thrill of it all. Finding people was easy and getting to them easier. No different than robbing a house. "Remember, Lady de Farone."

"Yes, yes." Maud shooed me away. "I did exist before you walked into my life. Go be Opal."

I grinned all the way to Willowknot. The streets were different by lantern light, sharper and louder. Crowds moved from building to building, shouting through tavern doors, and I slipped my hood from my head while watching them drift from bar to gambling table to bar again. With so many workers flooding the city, the shops were thriving.

I followed a group yattering about Alibi—best place to get dirt was from your target's competition. The place was flush with people.

Igna soldiers drank around the bar—their coats thrown off and weapons gone. A large crowd of women played drinking games I'd never heard of and cheered in one of the western languages from over the Blue Silk Sea that I didn't know. A couple at the back whispered to each other with the telltale harsh accent of Berengard from over the eastern mountains.

"Weapons to the bar," the person behind me said in Alonian.

"The bar?" I spun around, gripping my side, and eyed the older woman trying to herd me to the counter.

"No weapons inside. Drop them on the bar, you'll get a number, and they'll keep them locked up till you leave." She smiled, suntanned skin crinkling like the lines on a river map, and led me to a seat. "Check your weapons and have a drink or see yourself out."

I obeyed and traded my two knives for a ribbon with the number 247 looped over the end.

"You from down south?" my companion asked. She fixed herself a drink from the bar, winking at the barkeeper.

The barkeeper tossed a candied lemon slice at her.

"The coast." I smiled and nodded. "Rath da Oretta."

"Nanami Kita." She crunched the lemon between her teeth. "Most here call me Nana."

Neither of us was from Erlend or Alona then. I laughed and rubbed the back of my neck, copying one of the bashful musicians in the corner trying to talk their way into a free drink.

"I was looking to gamble, but..." I said and looked around like I was lost. Not a gambling table in sight.

"We've been known to have some of that." She leaned in toward me, bringing the scents of salt and seaweed with her, and poured out a decent measure of a nutty-smelling clear liquor into a cup. She set it in front of me and topped it off with golden tea. "You like dice or chalk?"

"Dice." I took a sip of my drink. She'd pulled it straight from the bar and couldn't have poisoned it. The woody tea did nothing to cover up the smooth burn of the spirit. "Friend told me Quick Silver's the place for it, but their tables look too good to be true."

Nana scowled, twisting the scars carved around her crooked

nose. "Quick Silver's a den of thieves playing at riches. Don't go there."

"All right." I poured more tea into my drink to ease it up. She was forceful. "That sounds like a good story."

"Not a good one for most." Nana flipped her short black hair from her eye. "They set up a few years back. Most of the place is travelers or people who've come looking for work, and they look it. House always wins if you look too poor to pay up."

"Sorry luck." I sipped my laced tea. Grell had done the same thing—pinpointed the cheapest looking of the lot, made sure they knew they'd have to pay interest on their debt if they lost, and then suddenly every gamble was unluckier and unluckier. Kept people paying up and earned you more than what they'd lost. And if they were poor? Defaulting left the house with a handful of options on how to collect, and none of them were fair.

I hated my few stints with his gambling rings. I'd moved onto mousing apartments and robbing coaches soon as I could.

Nana nodded toward the street. "That's what my illustrious competition says."

"Yours?" I turned to look. Thorn da Tonin, as bald and scarred as my note had promised, stepped out of a small covered coach and into the guarded door of Quick Silver. Even his horses were trimmed in the color.

"Part of it. Have to have somewhere to live when I'm not in Mizuho," she said. "Does give me the added advantage of saying 'drinks on me.'"

"Thank you." I grinned despite myself. Mizuho—they were a friend of Our Queen's, but I'd never met anyone from there. If Tonin was moving in on Mizuho's business interests and being an ass about it, she'd probably be angry. "Owners here always stay in the building?"

"I do rounds when I'm here. Tonin gambles—it's why he opened the hall—but he's got business partners that run it," Nana said. "He's got a nice little garden where he gambles with friends. All of them owe him money, but he keeps them liquored up to make amends."

So I wasn't getting at him unless he played without guards or till they left.

I shrugged. "If you've got the money."

She hummed in response and took my hand in hers, drawing a sharp little rune on my skin. The ink didn't burrow like when magic had run free—how it still did outside of our nation's borders—but I couldn't stop my shudder. The meaning was there even if the magic wasn't.

We were meant to sustain The Lady, not use her.

"Don't." Nana grabbed me before I could wipe it off. "It'll get you downstairs to the tables. You get caught without one, my guards will break your fingers."

"I don't like magic."

"It's not magic here." She dropped my hand.

I sucked in a breath and steadied myself, trying to maintain the easygoing calm I'd been using to get Nana to talk. I forced a smile.

If I looked it, eventually I'd feel it.

"Through that door, down, and to the left." Nana nodded toward the shadowy back corner of the room. "You keep that rune on you."

Slouched at the end of the bar, wrapped in a hooded cloak

that half-hid his face and nursing an amber spirit, Nicolas del Contes raised his glass to me.

As if that answered any of the questions I had for him. I'd other things to think about besides him and his spying. He had to know I'd killed Seve, but he'd done nothing about it. That meant he and Our Queen approved, or he wanted Seve dead for some other reason.

Either way, no time for him tonight.

"Will do." I slid out of my seat. "Thank you. I'm going to run back and tell my partner not to hit Quick Silver."

"As you should. Bring them. I'll be at the fights. My partner's up tonight." She gestured for me to turn. A muscular woman entering the building flipped her braid over her shoulder and waved. She was my sort—a street fighter's stance even in the middle of a crowded bar. "You look like you could throw some hits?"

"I'll stick to dice."

"Suit yourself." Nana sighed, touching her fingers to her lips and flicking them away. Her hand fluttered to her chest. "Luck on your side."

"Thanks." I nodded to her partner, who was returning Nana's hand signal with a love-eyed look. "And on hers."

I collected my weapons, downed the last of my drink—bad luck to leave a gift unused—and headed to Quick Silver.

Tonin could have some more fun. I could wait.

CHAPTER
FORTY

Quick Silver was a cacophony of Erlenian and clattering credit coins styled to look like real pearls. Drawling vowels as inaccessible and inescapable as nobles filled my ears. I was so tired of it.

How could people put so much loathing in their words?

The guards charged a single copper tooth to let people in, and I circled the building with a scowl. The windows were distorted glass. Useless.

The buildings around Quick Silver though were all tall fancy inns and eating houses—easier to keep your gamblers close. I snuck up the side of a white plaster building down the street—no guards and all the windows closed—and crawled onto the roof. The roof gardens were as expansive as the ones on the palace grounds, but these were filled with snap peas, garlic stalks, basil, and dozens of other everyday needs. I tiptoed around a trellis draped in huckleberries and stepped over the thin gap between the buildings.

Cities were the best for robberies. There was always noise to cover your tracks and alternate routes to get where you needed. I perched on the roof next to Quick Silver.

And these rooftop gardens were growing on me.

Tonin had a monstrously expensive garden with white and gray flowers blooming around the edge and silver furniture for his players. The table was dead center and framed by four chairs with cloud-shaped cushions. Tonin lounged on one with a stance entirely too relaxed for someone betting coin they cared about. His partner was ramrod straight and overcompensating, fancy slippers tapping out his nerves on the rooftop. The pair shared a pitcher of bloodred wine muddled with orange slices. Tonin downed the last of his glass, drizzled honey across the bottom, and poured himself another.

Good. Tonin was big, and he'd be easier to kill drunk. I didn't want a fair fight with anyone who'd forearms big as my thighs. The pair of them gambled more, drank more, and traded enough boring business chatter to put me to sleep. I spun one of my knives in my fingers, straining to hear anything of use. The only words loud enough to hear clearly were curses.

Lady, if this was what being Opal was like, I was in for a lifetime of boredom.

"You rat!" Tonin's partner tossed his dice into a carpet of woolly thyme. "No chance they're not weighted."

Tonin snorted. "You brought them."

I leaned forward, drawing my feet up and rising to my toes on the edge of the wall. Finally, something to do.

Tonin rose, muttering the whole time. The other man tossed a handful of credit coins—wood carved with his name and symbol as a promise he'd pay up—onto the table and downed the last of his drink. He straightened the merchant guild pin on his hat.

I leaned over the roof, hiding in the shadows as one of the predictable guards passed beneath me. "Come on. Leave."

Tonin's partner turned.

Shan de Pau looked as well fed and fancy on this roof as he did on his business posters.

Shan de fucking Pau. The man who'd sold Nacean goods while they were still warm and bloodied was Tonin's business partner. And I couldn't kill him.

I rammed my fists into my thighs, pain biting through the rage howling at me to follow Shan de Pau, rip him limb from limb, and sell the pieces like he'd done to us. He'd no right to still be standing. I groaned and wrapped my arms around my head.

This was worse, so much worse than Seve, who'd been right there. I'd made it an accident, but this was a trap. They were making sure I wouldn't kill him.

But why shouldn't he die? Why should he get to walk free when so many were dead? Homeless? Starving?

They'd trapped me. The Left Hand knew. They had to know what he'd done—everyone knew—and they'd let him stand. Now they were luring me into their complacency. But why?

Tonin gathered up the credit coins Pau had tossed aside. Pau vanished through the door.

More money exchanged hands.

Money.

We'd so little farming land left intact after the war that Our Queen had bought extra food from across the sea. She'd needed money.

But, Lady, the cost of it. There had to be more—there had to be—because she wouldn't sign away the murder of thousands so easily, not when she'd fought so hard to save everyone. There was more to it, and it was on Pau. Filth or not, he'd something she needed.

But he wouldn't for much longer.

I leapt to my feet and shook out my arms. He wouldn't live with it much longer because I knew where he was, and he wasn't going to live with it comfortably. Pau would pay. I'd make sure of it. As the ache in my chest grew with each step he took down the street, I gripped the trellis next to me to keep from chasing after him. Blackberries and thorns crushed under my palm. I let my blood fall to the garden beneath me.

"For what I've done and what I'm about to do," I said softly. The Lady's stars were gone tonight, too pale against the lights of the city and palace. I backed up from the edge, eyes fixed on my future, on Tonin, and double-checked that my path was clear. "And everything that will come after."

CHAPTER
FORTY-ONE

I landed hard on the roof of Quick Silver, stumbled forward, and rolled over my shoulder into Tonin. He opened his mouth to scream.

I shoved my fist into his mouth, knuckles caught in his teeth. He flailed and kicked, and I pinned him under me with my knees on either side of his chest. He howled.

I punched him. Hard. His eyes rolled back, and he went limp. I eased my hand from his teeth.

Bloody gouge marks lined my knuckles. I leaned back and rubbed the pain away, staring down at Tonin. Pau was a coward and opportunist, and he'd never fight Tonin or anyone head-on. He'd wait till they turned their back.

I couldn't kill Pau, but I could trap him like they'd trapped me. I just had to make them think he'd killed Tonin.

The empty glasses rimmed with silver glittered in the moonlight. I pulled the long, dull stirring rod from one and rolled Tonin onto his stomach. He moaned, fingers drifting toward his head, and I sat back down on top of him, pinning his arms with my knees. I glanced around and saw nothing better to use as a weapon, so I raised the rod. Pau hadn't carried a knife. He would kill someone with whatever was on hand.

And he could get a lucky hit.

"What?" Tonin slurred the word, still trying to grab his bruised temple.

"Shush." I pulled his signet ring from his finger. "You won't even notice."

I lined the rod up beneath the base of his skull and jammed it through his neck. He didn't even twitch.

Dripping blood and sweat, exhaustion tugging at my bones, I rose from Tonin and tucked the stirrer into my pocket.

Dead.

My mark was dead. I hadn't been caught, and I'd injured no one else. My final test for Opal had come and gone, and here I stood, one step closer to Shan de Pau and all the other bastards who'd buried Nacea in shallow graves and political nonsense. They'd finally have to pay up what they owed.

And it was going to be so *easy*.

I ripped the purse from Tonin's belt. He wore silver cosmetic dust on his face, sparkling in the night like some wayward star, and I smeared some across Pau's credit coins before stuffing them in the bag. I knocked over Tonin's glass and upended Pau's chair too. He'd be panicked.

A drunken brawl over gambling gone too far. A sudden stabbing. A frantic escape.

Careful not to step in the blood or wine, I made my way back to the edge of the roof. Every now and then, people and guards moved through the alley between Quick Silver and the building I'd leapt from. I shimmied down one of the decorative beams and waited for my path to clear.

The guards and crowds were none the wiser. I shoved my bloodied gloves into a pocket and straightened my clothes. Just had to find Shan de Pau.

A street kid that looked like me—young, dirty, racing away from a drunk man screaming about a missing purse—rammed into me as I turned a corner, and I grabbed her arm. "You want to make some money?"

She eyed me through a filthy fringe of hair and nodded.

"You seen Shan de Pau? Guards are looking for him." I slipped her one of the clean coins from Tonin's stash.

She turned the coin over in her palm, glancing from my hands to my face. At least the darkness hid the bloodstains on my clothes.

"Fancy inn with gold letters." She shoved me in the right direction. "You can't miss it."

"Thanks."

I grinned and took off, the wind at my back and joy coursing through my veins. This was as good. They'd trapped me, but I always find a way out.

The inn where he was staying was bright and welcoming, shutters thrown open in half the rooms and flickering candlelight breaking through the cracks. Pau, a silhouette more cliff face than nose, paced behind the half-shuttered window of a room spanning the entire upper corner of the building. Of course he had the largest, fanciest room. I scaled the building next door.

I waited for him to settle and snuff out his lights. Safe in the darkness, I made the short jump to the inn and balanced on the large sill sticking out from Pau's window. No one shouted at the clatter and the sill barely creaked. I nudged open the window.

A soft, fluttering snore met my ear. I held back a groan of disgust and slipped into the room. I laid still on the floor, listening to the footfalls in the hall and steady breaths coming from the bed, and waited for my eyes to adjust to the darkness. Pau's merchant pins—of course he'd more than one—rested on the bedside table. A guard's thick heels paced beyond the crack at the bottom of his door.

People depended too much on doors and guards.

Pau's chest rose and fell. I crawled toward him in an awkward half-slither and pulled out Tonin's coin purse. Dirt and dried blood crumbled to the floor, making a nice little pile of evidence next to Pau's boots. I dropped the bloodied stirring rod into one like a drunkenly hid secret. Pau didn't move.

I peeked over the edge of the bed. He'd a face that might've been handsome—large eyes closed and full lips open—if my hatred weren't clouding my vision. He was well taken care of with smooth unburned skin. All of it was paid for with money he'd robbed from corpses.

"Try to buy your way out of this," I whispered. He'd either be poor as dirt or walking to the gallows by the end of the trial.

He snorted and turned over. I dropped the bloody purse filled with credit coins into the pocket of his discarded over-robe and spat on my hands to dampen the blood dried between my fingers. Couldn't be too obvious or his servants would've noticed but still obvious enough.

I checked the size of his hands. Perfect.

I tossed one glove with his clothes, another behind the head of the bed, and cleaned my hands in Pau's washbasin. A few drops of wine were easy enough to dribble on his clothes. Tonin hadn't had time to fight back. The only ties to the murder Pau needed were a weapon, blood, and motive.

Check, check, and check.

What'd folks say? Death weighed you down? I'd not known the heavy pain of it till I was five and Erlend dragged its shadows to my home. This was nothing compared to my darkened childhood.

"I hope they hang you," I said to Pau's closed eyes.

Pau, snoring away the night in a drunken stupor, only rolled over.

I wiped all traces of me from his room, took one last look at his face, and pulled on my mask.

"And I hope I'm here to watch."

CHAPTER
FORTY-TWO

I'd a credit coin and Tonin's signet ring to give the Left Hand, and if that didn't work, they could wait for the news of Pau's arrest. Two debts for the price of one.

"Twenty-Three?"

I turned at the familiar voice, spying Dimas's willowy figure weaving between the palace gate guards. I stopped.

"The Left Hand is in the breakfast nook from your first meeting." He led me through the gate—there were more guards with weathered knowing faces—and through the old courtyard where I'd first met Ruby. "It would be unwise to approach alone."

"For me or the guards?" I asked as he opened the door.

He smiled. "You. Auditions are over. The palace patrols have returned."

"Over?" I slipped through the door he held open, grinning. "Sounds good to me."

"Should it?" Emerald's voice cut through the pleasant,

buzzing energy still coursing through my veins after Tonin's death and Pau's looming arrest. "I've gotten word of a rather bloody murder."

I nodded—news from Nicolas surely. "By who?"

She shrugged.

Ruby laughed. "You've been starting rumors."

"You gave me a job," I said. "But it was more trap than test."

"No, it was all test." Amethyst leaned forward. "Did you pass?"

"Thorn da Tonin is dead. I injured no one during, and I wasn't caught." I swallowed. That was every rule.

"Proof?" Ruby asked. "Your secrets can't save you tonight. Where were you?"

I glared at him, in no mood for his tone or reminder of my probation. "Alibi."

Amethyst let out a laugh.

"Alibi?" Ruby rolled his head back and sighed. "You can't invoke 'alibi' and expect us to take your word for it."

"I was at Alibi. Ask Nanami Kita. She saw me." I leaned against the wall next to the door. "Shan de Pau should be getting arrested for murder soon."

The Left Hand stayed silent, blank masks staring motionless at me. Then Ruby very slowly clapped and laced his fingers together. He leaned forward, chin on his knuckles.

"Shan de Pau. A murderer. Who would have thought? How will he be discovered?" Ruby asked. "And how convenient that a man so hated will be shuffled aside by the laws he's been so careful to abide."

"Gambling debts and bloody credit notes—merchants are very predictable about their money." I tossed the only credit coin I'd kept at Ruby. "You know what Shan de Pau did, and you sent me there—"

"Because not killing him would've been your job if you were Opal," Emerald said sharply. "Yes, we know. Our Queen knows every detail, but he bought his freedom by funding her."

My rage at watching him relax on that rooftop flared. She knew. Our Queen knew, and she'd let him off for money that wasn't his to give. "He's a citizen of Igna! Whatever is his belongs to her. She could've just claimed it."

"And the people of a nation barely born would never have trusted her." Emerald stood in one fluid motion, looming over me before I could blink, and held me against the wall. Her fingers closed around my arm. "Our nation is held together by fragile promises and fear. We are that fear, and we cannot jeopardize the deals Our Queen made after the war. Lord del Weylin has styled himself King of Erlend. He will take any chance he can to cast Our Queen aside and claim the throne. One moment of weakness or malcontent, and Igna is no more. You will not unsettle what little peace the civilians of this country have. Understood?"

I nodded.

I lied.

"Good." She let go and settled back into her chair.

Ruby sidled up next to me, flipping the credit coin back and forth across his fingers. "You should keep this safe. Interesting improvisation though."

"Didn't need a shield this time." I tucked the coin into my pocket. "So I passed?"

Ruby shrugged. The door swung open, slamming into the wall

next to me. Five stomped inside, blood dripping down his boots, and a frazzled Dimas followed him. Ruby danced back to his spot with the Left Hand.

"Done." Five dropped his slip of paper onto the table next to Emerald.

Ruby shrugged, flicking the paper aside. "Proof?"

Five pulled a severed hand from his pocket and tossed it onto the table.

Emerald picked it up by the thumb. "Well then."

"They won't question why it's missing." Five shifted, shaking out his filthy cloak. "They won't find all of him, and they won't know what to make of it."

I sucked on my teeth. Given his history and the memories he chose to keep, I'd have been suspicious if I were Ruby. Five's head snapped round to me.

"Evening," I said with a fake smile. Three's empty face flashed in my mind. "Nice night for a repeat of your shadow performance."

I nodded to the hand. Amethyst looked at me.

"Thief girl's here then?" Five asked, full lips pulling up into a sneer. He snapped at Dimas. "Towel."

I scowled. I wasn't "she," and he was rude. Lady bless, I'd gone to dinner practically styled as Ruby, and I looked more like Five than anyone here. I didn't want to deal with this, not when I was so close to having everything I wanted. I lurched off the wall.

"You can call me Twenty-Three or nothing at all." I handed him a plain handkerchief—stolen from Pau and still bloody.

Five shoved me away with one hand, not paying a lick of

attention, and I slipped his bracelet off. He wanted a thief, then I'd give him a thief.

"So touchy." I held up his bracelet and grinned. "I'll keep an eye on you then, little bird."

Five moved toward me and Ruby stepped between us. Five flinched away from him.

Dimas broke the tension with a towel on one arm and Two on the other. He handed the towel to Five. Two slumped against the wall.

I took the only open seat, tapping my nails against the wooden arms. I was too anxious to be tired but too tired to think clearly. I shouldn't have antagonized Five.

"Stop." Emerald laid her hand over mine. "It's annoying and noticeable, two things you've neglected to be until now."

I stilled—best I obeyed.

"Proof?" Ruby asked Two, beckoning her forward.

"Here." Two tossed a sack at him. "Unfortunate carriage accident by the river."

A head covered in matted hair and blood rolled out of the bag. I hid my grin behind a hand. I'd toss stuff at him too if I was tired and he was snappy.

"Perfect. That's what I like to see. So glad you all are so punctual and efficient." Ruby grabbed Two's mark and set it on the table next to Five's spare hand. "Although, I don't know why you keep tossing your proof of death around. You're going to need it."

"The night is yours. The competition is done." Ruby shooed Dimas from the room. "You may no longer attack each other, and there will be no more tests."

Amethyst stood. "The security around your rooms and grounds has reverted to normal. No more sneaking around. You will be caught and you will be escorted out of Willowknot and the running for Opal."

I couldn't see her eyes, but I swore she looked at me.

"You will meet the Queen before breakfast. Bathe, rest, and look presentable. A wardrobe will be provided, but it's up to you to choose appropriately." Emerald examined her brass nails, crossing her legs till her own green gown flared out around her like a sea of grass. "Do you understand?"

We all nodded.

"Good. Take these." Ruby gestured to the head and hand on the table. "Go clean yourselves up."

I followed Two and Five out of the room. Five kept his head turned with one eye on me, and I darted around him with a grin soon as I could. Maud and another servant walked toward us from the old archery courtyard, and I paused so Five could leave without me. His gaze followed me till he vanished around a corner with his servant. Two glanced at me.

"What was that?" Two asked as she shifted the severed head from hand to hand, jagged edges of spine scraping her skin before stuffing it back into the sack. "With Five?"

"He's an ass. Angry I messed with him a while back." I nodded to the scratch on her arm. "You're bleeding."

"Am I?" She didn't look at it, didn't even flinch, only hummed and stared at her approaching servant. "I'll see you at breakfast then?"

I nodded. "See you at breakfast."

She didn't turn her back to me when she left. I shook my head, going to meet Maud. Honor and trust were worthless when you were surrounded by folks like me, but I'd found Maud and Elise. They were nothing like me in the best ways.

"Twenty-Three?" Maud, hands clasped behind her back, bowed to me. "Ready to return to your room?"

"Lead the way." I scratched at the stitches running down my side. "So now that we're all tested out and corralled, what's the security like?"

Her lips twitched. "You're not to leave your room tonight."

Dropped security at a time like this—no wonder rumors about auditions were wild and untamed. It kept the truth quiet about what really happened and how unguarded the noble grounds were.

Maud even had to show a little bracelet to the guards.

"We didn't wear them while you were here, so none of you could steal one." She smiled as she opened the door to my room. "Only nobles, guards, and servants are to know about the passes and who can go where."

She still made sure the door was locked though.

"I suppose a one-in-three chance is still acceptable." She started unclasping my cloak.

"I aim to please." I moved her hands and shook my head. "You should let go."

"Why? What's wrong?" She pulled away, hands stained red.

"That's why."

She stumbled back and dunked her hand in the washbasin, gagging.

"That's what I thought." I finished undressing behind the screen and sunk into the shallow bath. "Can you wait and help me wrap my side? The stitches are getting itchy."

Slathered in salve and bandaged a while later, I crawled into bed with Maud's help. The sudden, crashing *everything* that had happened in the past few days slammed into my chest and dragged down my eyelids. I barely heard her leave.

It was my last night as Twenty-Three. The mask came off easily, sliding over my short hair. I took a deep breath and traced the bruises spilling over my chest in splotches of dark blue and deep red-pricked purple. The stitches burned.

I stared up at The Lady's stars, memory of doing this so close but hazy as a dream, and flipped the credit coin from finger to finger, rolling it across my knuckles. They could give me as many names as they pleased, but I was doing this for me.

I'd scrubbed and scrubbed, but blood still stained my nails.

"Don't be angry." I swallowed and clenched the coin in my hands. "You're all about balancing out the world and repaying debts. They owe you for Nacea."

The stars didn't answer.

Had I ruined it? I'd wanted to be perfect, but Shan de Pau drinking and gambling with money not his had awoken the rage in my blood born by Seve's death. I was good—no one had seen me, and no one would ever know Pau hadn't done it. Of course he'd protest, but anyone would.

I tucked the coin into the chest pocket of my shirt. I'd killed five people and more had died because of me, but it was all for nothing if I wasn't named Opal. Knowing the names of the Erlend lords was nothing if I couldn't get to them.

What was one more, five, five dozen when I'd so much blood on my hands I'd never be able to pay it back?

They were dead, blood drained and bodies burned, but they

were my deaths to carry and mine to remember, no matter how dark their pasts. Just like I'd made Seve remember. Just like I'd make the others remember.

North Star. Deadfall. Riparian. Caldera. Winter.

Grell. Eight. Seven. Seve. Tonin.

And tomorrow would come no matter how much blood I'd wasted. I fell asleep beneath the twinkling stars with the scents of lemon and ink filling my dreams.

CHAPTER
FORTY-THREE

I woke with the sun. Maud wafted the steam from a cup of tea under my nose and whispered my name till I rolled onto my back. Daylight burned through my eyes.

I was going to meet Marianna da Ignasi, Our Queen of the Eastern Spires and Lady of Lightning.

And I had to sit through breakfast first.

Two looked like the raging heart of a fire, dressed in deep reds and oranges, sunny yellows and golds, with a flicker of blue silk draped across her chest.

Five wasn't there.

"He went first." Two curled her bare hands around a steaming mug of tea, fingers shaking, and smiled. "The room feels larger without everyone else."

"I'm sorry about Three and Four." I poured myself a cup of tea, too afraid of getting food on my clothes to eat, and spooned enough honey in it to rile up Four from beyond the pyre. "Four was all right, even for trying to disqualify me."

"It was so fast," she said, not even acknowledging I'd spoken. "The last audition went on for two weeks."

"But you're alive."

"It doesn't bother you, does it? Killing?"

"It does," I said softly, "but we all signed up knowing we could die. Everyone has an ending."

I would remember them forever—their names, my reasons, the way their bodies slumped in death and their eyes stared through me. If I stopped, if I let their deaths weigh me down and keep me from being Opal, it was all for nothing. There was no going back.

I was what I was, and they were a part of me now.

Two opened her mouth, but Dimas bowed next to her. She twisted away from me.

"The Left Hand is ready to see you." He gestured toward the nook.

Two rocked back and forth on her heels, lingering behind Dimas, and said, "I didn't want them to die alone and leave me behind."

I stared at her retreating back.

They still had, and there was nothing anyone could do to fix that. Killing like Five did with Three was monstrous, like the lords did with the shadows as their weapon. That should bother people. This was nothing.

I dunked a roll in my tea. It would've been awful to see Rath here—watch him kill, tremble with the weight of something he'd not known, till one day, he wasn't at breakfast. He'd have lost himself. I couldn't have watched it.

I set the roll aside and stirred my tea to pass the time, forcing thoughts of Five and Two from my mind.

No use thinking of what I lacked and what they had. It was over.

"Twenty-Three?"

I jerked, knocking my chair arm into Dimas.

"The Left Hand would like to see you."

"Sorry I got blood on your floor last night." I kept pace beside him and studied the little lines crinkled around his eyes. A little older than Maud and me but not by much. Managing so many people and buildings took its toll. "Maud would've killed me for it."

"Thank you, but it was no issue." His jaw tensed. "Maud is very—"

"Lovely?" I sucked the last bits of food and honey from my teeth and straightened my coat. I helped Rath out enough times to know how this worked. "Trustworthy?"

Dimas stiffened. "Dedicated but avaricious."

"Who isn't?" I frowned. Everyone needed money, especially orphans and servants. Wanting wasn't bad. "Everyone's got their reasons."

He glanced at me, losing his calm expression, and rapped on the door. I took a breath.

"Our prodigal auditioner returns." Ruby's drawl, all feigned happiness and sarcasm, seeped through the cracked door. "You had a busy night."

"You would know." I sat in the only free chair in the little room off the dining hall, small and cramped. "Setting me up and keeping tabs like that."

"You're not as adept at hiding your hatred as you think." Amethyst leaned back in her chair, the tan leather armor with beautiful detailing back today. "But you didn't give into your anger this time. Mostly."

I flushed. "I do have some self-control."

"Hardly," Ruby said softly. "However, you're young and learning, and you got Shan de Pau out of the way quietly. He drank too much to remember the whole night, much less what really happened to his business partner."

That, at least, had worked in my favor.

"In a moment, we will take you to meet Our Queen Marianna da Ignasi." Emerald lingered over her name, voice dropping. "You will not approach her. You will address her by her title, and you will bow until she bids you to stand. You will not touch her. You will answer her honestly, and you will never turn your back on her. When she dismisses you, you will back out of that room in a bow so low your nose scrapes the floor. Do you understand?"

"Yes." I nodded, swallowing back the nerves and fear lodged in my throat. "What about our proof? The coin?"

Ruby shifted forward and held out his hand. "Whichever one of you is selected as Opal will formally present Our Queen with proof of your first contract."

"It will serve as your oath of loyalty." Emerald leaned her elbows on the table, resting her chin on laced fingers. "Any other questions?"

"If it's Two," I said carefully, "what happens to me?"

None of them looked at each other, but I could feel their eyes raking over me and glancing toward each other.

"You're free to go." Ruby spread his hands out in front of him, dropping them to his chair, and a muffled, tinkling laughter leaked from behind his mask. "Provided Our Queen doesn't take issue with your alternative agenda, you will be given an invitation for the next audition and compensated for your assignment."

"Enough to buy your uniform." Amethyst rose and held out her hand. "Come. Our Queen waits."

Lady, give me this. I'd repay the blood I'd spilled with my own. Let me have this life.

I took Amethyst's hand.

"Calm down." Amethyst led me to a plain-looking door guarded by soldiers too grim-faced to be real. She knocked twice—once with two slow beats and once again with two quick ones. "We'll be watching but not listening. It will be fine."

"Thank you," I tried to say, but my fear twisted the words into a whimper.

Amethyst laughed and opened the door. I glanced up, trying to get far enough from the door to bow fully, and my breath stuck in my throat.

I knew why those who'd worshipped The Lady had rebuilt their temples to honor Our Queen. She was power trapped in mortal form. I dropped into a bow to keep from staring.

"And you are Twenty-Three." Her voice drew out my name and rang in my ears. Silk and velvet rustled, and her nails clinked against the chair. "Come sit."

I rose, head still bowed, and folded myself into the chair at her feet. Her seat was undecorated but raised, set on a platform rising out of the ground and placing her a full head above me. She crossed her ankles, feet vanishing beneath her dark-blue gown.

"Now let's start at the beginning." She leaned forward, black eyes flashing, and the storm-gray chemise slid down her left shoulder. The lightning—twists of dark-brown scars against her warm, deep skin—curled around her neck. It was like everyone said, crawling up her flesh where the magic had left her body. She'd channeled all the magic of The Lady through her flesh and only been left with brittle hair and scars. "Who are you?"

"Sallot Leon, Our Queen." I glanced at her face and looked away.

"From Nacea." She'd salt-flecked eyes like Rath. The old runes, still dark as the day they'd been inked into her skin, lined her left eye and curled around her ear. They wrinkled with each word and blink, giving the illusion they still moved beneath her skin. "How many people have you killed and who?"

I swallowed. Here it was—my alternative agenda. It couldn't be different from hers. If she knew what they'd done to us, she'd agree. "Grell da Sousa, Eight, Seven, Horatio del Seve, and Thorn da Tonin. I got Shan de Pau arrested for murder, and I might've killed more when I was a street fighter, but I don't know for sure."

She tilted her head to the side. "Horatio del Seve fell from his garden and snapped his neck. A tragic accident."

She knew. Everyone knew, and yet here I stood.

I opened my mouth, stopped, and shuddered. She'd seen the monsters who'd created the shadows and turned them on civilians. She'd killed them to save us.

"Because if it were anything other than an untimely accident," she said softly, "the lords of what was once Erlend would have cause to challenge my rule and our nation's sovereignty, and we would be at war again."

"They shouldn't even be lords anymore. Not with Nacea—" I'd not spoken this aloud in years, and my tongue fumbled over the words. "They left us. Every single Erlend soldier left us before the shadows came. They didn't even warn us, just used us to slow down the shadows so they could save Erlend. They shouldn't get to be lords, alive while Nacea lies forgotten."

Our Queen leaned back in her seat, eyes narrowed, and laced her fingers in her lap. Light reflected off the four rings on her left hand, and red, purple, white, and green flickered over my feet. "The world is not so simple."

"They slaughtered us." I shook my head. This wasn't what I wanted. This wasn't what I'd dreamed. She'd known and she'd done nothing. "And you've let them live in comfort while I got tossed from town to town. You know how many orphans you've got with no place to sleep and no food to eat? While Erlends are running round rich?"

"Sallot," she said, voice caressing the peaks and dips of my name properly. "I have many regrets, but none so painful as what happened to Nacea."

"Regret does nothing but soothe your own guilt." I sniffed. "I thought you didn't know. You'd have done something."

"I bided my time." She beckoned me forward, eyes on my face and sad. Lady, they were as teary as mine. She cared—she had to. She couldn't fake this. "The lands of Erlend are fertile but wild, and the charges of the nobles are as stuck in their ways as anyone else. I couldn't erase a nation overnight. The lords had to stay if Igna were to thrive. We're thriving now though, and the old lords of Erlend are restless. I need them no longer."

"But you've never done anything about it?" I said. "I waited and waited, went to all your processions, and you never even mentioned us."

"I could not acknowledge Nacea without acknowledging what

Erlend had done, and my rule has been dependent on Erlend until now." She exhaled slowly through her nose. "I could not move against them without giving Lord del Weylin reason to attack Igna. More people would've died."

"And now?" I lifted my head and met her eyes. "What can you do now that you don't need them anymore?"

Her face didn't change—no frown or smile—and a high whine built up between my ears. I'd talked back to Our Queen. I'd talked back to her, and I wasn't even nice about it. I was dead. Disqualified or dead.

"I believe we want the same thing, Sallot Leon."

I jerked, mind reeling and nodded. "Truly, Our Queen?"

I froze. She'd spoken Nacean, and I'd responded in kind. It was clumsy and old, like an old door rusted shut and stuck, but it was there. I'd forgotten how smooth the words were on my lips. How my name really sounded.

"Thank you, Twenty-Three." She dismissed me and switched back to Alonian. "You may leave."

"Of course, Our Queen."

I bowed so low my head ached, but she said no more. The door slammed shut between us. I blinked back tears and sniffed. I still loved her.

But I did not trust her.

CHAPTER
FORTY-FOUR

I was either Opal or dead, but Our Queen was so steady that I couldn't make sense of what my chances were.

Great.

Maud and Dimas talked with each other in the corner, neither meeting the other's eyes properly. I slid behind her, and Dimas startled. He tore his gaze from her shoes.

"Maud?" I asked.

Dimas bowed to me and took off.

"Are you still in the running?" Maud turned to me, shoulders straightening despite the downward crook of her mouth.

I nodded.

She led me out the door. "Good, at least that's working out in our favor."

Maud had me unfancified and the clothes folded neatly faster than I could've done it, and I slipped out the door. She said I'd permission to be anywhere we'd trained. I headed to Emerald's greenhouse.

"You've seen her?"

I jumped. Two smiled from her perch in the branches of a tree above me. I nodded and raised my hand in greeting. I'd not even thought to look up.

"Our Queen?" I leaned back to get a better look at Two. She'd not bandaged the cut on her arm. "She's something different."

"She is." Two pried up a piece of bark and crumbled it in her hands. "I saw her once at the carnival. Even with the crowd between us, I stumbled when she looked at me. Dropped a knife on Four's foot."

"You all right?" I glanced around, pulling myself up so I could meet her eyes.

"Thinking." She shooed me off her branch. "Meeting you was nice. Don't ruin it."

"See you in the after." I grasped her wrist and bowed my head. "Or not. However they do it."

I passed two guard patrols before reaching the greenhouse. I picked the lock and slipped inside, inhaling deep, damp air. The deadly blooms nodded with each step, the wooden boards beneath my feet bending, and I sat next to the cleared table in the back. The dirt was soft and wet, smearing over my fingers. A bee landed on the sunny blooms of a poisonous shrub.

I couldn't fight the urge to move, and every bee and butterfly except the bravest fled to the other side of the greenhouse. I tapped holes into the dirt.

"I don't recall giving you permission to be here"—Emerald drifted before me, trailing her fingers along the petals of twining primroses—"and I distinctly remember locking the door."

"It was open, and no one told me I couldn't come here." I

shook a butterfly from my boot. Best it was gone if she attacked. "It's nicer than anything we've got in Kursk. And quiet."

She tilted her head, surely arching an eyebrow and scowling behind her mask. "And full of poisonous plants."

"It's my weakest area." I shrugged. "Not like I'll get a chance to apprentice with an apothecary."

She snorted softly, such a common sound for Our Queen's Emerald to make. "I'd say you're weaker at archery."

She gestured for me to stand and led me to the back of the garden. She pulled a hidden bow wrapped in oiled leather with a small bundle of arrows from behind a trellis, glancing to make sure I followed her. We ended up outside, off to the left of the building. She handed me the bow.

"I don't think quiet suits you." She pointed to a tree. "Practice."

I sucked in a breath and pulled back the string without an arrow—stomach in, arms up. A breeze ruffled my collar.

Emerald was gone. Figured. But she was right, and I'd never hold a bow so fine unless I stole one.

"Shoulder to the target and one finger above the arrow," I muttered.

My side burned holding this position. Maybe Two had the right idea, spending the last few moments tucked away where no one could find you. This was it.

North Star. Deadfall. Riparian. Caldera. Winter.

My first true shot went wide. Another three shots barely corrected the misfire, and I shuffled my feet and took aim. The arrow thwacked against the tree's neighbor. I fired another.

Wide again. I repeated this monotony of misses and barely-there hits a dozen more times till I reached down and the quiver was empty. The frantic panic in my chest eased with each shot, and I collected the lost arrows from the little forest she'd me shooting into.

My aim got better with time. I fired, missed, fired, hit, fired, and collected arrows till my muscles burned, my arms ached, and I'd no desire to run anywhere. I just wanted to know.

"Stomach in, shoulders perpendicular to your target." Emerald's brass fingers pressed my spine straighter, twisted me back, and pulled me into place. Her breath tickled my ear. "I already taught you this."

My arrow burrowed into the trunk—not center but closer than before.

"Your stance is still shaky." Emerald lifted a recurve bow from her back and held three arrows in her hand. "Bad practice, bad forever."

She shot three arrows faster than I could see, each striking the tree in a neat line.

"We've come to a decision." Emerald tapped my instep with an arrow. "Feet farther apart."

"Two is calm, followed the rules, got her fair share of kills." I let loose another shot, striking the tree closer to Emerald's shots. "Five's good but a risk."

"Yes, those were certainly things we discussed." She stared at me and fired another shot. "Your body directs the arrow, not your eyes."

I fired my last one. Emerald cocked her head to the side, green mask casting sickly light around our feet. She shrugged at my off-center shot.

"Still too tense."

"It's been a tense day." I moved to collect my arrows.

"Stand there. Don't move." She raised her bow and final arrow. "Trust me."

I froze, then faced her.

"Watch the arrow and don't turn your head. Tell me how it moves." She fired. The arrow, a blur of brown wider than the shaft, hit the branch behind my head. "See?"

I shook my head. "It wobbles?"

"But stays true to where you shoot unless it's windy or raining," said Emerald. "If you want to be better, you'll have to learn more than the stance."

"I will." I stopped next to her and raised the bow again. A wavering pain that had nothing to do with my exhaustion burned up my chest to my eyes. "Army'll beat proper everything into my head."

She hummed.

"There will be a more formal announcement at dinner." Emerald placed my feet in the dirt and ran her hands up my side till she was content with the line of my shoulders. She pulled my elbow up. "You are our new Opal."

I struck the tree dead center between her shots.

CHAPTER
FORTY-FIVE

T he Left Hand met me at the final door separating me from the nobles. The path there had been littered with guards, all wide-eyed and at attention, taking in everything before them. The sharp lines of my white outfit hung heavy over the knives at my waist and fading ink still clinging to my skin. No guards waited here.

A waiting room for only the Left Hand of Our Queen.

"And so we are four again." Ruby beckoned me forward, a bright slice of light cutting across the shadow of his outstretched hands, and pulled me into a tight, uncomfortable hug.

"No hard feelings?" I asked.

Emerald laughed. "He's too fickle for feelings."

"Your probation was the most interesting thing to happen to me in ages. But no more back talk." He let me go and patted my cheek. "Come. I cannot call you Opal until after the ceremony, and I'm not calling you Twenty-Three one more time. Such a mouthful."

"How do you feel?" Amethyst asked softly. "Don't be scared."

"I'm not." There were no words to explain the settled feeling of accomplishment and anticipation coursing through my veins.

"Good." Ruby grinned, his ears shifting with the hidden expression. "You are to be our Opal, and we are to be your new family."

Family. I'd never even tried to form a new one, but if I was to kill beside these three and trust them, I'd have to think of them as more than accomplices. A bond as deep as the blood we'd spilled.

"Ignore him. Poetry runs in his blood, and I've never been able to drain enough of it to spare us." Emerald pulled a thin, wide box from the folds of her green skirts and opened the lid. A bone-white mask with vertical slits for eyes and a crooked smile stared back at me. "Our previous Opal's mask will serve you until yours is made. What would you like it to be?"

"Nothing." A new life, a clean slate. I could be anyone and everyone. "Solid white, no eyes and no mouth."

Amethyst nodded. "The crafter will meet with you tomorrow."

I stroked the black ribbons dangling from the mask. Amethyst's hands moved to my old one and eased it from my head, revealing my face.

Sallot Leon's face.

"Now we know you." Amethyst studied my face and tucked my old mask in her pocket.

Each of them reached behind their heads and undid their own masks. The metal fell away, and Amethyst's smiling face met me first. She was pale, golden tan beneath the purple, face unused to the sun, a few splotches marring her skin where the color had been sapped from it. Easy amber eyes crinkled when she laughed.

"And you know us." Ruby grinned, and it was like his

voice—crooked and sharp. His chestnut hair came to an even peak above deep-set gray eyes darkened by faded runes, and freckles dotted his long crooked nose.

"So." Emerald lowered her mask last, metal giving way to gems. Three deep scars cut through the right side of her face and down her cheek, wrinkling when she smiled. A delicate green glass orb with an emerald at its center sat in place of her right eye, and runes, small and dark as night, lined her upturned lids. "Don't make us regret it."

"I won't." I shook my head, fingers painfully tight around Opal's mask—my mask—and pressed my lips together. My eyes burned.

Ruby winked. "I cried too."

That threw me over the edge. Amethyst wiped the tears from my cheeks as Emerald straightened my hair and settled my mask into place. Ruby turned to the great doors before us.

"You have the coin?" he asked and waited for me to nod. "When the doors open, walk straight to Our Queen and kneel. She'll direct you from there."

Silver stars sparkling in a cloud of onyx storm clouds dripping raindrop sapphires shivered as the doors creaked open.

"It will be fine." Amethyst squeezed my arm. "You'll sit next to me at dinner, with Emerald on your other side. Always be in the order of the rings."

The doors opened. I rolled my shoulders back and lifted my chin, letting out a breath. I was Sallot Leon, Twenty-Three, Opal. I was chosen for my skill, and I'd no need to fear the high court. They'd every reason to fear me.

I strolled through the doors, eyes only for Our Queen. She was a vision of death draped in black velvet. Snowdrops fresh from the gardens were woven into a crown atop her shaved head, and a dusting of silver sparkled on her eyelids and in the hollow of her throat. She'd a corset of black velvet laced with steel, the stamp of the imperial army across her chest. Her long, delicate hands curled over the arms of her throne. A metal gauntlet tipped with bear claws covered her right hand. She held out her left to me. I kneeled.

"My new Opal." She beckoned me forward, rings flashing. Her fourth finger crooked, the opal ring flashing. "And you've brought me a present."

I pressed a kiss to the opal and placed the bloody credit coin in her hand. "Of course, Our Queen."

"Of course." She smiled and covered her laughter with her gauntleted hand. "You are eager to please, and I am eager to accept. You are mine and mine alone, and you will clear away all who stand in the way of Igna."

"Yes, Our Queen."

"Good. Stand."

I did, and she pulled my face to hers, her lips pressed to my forehead. She smelled of lemons and lavender.

"I didn't think you knew," I whispered. "I thought you were justice."

"There is no true justice, and I have let you down, my darling." She raised a hand to my face and cupped my jaw, fingers cool beneath the edges of my mask. "But I will make it up to you—the traitors are out of time, and their deaths are overdue. Make them pay, quickly and subtly, as you did Seve and Pau."

She dropped her hands and swept by me, leaving a wake of perfume and confusion.

"My court." Our Queen raised her arms wide. "My new Honorable Opal is upon us. Behave yourselves."

And with that, I was Opal—noble and deadly.

A servant led me to a long table, and I sat next to Amethyst. Her hand found mine under the table.

"Relax." She squeezed my hand and let go. "We'll have our own party later."

Ruby was talkative, making up with his body what he lacked in facial expressions, and Isidora dal Abreu nodded to me from her seat across him. They were engaged in a loud, exaggerated argument over poetry I'd never heard or read, with several other nobles I'd never met. Elise listened intently, too far away to speak to me, and I half-listened. The art others heard in poetry had never spoken to me.

Nicolas del Contes cheered his wife on quietly in the argument. His wide brown eyes followed her gesturing hands, and he lounged back in his chair, long legs splayed out under the table. He grinned when he caught me staring.

I'd have to deal with him tonight.

A long high note drowned out Ruby's latest poem, and Isidora dragged Nicolas to the dance floor in her haste to escape Ruby. He only laughed.

Amethyst spun an older lord with silver-streaked hair around the edge of the dancers, and Ruby vanished into the crowd with a blushing Alonian lord who stumbled over his own feet. Emerald glanced at me across Amethyst's abandoned chair.

"Not a dancer?" Emerald asked. "I'm sure your young love will sweep you off your feet soon."

"You watched everything, didn't you?" I ducked. Elise was

off somewhere, and I'd lost track of her. "Dancing not your style?"

Emerald shook her head. "I'm not really the romantic partner type, but much like you, I'd rather not explain my existence every time I step out in public. You'll learn about us all soon enough—we share common quarters."

She pointed over my shoulder. I turned.

Elise, dressed in starry silver cotton draped like rose petals, bowed. "You look very handsome, Your Honor."

"Thank you." My ill-fitting mask halved my vision, but nothing could hide Elise's grace. "You look lovely, Lady de Farone."

She blushed and held out her hand, foot tapping to the tune of an archlute. I swallowed.

"I'm afraid I have to disappoint you." I gestured to my feet. "I have no idea how to dance."

"I'll lead, you follow." She pulled me from my chair and placed one of my hands on her waist as we walked. The other she held tight in her own. "I had to bribe Ruby to find out you were Opal. You owe me a dance."

"Well, I have to repay a debt." I scrunched my nose till the mask rose, and I could see the high spots of color on her cheeks and how her eyes searched for mine through the mask. "What's wrong?"

"I miss your eyes." She led me through a series of turns, fingers lacing through mine.

"I could rob you." I laughed and splayed my hand over her side, taking in the warmth of her skin. I'd not been this close to her since that night, and we'd only those simple memories, but I missed the press of her against me and the flutter of her lips against my neck. We'd so many memories to make. "A bit of familiarity might make you feel better?"

She smiled. "Probably not the best idea. We'll have to settle for dancing."

"Yes. Settle."

We turned, Elise still leading, and her fingers crept up my collar. I stumbled over her feet.

"Sorry, sorry."

It was all new and happening so fast, but I was here and she was with me. I played with the ends of her hair, the soft strands escaping her intricate crown of braids and curling around my fingers. She shuddered.

"This isn't so bad though." The crowd hid us from prying eyes, too many loves and friends caught up in their own lives to care. Elise's fingers crept farther up my neck with each step. I leaned forward to ease her grip. A spot of ink freckled her nose. "What was the poem?"

Elise blushed, eyes widening. "What?"

"You wrote a poem on my arm." I trailed my fingers down the arch of her neck, her shoulder, her wrist, and laced our fingers. The music pitched and we spun into the press of bodies. I pulled her closer. "I want to know what it said."

Whatever I was now, whatever Our Queen had made me, I had Elise, and she would have me. The ink was washed from my skin, but the memories would never fade.

"It was only part of one." She ducked her head into the curve of my throat. Rosewater and lemons lingered in her hair, sharp and fresh and clearing the scent of death from my new mask. "It's not even from Igna."

I laughed. "You wanted me to translate a poem in a language I don't know and wasn't learning?"

"I'm still learning it. The poetry was for practice." She exhaled, breath fluttering against my throat. "Under the moon alone, I broke as ice breaks."

I slid to a stop in the middle of the dance floor. "What?"

"It's only one line," she murmured.

"But it's sad." I spun her as the dancers swelled around us, heels whispering across the tile with each pluck of the strings. "Breaking—it's dying, isn't it?"

"It's not literal." Elise laid her cheek against my shoulder. Hidden in the crowd and by the twisting collar of her dress, she kissed the skin beneath my ear. "And sometimes a little death is a good thing."

I'd have to ask Ruby about poetry.

The song died and the crowd stilled. Elise brought us to a stop, and I brushed her cheek, straightening, no better at dancing. She dropped her hands, and I bowed slightly as she stepped back.

"I want you to meet my father." She smiled, tugging me from the dance floor. "He's still sick, so he won't talk long. Don't worry."

I pressed the mouth of my mask to her cheek. "Anything you want."

She shook her head and darted off. Meeting him wouldn't be bad so long as she was at my side. A servant drifted past with a tray of drinks, and I followed them, picking up a cup of mulled wine to warm my hands. I settled into a window seat, a cold breeze at my back.

"Beware the Erlend winter," a soft voice said to my left. "It will come quickly and quietly if we're already getting northern winds."

CHAPTER
FORTY-SIX

O ur new Honorable Opal." Nicolas del Contes bowed
next to me, tall frame barely fitting in my small nook.
"Welcome to court."

"Lord del Contes." I nodded back. He was predatory up close,
and the runes peeking out from under his clothes set my teeth
on edge. A Master of the Soul—one of the only ones left, the
only one who'd nothing to do with the shadows—with the ink
beneath the thin flesh of his hand and feet to prove it. During
the old days, he could've transported himself from place to
place no matter the distance with just a rune. And now he was
stuck here.

"What's that mean?" I held my hand out the window, the
current of the Caracol rushing far beneath us. "About the Erlend
winter?"

"Old saying—Erlend winters are bitterly cold." He leaned
against the wall, gaze scanning the dancers. "Sooner the wind
blows in, longer and colder the winter will be. Makes it hard to

counter Lord del Weylin, but he should be easier to manage now that you took Seve out of the equation."

It took everything within me not to tense and deny it immediately. I cocked my head to the side, turning slightly to him. "Didn't he fall out a window?"

"Well, off the roof but only after you pushed him." Nicolas stared at me, face even but eyes cold. "Please don't insult me by playing the fool. You're after the people who allowed Nacea to fall, a list nearly identical to the list of noble Erlend houses, I'm sure."

"If you'd cleaned up your messes, Lord del Contes, I wouldn't have to be." Rage straightened my spine and forced me to stand taller. I was already Opal. He couldn't touch me. "You let your fellows get away with it."

"You should call me Nicolas. We'll work together often enough." He raised his hand to his mouth and held it there in the telltale sign of keeping a secret. "The art of keeping a very fragile, very new country intact without falling back into the violence that preceded it is that you must separate your personal feelings from your nation's needs. Which is why Our Queen designed your final test—do not kill anyone but Thorn da Tonin."

That didn't make it any better. I shrugged.

"Why was Three flayed? In the forest?" Nicolas leaned down so he could look me in the eyes. "Exactly like the shadows. Why?"

"To scare me."

"No, to scare everyone." Nicolas set his glass down on the window ledge behind us and wiggled his fingers, casting long shadows on the stones. "Our Queen's claim to the throne, to the nation she created, is based on her history as the mage who cast out magic and destroyed the shadows to protect us. But if there were proof that magic still existed, that the shadows still lived, that she had not truly gotten rid of them, no one would have cause to listen to her. She would just be a woman with a crown. The only reason most Erlend nobles bowed to her rule was because they feared her, and we needed them because we needed their land to prevent famine and revolts."

"They *were* the war," I said. "They were the whole reason we were at war."

"And it is much better politically for us if they start the wars." He straightened up and dropped his voice to a whisper. "It's true though—Erlend culture is a river overflowing with violence. It may be dammed, it may be guided and useful, but it wears away at the rest of the world. I was born in its currents and know its path, and while I may leave its waters, I will never be free of its pull. But all rivers have a source. If you want to stop Erlend from committing such atrocities again, you must stop Erlend at its source."

"Lord del Contes, why are you telling me this?" I asked, finally finding the words I wanted to say amid the swirling mess of uncertainty and anger within me.

He grinned. "Because we don't need them anymore."

I shifted, not at all happy with that answer but no longer as angry. "That's it? You just don't need them anymore?"

"We. You're a part of this nation too." He took a sip of his wine, completely at ease. "Did Seve tell you anything?"

I hummed, weighed my options, and shook my head. "Nothing I can't tell you tomorrow."

Wasn't necessarily a lie—I got some names, but I couldn't do anything with them. Nicolas might know what they meant. Still, would be impossible to handle those lords tonight.

Isidora and Ruby stopped next to us. Isidora glanced from my clenched hands to Nicolas's face and sighed, glancing away long enough to flag the closest server. He bowed, blond hair falling over his pale eyes. She whispered a request to him.

"Are you corrupting my new protégé?" Ruby asked before plucking a knife from the server's tray as he ran off and brandishing it at Nicolas. "He's mine. You can find some other terrible swordsmen to teach your terrible ways."

I scowled and turned to him. "I'm not terrible."

"You're appalling," Ruby drawled.

"We were talking." Nicolas pressed a kiss to Isidora's offered hand, completely ignoring Ruby. "Are you leaving?"

She darted up and kissed his cheek. Ruby made a guttural sound of disgust next to me, and Isidora whipped her head to him. He raised his hands in surrender.

"Ruby's doing my rounds with me." She patted his shoulder and glanced at me. "I do house calls with the other physicians at night once everyone is home from work. You should come once you're settled. It's a good learning opportunity considering you skipped every day of my training."

I nodded and smiled, glad my conversation with Nicolas was done but feeling oddly guilty. I'd been doing other important things.

The server appeared at her side, one glass of orange blossom water and another filled with mulled wine. She thrust the wine into Nicolas's hand.

"You need to relax and eat something before you get back to

work." She moved away, sipping her water till Ruby snatched it from her hands, and beckoned Nicolas.

"Opal," Nicolas said softly as he bowed goodbye. "Beware the Erlend winter."

And in the space of a breath, he was gone and the familiar scent of spring washed over me. I turned.

Elise stopped a few paces from me, with her father on her arm.

"Opal." Elise politely bowed a little, and I returned it with a slightly deeper bow. With her father's eyes on us, I'd no desire to make him dislike me more. "I'd like you to meet my father, Lord Nevierno del Farone."

I bowed even deeper and ignored the prickling sense of recognition at his name. Of course I'd heard it before. He was Elise's father.

Nevierno was old Erlenian, and I was a fool. A traditional name for a traditional man.

Beware the Erlend Winter.

"Lord del Farone." I stayed bowed, with his damned name chilling me down to the bone, and held back the growing ache for Elise in my chest. "It's a pleasure to meet you."

Nevierno. Icy peaks and snow-encrusted forests, the old Erlend name for a winter as harsh and as cold as death itself.

Lady help me, he'd not even used a good secret name.

Elise hadn't hated me before, but she certainly would now, no matter how monstrous her father. He had to die.

"Welcome to court, Opal." He returned my bow, neck bared. It would be so easy to kill him here. I could jam my blade through the back of his spine and watch the life leave him. Quick and simple. More than he deserved. "I hope my daughter is being welcoming as well."

Elise glanced at him, nose wrinkling. He was ill—a pink flush covered his neck and cheeks no matter how he tried to hide it with his high collar, and each word escaped his throat as a dry rasp.

"She is," I said carefully, not sure what was off but sure that something was.

Maybe he was too sick to be particular.

"Excellent." He coughed into a handkerchief, hacking up blood, a lung, and Lady knew what else.

But he was Elise's father, and better that illness take him than me.

"I wish you'd go catch Isidora before she does her rounds," Elise said, glancing at me and rolling her eyes back to him. "She's bound to have something for that cough."

"I am not so old that a cough will kill me." He straightened up, folding his handkerchief into squares. A smear of red was bright between the folds.

Bright as the red cosmetic cream Maud had used on my lips.

Elise smiled. "Of course not, but I'd rather be safe than sorry."

"Of course, darling." He tucked his handkerchief into the coat pocket at his hip. Perfect. "I'd hate to ruin the festivities as well as your expectations."

"Lord del Farone." I bowed again, as close as I could without touching him, and handed him my handkerchief. "I insist."

He nodded to me, and I let my free hand drift toward his side, as natural as any of Ruby's wandering gestures. His handkerchief vanished up my sleeve.

"How generous of you."

I glanced at the speck of red on white. Definitely cosmetic cream.

She stared at his retreating back. "I thought he'd put up more of a fight. Do you think he is that sick?"

"No." I handed her my wine. He wasn't ill in mind or body, only in his soul. You had to be to do what he'd done. "I'm sure he's tired of getting told off for not seeing her."

He wasn't ill. He'd agreed to see Isidora too easily, and he was Winter. That was a plot if I'd ever heard one—a long game coming to a head.

Missing this party to see Isidora was either the beginning or the end.

"I suppose." Elise took a sip, drifting closer to me with each breath. "I knew he wouldn't argue with me over it because you're Opal, but he'd never be—"

"Generous and understanding?" I curled an arm around her waist and savored the warmth of her body against mine. "How long's he been sick?"

Let it be the start. Let me not have to shatter her memories of him so soon, and let Our Queen learn of it quickly.

"Since summer." She drawled the word like Ruby. "I hate it. He works all day and night, never speaking to anyone but his assistants and won't see Isidora because it's unseemly for a man of his stature to show weakness. Traditions have their place, but this is ridiculous."

Erlend's ideals had ruined more families than Nacean ones.

Horatio del Seve's notes had mentioned waiting for winter, but the north wind at my back had nothing to do with the chill running down my spine. I had to get out of here. "I have to talk to Ruby."

Elise frowned. "What?"

"I'll be back. I promise." I held her close, comforted in the fact that I'd see her again no matter what. "Talking to your father reminded me of something I meant to ask Ruby before he left."

Even if I was wrong, he'd understand. And if I was right, hopefully it wasn't too late.

"Go." She sighed, long and sad, but smiled. "I should've realized I'd not have you to myself yet."

I laced our fingers together, brought them to my false lips, and pressed our foreheads together. "I'll make it up to you."

I'd all the time and resources to do that. Soon as I figured out what Winter—her father—was up to, I could let Nicolas and Our Queen do as they wanted with it. It wasn't my fault or Elise's that her father was what he was. It wasn't my fault that I had to do what I was about to do, but she couldn't know my part in it. Not yet. Not if I was right.

Lady, let me be wrong.

CHAPTER

FORTY-SEVEN

Winter walked for ages. We passed through a dozen different buildings and wove our way toward the outskirts of the palace where the number of servants and guards thinned. He shared Elise's round frame and dark curls, hair bound by a forest green ribbon trimmed in gold, and wore Erlend's old colors hidden in the pleats and stitches of his clothes. He was easy to follow through the open walkways high above the forests where I'd lived as Twenty-Three. He finally stopped in a hallway populated by unlabeled, locked doors.

He slipped through a door and locked it behind him. Muffled voices echoed behind it.

I sighed. His faked illness, Seve's note, and his life as Winter all pointed to some nasty plan brewing. Seve had been told to wait for Winter, but there'd been no notion of what the waiting was for. I darted back to the open-air path I'd followed and glanced over the edge. I'd not thought to bring lock picks to a party.

The ends of supports jutted out from the building, a broken pathway three stories above the swirling waters of the Caracol.

Best not fall then.

I leapt over the wall and onto a beam. Dimly lit windows shone in the darkness, and I stepped onto the next support. The remnants of an old bird's nest crumbled under my feet, falling off the metal-enforced wood, and a handful of bird bones tumbled into the river. I focused on a far window as Winter's voice leaked through the paper screen. A line of marching turtles decorated the bottom of the screen.

Turtles meant a Royal Physician—Isidora dal Abreu.

"Remarkable," Winter said, Erlenian polished as Elise's but the drawl all his own. His voice wasn't rough or weak. "How did you notice? I can hardly tell when they speak, much less drink."

"Noticing things you miss is my job." Five's familiar voice cut through any lingering doubts in my mind. Winter had bad intentions, and this was his endgame. "Celso and I used to do the same, and with him at her side, no one would ever think to poison her."

I tilted my ear toward the window. Five was working for him, with him, and had to be talking about Isidora and Ruby. They did share drinks—they'd shared water tonight.

Hand-delivered by a blond, pale-eyed server.

A body hit the floor. Isidora let out a slurred cry, and Five laughed. I bit back the anger bubbling up my throat. Whatever he was plotting, she'd no place in it. She was a physician.

One of the good ones. One who'd never broken her oath and harmed someone even in the middle of war.

"Restrain yourself." Winter crossed the room. "Your little

revenge fantasy has already forced me to move well ahead of schedule. We need to make this believable."

"Fantasy?" Five's voice pitched, and metal clattered against metal. "I've already done this once. You messed up your end. That's your problem."

I curled my fingers around the window's edge and pulled myself up. Memories and finger bones weren't enough for Five. He had to have more, had to have revenge for a mage who didn't deserve it. But Rodolfo da Abreu was dead, and Isidora had nothing to do with her brother's actions. Why take it out on her?

"Lay her here." Winter picked something up from the floor and snapped a piece of cloth. "Box there—opened."

Cloth whispered over the stones, heels smacking wood. Five's familiar quiet steps drew closer to me. The memory of Amethyst's training still in my muscles, I pulled myself up by my fingers and peeked under the window screen.

Five stood over the prone Isidora dal Abreu. He was dressed as a server, but his tray had been traded for a sword. The room was plain and efficient, a writing desk in one corner and the walls lined with bookshelves. Isidora's orange blossom water rested on the desk. Ruby's limp body lay next to it.

He groaned. Five was on him in a heartbeat, crushing Ruby's fingers under his heel.

"Nothing to protest yet." Five leaned over him. "Haven't even started."

Shit.

I'd missed it. The runes lining his eyes, the shared freckles and eyes, the closeness, the anger at my outburst when he'd changed my disqualification to a probation. Ruby had lost everything.

His life as Rodolfo da Abreu.

He was the perfect Ruby—unquestionably loyal to Our Queen, prepared to do anything for her, and undoubtedly had been living locked away on family lands, keeping his entire existence a lonely secret. Being Ruby gave him back his life, gave him back a purpose.

And meant Five had every reason to want him dead.

Winter rolled his eyes at Five and sighed. I couldn't think of him as Elise's father any longer, not if this would end with his blood on my hands. I'd expected something suspicious but not this. Not tonight. "No broken bones. Shadows only take the flesh."

Five turned, eyes bright and fingers twitching. "I know."

"Then stop." Winter picked up the water glass and turned toward my window. "We need this set before Nicolas arrives."

That was it then. The last folks who knew how to create the shadows were to be killed as though they'd lost control of one they'd made. If the people thought Our Queen was a fraud who'd never banished magic and shadows in the first place, and she was making shadows on top of that, they'd tear Igna down before she could even mount a defense. Weylin and his lords could swoop in and take over without a fuss.

I ducked and flattened myself against the wall. Winter opened the window screen, tossed the water out, and took a deep breath of the breeze. I slid my hands over my head slow as I could. The orange slices splashed into the water far beneath us.

"You said I could do it!" Five's voice pitched, wilder and more frightening than I'd ever heard it, all his careful cleverness gone. Metal clattered against stone—Ruby's mask hitting the ground. Hard. "I suffered through days of your 'stay low and stay alive' shit with those fools you foisted on me, and I'm not walking out of here without his head and hands."

Winter whipped around, window screen falling. I jammed one finger in the way before it could latch shut.

Five was replaying his brother's death. When Ruby had been Rodolfo, he'd gifted the Erlend mages with a taste of their own medicine by flaying them like the shadows flayed their victims, and now Five would return the favor.

Two on one weren't the worst odds, but I had to look after Isidora and Ruby. And Five wasn't well.

The hitch in his voice, I knew too well. Ruby would not leave alive so long as Five still breathed.

"You'll leave when I say you leave and with what I say you can have." Winter moved away from the window. "He'll be dead either way."

"Shadows flayed the living." Five grinned, pulling off his coat and revealing the paring knives strapped to his side. He pulled back his sword. "Three thrashed, but I'm going to pin you."

I lurched up, muscles burning, and quietly shoved the screen out of the way. Ruby swatted Five's sword aside.

"I've been to worse parties." Metal muffled Ruby's voice, and blood dripped out from under his chin. "You finally figured it out then?"

Buying time. Good. I dragged myself onto the windowsill, legs dangling out, and paused. Winter and Five faced Ruby, and I'd no weapon. I picked up the empty glass.

"This is it." Five kicked Ruby onto his back. He punctuated each word with a well-placed kick to the kidneys, ribs, stomach. "Don't be predictable, don't be predictable, don't share the same drink every single meal and have the same damn schedule every night. You made me give up my brother when you couldn't even do the same for your sister, and look what your carelessness has done to her. You're bad at hiding your tracks, Rodolfo."

"You're bad at kicking." Ruby struggled to rise but tilted his head toward Isidora. "I suppose this is about that nonsense with your brother then?"

Five slapped Ruby with the broad side of the sword. Ruby went flying, arms weak and legs trembling. I inhaled, drawing myself fully into the window, and gripped the glass tighter. Ruby collapsed.

"Nonsense!" Five yanked Ruby's hands in front of them and crushed Ruby's wrists under his boots. "You stripped his arms before you took his head. He was alive."

"Yes, he lived through a flaying like the victims of his shadows did. Very poetic of me." Ruby beckoned Winter forward and away from Isidora—never looking at me, but he had to know I was here, had to be hyperaware of everything happening. "But what are you doing here?"

Good. Keep talking.

Winter shook his head. "It doesn't matter."

Five ripped off Ruby's mask and punched him.

"This is it?" Ruby laughed and spat out a tooth. "We at least thought you were going for an assassination, but revenge?"

Five punched him again, and Ruby's neck snapped back.

"This is petty!" Ruby cackled, a spray of pink coloring the air with each word. "All that work for this?"

I shuddered as Ruby's high-pitched, echoing laughter rang in my ears. Five sucked in a breath, shoulders rising, and I knew that look, knew the tightness of his muscles and shuddering desire for vengeance in his fingers. I lunged, and he slashed his sword. Blood splattered across my face.

I slammed the water glass into Five's temple, ducked, and ripped a knife from his side. He crumbled.

"I'd scream, but you'd like that, wouldn't you?" Ruby slammed a shoulder into Five, knocking him back to the floor, and rose to his knees. His right hand hung from his wrist, fingers still and tendons snapped. The left arm was red as dawn and soaked. No magic left to stitch the artery shut. No chance he'd live through this night. "Your brother Celso screamed. I thought his throat would tear with so much sobbing, but he kept going, one new curse for each new cut till I took his head. And not one word was an apology to his shadows' victims."

I kicked Five's sword away from him. He opened his mouth, hands reaching for his knives, and I jammed my stolen blade into his neck. He fell to his knees, gurgling. Ruby turned toward the sword.

"You're terrible." Ruby groaned and collapsed against me. "Never discard better weapons."

"Knife down." Winter leveled Five's sword with my heart, stance perfect—everything Ruby always demanded I be—and stepped forward. "You're what happened to my handkerchief, aren't you?"

Ruby sighed. No world without magic could return the blood he'd lost. He looked at me, mask gone and face smeared with red, dark eyes glazed. He mouthed, "Improvise."

Winter raised his sword.

Lady, let Elise understand.

I shoved Ruby in front of him. The sword tore through his

stomach, ripping a hole from navel to spine. Winter paused, stunned with the blade stuck in Ruby, and I punched his throat. He stumbled. I ripped the knife from Five's neck and lunged.

"Stop!"

We froze. Winter turned slowly, mouth open in shock. I didn't, couldn't look.

"What is this?" Elise asked, breaths coming fast and scared. "What have you done?"

CHAPTER
FORTY-EIGHT

T he cloying scent of blood-soaked silk seeped through my
mask. A steady drip echoed in the silence, keeping my
eyes fixed to the growing red stain on Winter's shoulder. My
knife trembled against his neck, nothing between him and death
except Elise's voice. I couldn't look at her, couldn't see her face
twisted into rage. Winter dropped his arm.

"Elise," said Winter as Ruby slid off his sword and collapsed
at his feet.

"What is this?" She stepped forward, voice breathy and small.
Her footsteps were loud in my ears. "Opal?"

I shifted, still and cold under her gaze. Winter sighed.

"Darling, this brute—"

"No, not you," Elise said quickly. "He knows me better and
wouldn't insult me by lying. His knife may be at your neck, but
your sword was in my friend. I know this has nothing to do with
Opal or me. Nicolas was the one who was called, but he sent me
in his stead."

Winter stiffened. A flutter of warmth grew in my chest. Of course Elise was smarter than him—she hated politics, but she studied it. She'd know every trick ever used, and she'd handed me the missing piece. They'd wanted Nicolas too.

He'd been right. The shadow kill in the woods was only the start. This was all planned, all connected, and Erlend was making a play for Our Queen's crown by making her look weak. If she'd never banished magic, if she'd never freed us of the shadows, if she'd let her most trusted advisors bring back those horrors, everyone would hate her. Igna would be no more.

The one person we'd trusted to protect us from monsters had lied all along. That was all Erlend would need to say. Anyone unhappy for any reason—Our Queen's fault or not—would lose faith.

"So your daughter or your plot?" Elise asked, squaring her shoulders at him.

Winter sighed. "You are too young to remember life under a good ruler. You will understand with time."

"I'm too young to remember?" Elise laughed, hollow and high, and let out a shuddering breath. "My childhood memories are of soldiers and funeral pyres, air so thick with ash I could taste their souls. And you would bring that back? For what?"

"For us!" Winter stepped back, forcing me to step farther away from Elise too. "We are worse off under that woman than we have ever been, and sacrifices to repair the balance must be made. She would see us ruined."

"She would see us equal." Elise, eyes narrowed to furious slits and cheeks flushed, glanced at Isidora. She stared at her, unable to look at Winter. I knew that look, that disgust. "You would throw aside peace hard-won for personal gain, and I will not help you."

She'd understand.

"Tell her what else you did." I licked my lips, heart heavy but so ready to draw out my second confession, like pus from a wound. "To Nacea."

Winter and Elise both looked at me, confusion clear on their faces. He shook his head.

I scraped the knife up his jaw, drawing blood. "Tell her about Nacea, Winter."

He flinched at the name. Elise moved toward us.

"Nacea? The old coast territory?" She shook her head. "What does he have to do with it?"

"Everything." I flicked my blade up and scratched a thin line along the edge of his face.

"I don't know what you're talking about," said Winter.

"I found your name with Horatio del Seve's, and I know your circle was in charge of directing troops." I looked at Elise, fully seeing her for the first time, and wanted to rip off my damned mask so she could see the hurt and truth in my eyes. See my apology for what I wanted to do to her father. "Tell her, or she'll hear it from me when you're dead."

"The shadows were drawing closer to Erlend—"

"The shadows you released among Alona's civilians." I swallowed, unable to stop my disgust from seeping into the words.

"And we chose to withdraw a few troops from Nacea so they could protect Erlend." He leaned away from my knife. He was too calm, too steady with this happening, and he stared over my shoulder, never at me. "Nacea's lack of an army unfortunately meant they were ill prepared, and many failed to evacuate in time."

"Yes, we were very ill prepared for the shadows you didn't warn us about." I glanced at Elise, trying to say as much as I could with the motion since I still wore my mask. "I'm sorry."

"You shouldn't be," she said. "He should. I might be too young to remember the politics, but I remember our agreements with Nacea."

We both fell silent under the cutting, cold voice of Elise. She was utterly unrecognizable in her horror—eyes wide, lips twisted into a sneer, and body reeling back from her father like physical distance could erase the past between them.

"Darling." Winter recovered before me, sweeping the sword he'd gutted Ruby with to one side. "You really can't believe—"

"I can believe whatever I damn well please, and if it's anyone's fault for making your hand in a massacre seem plausible, it's you." She glanced between him and Isidora, gaze falling on Ruby's crumpled body, before finally looking at me. "Nacea?"

"Nacea had no protection except Erlend soldiers." I swallowed, the words heavy on my tongue. "And the Erlend lords decided that when the shadows got close, they'd buy time to fortify their lands by withdrawing their soldiers and letting the shadows tear through us like battle fodder. And the names in the letters planning the massacre were North Star, Deadfall, Riparian, Caldera, Coachwhip, and Winter."

Elise sniffed. She shook her head and leaned back, failing to keep the tears at bay.

"I'm so sorry," I said quickly. "I never wanted to take your father from you. I never would, but he took my whole family, my whole world. I'm sorry. I am. And this, I didn't do this."

I gestured weakly to Ruby's blood splattered across the room, praying she'd understand.

"I have always done what is best for you and our family, and that woman is not it!" shouted Winter.

Elise shook her head, tears dripping down her face, and eased back toward the door. "The worst part of this is I'm not surprised at all. But thousands. Do you even know how many you killed?"

The tiny little piece of me that still woke up screaming at night and pushed Seve off the roof was shrieking in my mind, anger and need coursing through my veins like blood. I wanted him dead, and I wanted him to suffer.

Elise would hate me. I wasn't fair at all.

"Winter." I turned to him, pushing Elise from my mind, and felt the cool wind of autumn whipping through the window at my back. Eastern winds dragging the scent of the sea with them. They'd crossed Nacean lands. Nacean graves. "You want to tell me anything else?"

"No." Elise shifted toward me, gaze stuck on the bloodstained knife in my hand. "You can't kill him."

I sniffed. This was the end then. A home for a home. Life without Elise wouldn't be pleasant, but I'd live. I could live with her hating me.

Hopefully.

"I'm so sorry," I said and lunged.

Winter jerked his sword toward me. I raised one arm to take the hit, rearing the other back to tear through his arm. Elise slid between us.

"Stop!" She grabbed my wrist and squared her shoulders, neck even with her father's blade. She took a step back and forced us farther apart. "Just stop."

The two of us froze, but Winter didn't drop his arm. He didn't even tremble as he held a sword to his daughter's neck.

"Don't kill him." She rubbed her thumb along my wrist, the memory of her warmth and words on my skin rising to the surface. "Trust me."

"Elise," Winter started, but she cut him off.

"You don't speak. I can't even look at you." She stepped from between us. "Don't kill him. People need to know what he did."

"What?" My knife dropped to his shoulder.

Elise turned to her father slowly and said, "We failed Nacea and you, and I'm sorry, but he can pay with his life in court. Let everyone find out what he did and know it was wrong. You can have justice with that. Trust me. If you kill him like this, no one will know and nothing will change."

Would it be justice if his death wasn't by the last Nacean hand? They'd hang him. They'd have to. But she'd be sending her father to the gallows.

"It's what he deserves," she said softly to me. "Please, for me."

She'd no part in this. This was justice, vengeance, everything I'd been breathing for laid out right in front of me, flesh beneath my blade and heart beating at my command. I could stop it. I could end this.

And it was only the beginning. His death would give me everything.

Except Elise. Except Maud. Except my new place at court. No matter what he'd done, they'd never forgive me for killing him. And Elise, Lady, she'd never forgive me for murdering her father. Not after she'd asked me to stop.

Nacea for Elise. A home for a home.

A home Winter didn't deserve. A comfortable, wealthy lordship he hadn't earned and should never have kept. He deserved a thousand deaths, the skin stripped from him and a decade of haunting nightmares filled with faceless friends all clamoring for attention. For revenge.

They'd bled me that morning while I watched my siblings die and heard my parents murdered, and there was nothing left in my veins but vengeance.

Till now. Till Elise had seeped under my skin like ink on paper and swept my loneliness away. I could have the home that was taken from me. I could have Winter paraded out for all of Igna to see and watch him hang. I could be Opal, he could be dead, and Elise wouldn't hate me.

I'd have someone who cared about me—what Winter stole. I could have that back.

I opened my hand, knife clattering at my feet. "I trust you."

She stepped away from me. Her father surged forward, arms outstretched and sword slashing through my stitched side. I stumbled back, crashing into the windowsill, and he grinned. He tipped me up and over.

And I fell and fell and fell, the image of Elise's terrified face framed against the night sky scorched into my mind.

CHAPTER
FORTY-NINE

There was ash on my lips and blood on my hands, and no force in this world could cleanse me. The fire burned lower and lower, embers red as the rising sun, and the last support beam snapped. I shuffled forward, all fractured bones and stitched-up skin. Heat licked the hem of my funeral clothes.

The brimstone stench of burning hair and the bitter taste of bone dust crept under my new mask till each breath was thick with death. I'd never attended a proper pyre—no funerals for Nacea and no money for the felled members of Grell's gang. I'd never known the taste of ash.

Not like Elise had.

"He hated tawny wine," Emerald muttered.

Amethyst tossed her glass of it into the fire, mask streaked with soot. "He loved wine. He hated funerals."

I poured my wine on the ruined shirt in my hands, Ruby's dried blood dark as night against the white silk, and threw it into the fire. It caught in an instant.

Dead and gone and never coming back.

I peeled back my sleeve and took out my knife, scoring seven long marks down the inside of my arm. Seven dead by my hands, seven bodies left to burn, and seven ghosts howling in my head. It wasn't justice.

It was necessity.

There was no peace without death, and there was no justice at all. Nothing true. Nothing real. I was what Erlend had made me—killer to Our Queen—and they were what history made them. The lords screaming for my head were what I'd made them with Five's death.

Fernando.

His name was Fernando. He was like me, and he was dead.

I dropped my arm, blood dripping around my feet. I could bleed for years and never clear their names from my soul. I deserved nothing but the weight of their deaths. Elise deserved so much better.

"How do you live like this?" I asked. "How do you live and look at other people when they *know* what you've done?"

Elise was too caring for me. For the callous lands of Erlend.

They'd eat her alive. They'd break her down bit by bit, till she was jaded as they were, and she'd never recover. Winter might not kill her, but he could use her to further his needs, and they knew what she meant to me, and that might...

I shuddered. Elise couldn't die—not yet. She'd so much to do, so much she deserved. She'd be a better noble than her father ever was, and she'd turn the old Erlend traditions on their heads. She'd do everything to stop a war.

Elise had fought. Claw marks lined the wall where her father dragged her away, nails tearing through paint till she bled. I'd so many better memories of her—ink and ice and orange blossoms— but all I dreamed of now was her face framed against the stars. Her screaming.

And unable to escape the never-ending echo of her crying my name, I broke as bones break.

"Carefully. Sadly." Amethyst wrapped an arm around me, pulling me to my feet, and wiped away the tears dripping down my neck. "Because we must. Because those who care to know us understand."

"Because if it wasn't us, it would be someone else." Emerald unclenched her hands, copper nails now tipped with red.

I sniffed, throat tight, and nodded.

Amethyst sighed. She lifted my new mask to the top of my head and wiped the sticky mess of tears and wayward ash from my face. "We are the Left Hand of Our Queen, no one else. You are Opal. We've a sad, sorry job that should not exist, but this is our world and we are what we are."

And I was what I was—what Nacea had made me, what Erlend had made me, what Our Queen had made me. There was no innocence left in this world, left in me, not after all we'd done. I'd killed seven people, wiped them from this earth, and I'd kill more. I had to.

I could not let someone else, someone clean, someone who didn't wake at night with a weight on their chest and no air in their lungs, the ghosts of those they'd killed clawing at their throat, know the terrible unease deep within my bones.

I would be Opal from now till I died so no one else had to be. I would kill the lords whose heritage was built on war and

LINSEY MILLER

hate, and I would never be free of it, but the world would be free of them.

Amethyst slipped my mask back on and squeezed my shoulder. She turned me around.

Our Queen nodded to us. "Are you well enough to be walking?"

"Well enough, Our Queen." I knelt, Amethyst on my right and Emerald at my left, the only three to stay by Ruby's side till the sun rose and his pyre crumbled to smoldering ash. Our Queen's voice and quiet footfalls left me shivering. "I had to see him off."

The three days since my fall and Winter's betrayal felt like three decades to my shattered arm and fractured ribs. I moved so slowly that the world passed me by with each blink.

"I'm glad you are well." Her fingers traced the edges of Ruby's bloodstained mask. "You are new, my Opal, but you know the troubles that plague our young nation and threaten the peace so many died for."

I winced. My blank mask only twitched. "Yes, the war criminals you let fester in your court have finally risen against you."

Emerald's hand closed around my arm. I swallowed. Elise had been spirited away by Winter to the ice-ridden peaks of old Erlend for some last-stand war she wanted no part in, and if Our Queen had even tried, Winter and his cohorts wouldn't still be alive. No forgotten Nacea, no lords threatening chaos and war, and no civilians left floundering under Erlend rules.

"Yes, they have." Our Queen waved Emerald off. She wore no gauntlet today, no metal corset. Soot and mud hemmed her plain gray funeral dress. "And it is time they were purged from our lands. You will bring me their heads."

332

Emerald and Amethyst nodded. I only stared, bones aching and rage gnawing away the last of the fear within me.

"Emerald, tell Nicolas and Isidora I need to speak to them." Our Queen dismissed her with a nod and a frown, not taking her eyes off me. "Please wait by the gate, Amethyst."

She might've freed our land from the grip of magic, but she used us as a substitute. We were little different from her shadow, taking her every order, killing who she pleased, and whispering secrets in her ear. She'd lost nothing and gained a throne.

"I have a job for you, Opal."

"Your wish is my command, Our Queen." I bowed, back straight and broken arm snapped to my side despite the pain.

Eight out of ten, surely, if Ruby were not ash and bone.

"Is it really?" She shifted forward, dark dress littered with dried ash. The runes across her eyelid folded. "You've lost so much, Sallot, and I—"

"I used to love you." I shuddered, memories of runes and shadows and paring knives slipping under skin fresh in my mind, and shook my head. "I adored you. I would've died for you. I thought you were Lady-sent to save us, to pull us from the chaos magic and greed had brought down upon us, but you're just like us. You're not any different from them, maneuvering people like pieces to keep your power."

She flew at me, fingers curling around my collar and pulling me close. My mask clattered to the dirt at our feet. "I am nothing like them. The decisions I made, everything I gave up, I did it for you, for each and every one of you, and you have no idea of the costs. You may be able to repay your debt in blood, but I'll take mine to the pyre. I will never be free of what I did for this country."

And I would never be free of what her people did to mine.

I grabbed Our Queen's hand, prying her weak fingers from my throat one by one. Weaker than me, and poppy tincture still flowed through my veins. Her last act of magic had left her with more than scars. She stumbled.

"None of us will." I let her go.

She picked up my mask with trembling hands, gaze stuck on the rough interior. "We cannot let our people suffer through another war."

"Your people." I helped her to her feet. "My people are dead."

"Lord del Weylin has made himself a king and raised an army of drafted civilians and Erlend allies. His rebellion must be crushed before it becomes a war, and the people he would throw unprepared into battle must be freed." She held out my mask, the finish bone-white and blank. "And our Elise was taken against her will. We cannot abandon her."

The brittle calm my wrath had brought broke.

I took my mask and hid my face. "You've never managed to kill Lord del Weylin."

The last Erlend lord clinging to the past. To tradition.

The source.

"No, it was our previous Opal's final assignment. The three of you will go to Erlend. Weylin and his allies will die." She gestured for me to turn and tied my mask back into place. "Understand?"

He expected assassins. He expected the Left Hand and Our Queen's attempts on his life, but they'd never kill him like that. He'd sent Five here and knew even more about the Left Hand's tactics now. Emerald and Amethyst would fail. But I was more than Opal.

I was a thief and a killer, trained by a childhood of fear and violence, and Weylin was not prepared for me. No walls or armies could protect him.

"Understood." I tried to pull away, but her nails dug into my skin.

"And Opal, my Opal," she whispered in my ear. "I will forgive your bitterness today, but if you ever treat me like that again, you won't make it out of this city alive." She released me. "Now kill them or die trying."

"Of course, Our Queen." I turned and swept into a bow, the names gouged inside my mask pressing into my flesh like brands. *North Star. Deadfall. Riparian. Caldera. Winter.*

They would know me. They would know Nacea, and they would never forget it again in the short, short lives I granted them before they died.

They'd taken my country and my life, and I would take their heads.

For Sal

The history of Igna is long and divided—by people, by religions, by language—and Our Queen has tasked me, as well as many others, with connecting this history. I have attempted to distill it into one shortened time line for quick reference and one historical analysis detailing what I believe are formative events. To ensure that all who have need of this history are able to make use of it, I have decided to use the common as opposed to the academically accepted terms in the time line. The expressions most commonly used by historians will be expanded upon and their origins explained in the book proper. Versions in both Erlenian and Alonian reside within the same binding to, I hope, promote a common understanding between readers of various backgrounds.

Erlend and Alona exist no longer, but the division remains. The last ten years have been wrought with skirmishes, battles, and one-day wars between Our Queen and Lord Gaspar del Weylin, and few are of note when the larger picture is not taken into account. Many of these clashes I have left out of the time line because they are as frequent as they are repetitive, and we have neither the time nor the presses to list them all within this brief time line. Given the increasing appearances of ghost towns and increased nighttime raids by the north, a number of favorable and sensational rumors have taken root within Igna. I will state what is known and not theorize given that these events are still unfolding. For now, it is simply important to know that the struggle between Igna and Erlend—or some would say between Alona and Meredan's displaced—is still ongoing.

—Elise de Farone

Spring 295 RA	The monarchy of Lona—the precursor to Alona—is formed from the Sun-drenched Coast and its city-states.
Summer 308 RA	The Great Migration—Meredan refugees travel through Berengard and are granted land north of Aren after Berengard denies them asylum due to their role in the Whispered War.
Spring 346 RA	The War of Twelve Gods begins between Lona and Berengard.

Who needs twelve gods? I can barely keep up with your Triad.

Winter 354 RA	The War of Twelve Gods ends when the Religious Rights treaty is signed by the three Head Priests of Lona and the Queen of Berengard.
Winter 397 RA	The northern lords of Aren—del Weylin, de Seve, de Farone, and del Aer—withdraw from the country and form the new nation of Eredan.

Of course they did.

Spring 398 RA	The last surviving noble house of Aren, the de Contes family, surrenders to Eredan. Lona declares war on Eredan after a series of border skirmishes to the east of Nacea.

Winter 398 RA	The Three Stars of Nacea agree to pay tribute to Eredan in exchange for military protection. Nacea becomes a territory of Eredan.
Spring 400 RA	The first civil war ends with the Eredan-Lona Treaty outlining the terms of surrender.
Autumn 400 RA	The Thrice-Blessed School opens on the border of Eredan and Lona to promote civility between the nations.
Summer 405 RA	Lona becomes Alona after the monarchy of Lona is dissolved and the High Council elected.
Summer 435 RA	The first victim of the Ash Plague dies. Alonian citizens head north to avoid the plague. The Eredan town of High Water allows them to settle outside of the city gates. Nacea stations quarantine healers along its borders to monitor visitors. Mizuho closes all its ports and recalls its ambassadors.
Winter 436 RA	The plague spreads through the Bay of Glass. Eredan closes its borders but continues to send aid.

Autumn 438 RA	The First Star of Nacea succumbs to the plague. The northern cities are isolated to prevent further spread.
Spring 439 RA	The Royal Physician system of medicine is adopted from Berengard after Physician Serrat Ansleigh visits Alona during the Ash Plague and trains with the Priests of the Body at the Thrice-Blessed School.
Summer 440 RA	The Third Star of Nacea sends ten handpicked students to the Thrice-Blessed School to study medicine and quarantine procedures.
Autumn 501 RA	During this century of peace, Eredian undergoes several small linguistic alterations (detailed more thoroughly in my passages on how language widened the Erlend-Alona-Nacea divides) and the name "Eredan" begins appearing as "Erlend" in historical documents.
Winter 502 RA	Mizuho reopens its ports for foreign trade.
Summer 542 RA	The Berengard borders along the eastern mountain line are activated. Mages

attempt to penetrate the borders but fail. All contact with Berengard is lost.

Spring 543 RA — Lord Gaspar del Weylin claims Alona's northern territory of High Water is unfairly claimed Erlend land.

Summer 543 RA — Erlend's army occupies High Water. The Third Star of Nacea Namrantha Brielle withholds yearly tributes to Erlend in protest of High Water occupation. The First and Second Stars follow in kind. The second civil war begins.

Autumn 543 RA — Mizuho denounces Erlend's invasion as a violation of the Erlend-Lona Treaty signed by the nations after the end of the first civil war. It announces intentions to support Alona.

Winter 543 RA — The southern Erlend town of Bosque de Lex vanishes. Erlend demands retribution, but Alona denies involvement.

Nothing just vanishes without a little help.

Spring 544 RA — Lord Mattin del Aer attacks Caldera Lake in Alona, claiming that they must "even the scales of justice after the massacre of Bosque de Lex." There are no survivors.

Summer 545 RA	The Mizuho navy assaults the coasts of Erlend, forcing a withdrawal from the eastern lands.
Autumn 546 RA	Lord del Weylin leads a successful attack against the Alonian army stationed in the Snakespire Mountains.
Autumn 546 RA	High Mage Celso de Lex announces the successful creation of mage shadows and their addition to the Erlend army.
Winter 546 RA	During the nine-day battle in Poppy Green, fifteen-year-old Isidora da Abreu becomes the youngest person to achieve Royal Physician rank in the lands east of the Blue Silk Sea.
Spring 547 RA	Priestess of the Mind Marianna da Ignasi refuses to surrender her students as combat mages to their respective countries of origin. Alona withdraws request. The siege of the Thrice-Blessed School by Erlend begins.
Summer 547 RA	The last remaining member of the Alonian High Council, Arleen dal Oretta, is assassinated.

Autumn 547 RA	Rodolfo da Abreu assassinates High Mage Celso de Lex and his assistants.
Winter 547 RA	The Erlend army loses control of the remaining shadows. The areas from the western Field de Contes to the southern tip of the Bay of Glass are quarantined and considered lost. Only seven survivors are recovered after Priest of the Soul Nicolas de Contes bilocates across the border.

Quarantined my ass.

Spring 0 EA	Priestess of the Mind Marianna da Ignasi banishes magic and its creations from Alona and Erlend. The Runed Age ends and the Empty Age begins.
Summer 0 EA	Erlend surrenders and the civil war ends under the agreed terms of the Last Words Treaty. Lord del Weylin refuses to surrender and withdraws from Erlend.
Autumn 1 EA	The nation of Igna is officially formed and its borders secured. Marianna da Ignasi is crowned as Our Queen of the Eastern Spires and her Left Hand selected. Lord del Weylin's "Freedom Fighters" lead a series of attacks against the northern Igna borders in protest.

Winter 2 EA	Lord del Weylin captures the northern city of Merebrook.
Spring 3 EA	A new Ruby is selected by Our Queen for her Left Hand.
Summer 3 EA	The city of Merebrook is retaken by Igna forces. Lord del Weylin withdraws his forces to the borders of his land.
Summer 5 EA	A plague sweeps through northern Igna and the lands north of it. Lord del Weylin refuses aid.
Spring 6 EA	Our Queen attempts a raid on Lord del Weylin's forces but finds the south-ernmost territories empty. Soldiers are stationed in the ghost towns.
Winter 7 EA	A new Amethyst is selected by Our Queen for her Left Hand.
Summer 10 EA	A new Opal is selected by Our Queen for her Left Hand.
Winter 10 EA:	The last traitors of Erlend die.

ACKNOWLEDGMENTS

There are not enough words to express how thankful I am for the people behind this book's creation. My fiancé Brent suffered through the rough drafts and world building ramblings before Sal was even named Sal, and without his support and superior coffee skills, *Mask of Shadows* would never have been written. Thank you to my mother and grandmother who fostered within me a love of reading and baking that so often overlapped and kept me alive while writing.

My mentor and writing partners were invaluable. Jessie Devine was the best mentor a person could ask for; Kerbie Addis was a constant source of strength, knowledge, and puns; Carrie DiRisio believed in Sal's story even when I didn't; and my favorite dragon Kara Wolf was one of the first to read about Sal and love them.

Thank you, too, to the amazing readers who helped make this as safe and enjoyable a read as possible—I can't thank all of you enough.

Thank you Brenda Drake for creating Pitch Wars and ultimately introducing me to the Pitch Wars 2014 group where I met so many writers and friends who made the last three years spectacular.

Of course, none of this would have been possible without my awesome agent Rachel Brooks at the L. Perkins Agency. She believed in Sal and me from the very start, and working with her has been one of the best parts of publishing.

Annie Berger, thank you so much for taking the little assassins book I wrote and turning it into a real novel. I still remember getting the call that you wanted to work on *Mask of Shadows*, and I'll never forget that moment. Thank you Elizabeth Boyer, Katy Lynch, Alex Yeadon, Stefani Sloma, Heather Moore, and the whole Sourcebooks team for all of the work put into this book.

And thank you especially to Nicole Hower and the amazing art department who designed the cover. It's more beautiful than I could have ever dreamed.

None of this would have been possible if not for the dozens and dozens of people who helped *Mask of Shadows* every step of the way, and I am forever grateful to all of them.

ABOUT THE AUTHOR

Linsey Miller is a wayward biologist from Arkansas who previously worked as a crime lab intern, neuroscience lab assistant, and pharmacy technician. She is active in the writing community and can be found writing about science and magic anywhere there's coffee. Visit her online at linseymiller.com.